Petrichor
A Contemporary Romance
Helene Gadot
© 2018

To coffee - without you, I wouldn't be able to get through the day.

Playlist

Petrichor - Tall Ships
The Funeral - Band of Horses
Your Ghost - Greg Laswell
Running Up That Hill - Placebo
Shattered - Trading Yesterday
Make This Go On Forever - Snow Patrol
Please Take Me - Beth Crowley
Sad Song - We the Kings, Elena Coats
9 Crimes - Damien Rice
One More Day - Vast
Faded - Alan Walker
Hold On - Chord Overstreet
The Sound of Silence - Disturbed
Better Now - Post Malone
Walk Through the Fire - Zayde Wolf, Ruelle
Bohemian Rhapsody - Queen
No One But You (Only the Good Die Young) - Queen
Hurts Like Hell - Fleurie
Losing Your Memory - Ryan Star
So Cold - Ben Cocks
River of Tears _ Alessia Cara
Rain - Breaking Benjamin
Corners - The Fray
Light - Sleeping at Last
Carry You - Ruelle, Fleurie

PETRICHOR - "*A pleasant, distinctive smell frequently accompanying the first rain after a long period of warm, dry weather.*" (Oxford English Dictionary)

Chapter 1

Poppy didn't want to associate the death of her brother with the petrichor rising from the dry soil as rain pelted the ground. It was her favorite scent, her favorite word. Perry was the one who told her what it was she was smelling every time it rained. He'd even had a gorgeous print made for her and displayed it behind the counter in their coffee shop.

She welcomed the gray clouds cutting off the bright sun who shined down on them with its happy rays like her world hadn't just ended.

It was supposed to rain at funerals. All the movies said so.

Seeing and feeling the sun while she buried her twin brother just felt wrong.

As the minister finished speaking his canned remarks, Poppy barely heard the other mourners murmur their apologies and platitudes, hurrying away as the rain lashed harder.

She wanted to crawl into the grave with him, her heart breaking all over again as the diggers filled the hole in. There was a metaphor in there somewhere, but she couldn't be bothered to figure it out.

Perry was the one who liked puns and metaphors and words. With him gone, what was she supposed to do?

Her knees buckled and a firm grip on her arm kept her from crashing to the ground in front of her twin's grave.

"You can't go with him, Poppyseed."

The tears she'd refused to shed during the funeral streamed down her cheeks at Gavin's broken voice calling her by Perry's pet name for her. Her eyes squeezed shut as sobs quaked through her, Gavins's grip the only thing keeping her upright.

Rain soaked her, washing the tears from her face. The petrichor made it worse. She would forever relate it to this day now. It ruined her favorite smell.

Hell, everything was ruined with Perry gone.

"I know, sweetheart. I know." Gavin swept her into his arms and cuddled her to his chest.

She struggled against him when he turned and walked towards the line of cars, leaving Perry behind. "No. No. I can't leave him here. Let me go. No." They'd never been apart their entire lives for more than a night or few hours. She couldn't leave him alone, she couldn't leave him behind, without her.

Gavin held her tighter, with almost bruising strength, accepting the nail marks she gouged into the flesh of his arm without a wince. "You have to, sweetheart. You have to. I'm so fucking sorry."

Her brother's other two friends, Dean and Flynn stepped into place behind them, cutting off her view of the grave and the hideous tarp with fake green grass mats being dismantled, removing all the signs of grief and pain of those who came to tell her twin, the other half of her soul goodbye.

Dean and Flynn's eyes were red and wet with their own suffering.

She slumped against Gavin's chest, closing her eyes, only able to handle her own agony at the moment. "I can't wake up. I just want to wake up."

"Me too, sweetheart. Me too."

Gavin stopped at a sleek black car and Dean hurried to open the back door so they could place her inside. Usually, she would have grumbled or objected at all the chauvinism and manhandling, but right now she didn't give a shit about anything. Her brother's three best friends had been helping her every step of the way through the whole process of preparing for today. She'd be strong again and stand alone tomorrow.

Flynn and Dean squished her into the middle, their warm sides pressed against her freezing ones while Gavin jogged around to the driver's seat.

Her trembling hands were caught in strong, comforting grips as her head fell back against the backseat of the car.

Fuzziness crawled towards the edges of her vision, and she wanted nothing more than to succumb to the numb darkness it promised, but she still had the wake to get through.

At the coffee shop she and her brother bought and ran together. At the coffee shop she now had to run alone.

Chapter 2

The rain shower had passed by the time Gavin stopped the car in front of her shop, but the remains of the quick storm left behind ugly puddles and a sad sky.

Flynn helped her from the car, his light green gaze searching hers. Poppy threw back her shoulders, determined to get through the next hours with what little calm she had left, even though all she wanted to do was crawl into her bed and sleep for two weeks, pretending like none of this had happened. Like she hadn't lost her only remaining family.

The whole idea of wakes was stupid to her. It forced those wracked with pain, to plaster on a sad smile and accept words from people who had no idea what true grief felt like.

She frowned when Dean pulled a gym bag from the trunk. Did they think they were staying over?

He noticed her interest and shot her a strained smile. "We brought extra clothes so we could get out of these suits."

She nodded. "You can change in my apartment while I finish getting everything set up." Her voice was hoarse with swallowed tears.

"Thanks."

Poppy shrugged and opened the door to the shop, the scent of coffee and pastries almost sending her to her knees. She sucked in a deep breath and swept inside.

The store already teemed with mourners sampling the appetizers and baked goods she'd been cooking for days. She and Perry had recently hired a couple workers once they could afford to, and they got too busy to handle it all alone. Tam and Marie rushed back from the funeral to get things set up, promising to handle everything so she didn't have to worry.

What they didn't understand was she didn't worry. She didn't give a shit how perfect this wake was. Perry was dead. He wasn't here to care about the flowers or cookies or cakes or mini paninis.

If she hadn't been running on autopilot ever since the phone call informing her of the accident, she wouldn't have thrown a wake. Especially here. Where all her memories of him were fresh and deep.

Signs of him, of his touch were everywhere, tormenting her.

A warm hand pressed against her lower back, making her startle. She turned to see Dean looking down at her, Flynn and Gavin at their backs.

"What?"

Dean brushed rain from her face. "You're still soaked. You should change too."

"Right." Except she had no more black clothes. She hated black, so she'd run out to the closest store and grabbed the first funeral appropriate dress she found in her size.

Flynn nudged her, making her realize she still hadn't moved. "Come on."

Poppy pasted a fake smile onto her face as people she barely knew stopped her on her way to the door at the back of the shop to express their condolences.

She let out a shaky breath when they pushed into the kitchen where more food waited to be taken out to the main shop. She'd made a lot. It was all she could handle between phone calls and visits to the funeral home. She just kept baking.

Thankfully, Marie and Tam were still handling the mourners in the main part of the shop, so there wasn't anyone to stop them or ask questions as Perry's friends and roommates hustled her through the next door to the steps leading up to her apartment.

Inside, she kicked her mud and grass covered ugly shoes into the corner and padded to her bedroom without a word to the men in her place.

They'd been here before. Tons of times. They knew how to make themselves at home. It wasn't huge, but there was another bathroom and a guest room she used as an office they could change in.

She stared into her closet, hoping something proper would jump out at her, but everything was bright or pastel to match her unicorn hair and lavender themed coffee shop. Nothing in there said funeral.

With a shrug and a sigh, she pulled out her darkest dress, plum-colored with a sparkly unicorn painted across the front. Perry had bought it for her and he'd love her wearing it today. She didn't care if the people downstairs didn't approve. None of them mattered. Only Perry did.

After twisting her damp, multi-colored hair into a bun at the nape of her neck and sliding her feet into a pair of lavender ballet flats, she emerged from her room.

The sight of Gavin, Dean, and Flynn in ripped jeans and graphic tees made her sigh in relief. Those three were the only ones who had even an inkling of how much she was hurting. They were the only ones who loved Perry almost as much as she did, who had known him almost as long.

Flynn looked her up and down with a sad smile. "You look perfect, Poppy. Let's get this bullshit over with and we'll help scare everyone off."

Poppy smoothed down the skirt of her dress, a little bit of gratitude warming the edges of the cold numbness spread through her. She could do this. She could do it for Perry.

Pain ripped through her, but she swallowed it down and swept back downstairs.

Chapter 3

If one more person told her how kind and amazing Perry was, she swore she wouldn't be able to keep the scream building in her chest inside.

Perry was kind and amazing, but he could also be selfish and cutting and cheap. Why were dead people always lauded as saints? Why were people scared to speak the truth? She knew Perry better than anyone, so she wasn't afraid to hear stories of him acting like a jackass. She could use the laugh.

Most of the people here were firefighters Perry and the other guys worked with, other small business owners who ran shops on their same quaint street or friends from Perry's neighborhood where he lived with Dean, Flynn, and Gavin.

No one was here for her.

She and Perry had no family they were still in touch with, their father left them long ago and their mother passed last year. And neither one of them were big on trust or making friends. The only reason Gavin, Flynn, and Dean had gotten past their walls was because they'd known each other since they were kids. And they were more Perry's friends than hers. She wasn't as close to them as Perry was.

They all grew up in the same neighborhood, on the same street, same schools, two of their moms were best friends. Perry and the guys even went to college together, they became firefighters together.

Poppy hadn't bothered with college, instead she went to a couple years of culinary school close by the college Perry and the guys chose. She focused on cooking while Perry learned the business side of things, and once they were finished and saved enough, they opened Cool Beans.

Since Poppy was the chef, she moved into the apartment above the shop so she could stay on top of the baking and Perry moved in with the guys a few blocks away since there wasn't enough room for both of them in her apartment and he and the guys were on the same schedule at the fire station.

Since they were in the womb, she and Perry hadn't spent a single day apart.

How was she supposed to survive without him?

Gavin's mother appeared suddenly in front of her and Poppy wanted to shove her away. She couldn't handle her. She couldn't handle her and Perry's second mother, the one who babysat them when their mom had to work late, whose house she knew as well as her own.

Stacy seemed to realize it because she didn't pull Poppy into a hug or say anything about Perry and how sorry she was or how much she missed him. Instead, she cupped Poppy's cheek and handed her a plate of food.

"Eat something, sweetheart. I'll keep everyone away from you so you can have a moment away from the horde."

"Thanks." Poppy's voice came out hoarse and raw.

She turned away before she saw Stacy's reaction. Not today. She couldn't handle Stacy today.

Poppy ducked away into the kitchen with her plate of food, watching everything through the window in the door. People chatted and laughed, like this was some kind of party. Because their lives hadn't changed. They hadn't lost something precious. She wanted to shove every last one out of her shop.

She recognized one man there as one of her usual customers. Why was he here? He usually came in on the days Perry was working at the firehouse. And he definitely hadn't been invited. Weird. But there were several people milling about she barely recognized and hadn't invited. Maybe one of the guys or Tam or Marie asked them to come. It didn't matter.

Gavin, Flynn, and Dean stood in the corner, barely talking as they poked at the food on their plates. They understood.

She turned her back on everyone, the food ashes in her mouth. Could she escape upstairs and hope everyone left without noticing she was missing?

Nope. Someone would probably just come knock on her door. Or they'd never leave.

She dropped her plate in the sink and pushed back into the shop, immediately swarmed by apologies and tears.

Finally, the last mourner walked out the door, leaving her alone with the guys and her two employees.

She wished they'd leave too. She wanted to be alone so she could peel off the mask.

Marie shooed her away from the tables she tried to clear. "We'll handle all of this. You go take a nice bath and get some sleep."

Yes, a bath would fix everything. She held back a snort and harsh words. Marie didn't deserve it. She was trying to help.

Tam stacked plates on trays. "She's right. You don't worry about a thing. We'll clean up and put the sign up letting everyone know we're closed until next week."

"All right. Thanks, guys. I'll see you Monday." There. That was polite.

Tam hugged her. "If you need more time, we can keep things going for you for a while longer. Just let us know."

"I will." Poppy turned to the guys. "Thanks for helping with everything. I'll see you later."

Gavin opened his mouth to say something, but Flynn elbowed him in the stomach, cutting off whatever he planned to say.

Dean reached over and squeezed her arm. "We'll come check on you tomorrow."

Poppy shook her head. She would not be up for company any time soon. She just wanted to be left alone. "That's not necessary. I'll be fine."

Flynn frowned. "Call us if you need anything. Anytime."

"Sure." Please just go away. Seeing them hurt. They were all twisted up with memories of Perry and it was too much. They needed to leave her alone.

Perry's voice in her head reminded her how much they loved and missed him too.

She knew. But she didn't have it in her to care right then. She shot them a brittle smile and turned her back to head upstairs.

Poppy made it into her room before the dam broke. Barely.

FLYNN RAKED HIS HANDS through his hair as he left the coffee shop with Gavin and Dean. Loss roared through him, so powerful it almost sent him to his knees. Fuck. He couldn't get the empty look in Poppy's eyes out of his mind. It wrecked him seeing her so lost and hollow. The way she'd looked like she wanted to join Perry in his grave. The desperate way she fought Gavin as he carried her away.

Like the woman hadn't been through enough in her life, she needed this last stab to the gut? The worst one yet?

Gavin's hand clapped down onto Flynn's shoulder, grounding him. He looked over at his friend with an appreciative smile. Gavin met his eyes with complete understanding. He and Dean knew the helpless rage and grief inside him because it thundered through them too. Their friend was fucking dead. And killed in a damn car accident instead of fighting a fire like they all half expected. It was bullshit. All of it.

"We shouldn't have left her. We should have brought her with us." Flynn's fists clenched at his sides, desperate to sink into a heavy bag or someone's face.

Violence brimmed beneath his surface and he needed to let it out soon.

Dean shook his head as he opened the driver's side door of the car. "She was a breath away from shattering, and she doesn't want to do that in front of us."

Flynn slid into the backseat, needing room to breathe. "She shouldn't be alone."

Dean pulled the car out of the parking space and onto the street. "It's what she wants. We just need to give her a little time and space. But we'll come back for her."

Chapter 4

Poppy frowned into a cup of coffee with swollen eyes, exhausted and shaky. Every time she tried to sleep, she saw Perry's body laid out on the metal table when she'd been brought to identify him.

So for three days since the funeral, she'd barely dozed, lost in a fog of grief and pain, waiting to wake from this nightmare. Three days, she'd remained hidden in her apartment, ignoring the knocks on the door and ringing phone.

Why couldn't everyone leave her alone? Let her grieve and come to terms with this loss in peace?

No longer in the mood for coffee, she left it cooling on the kitchen table and returned to the cocoon she'd built herself on the couch. Wrapped up in blankets, she turned to face the back of the sofa, staring blankly at the green fabric.

She fell into the space between asleep and awake, remembering her and Perry's last conversation. It was so stupid, nothing profound. Just chatter about bills and vendors and a new recipe she wanted to try. He invited her to Flynn's bar. It was an everyday conversation. She couldn't even remember if she told him she loved him. Or if he told her.

A buzzing sound vibrated in her head and her chest tightened as she fought off the tears. She didn't want to cry anymore. She didn't want to feel anymore. She wished she could sleep and forget. But waking up brought its own special level of hell. She had to remember all over again how alone she was.

She clutched Perry's hoodie tighter around her beneath the blankets. It still smelled like him, but her unwashed scent was fast overtaking it. her hair flopped in greasy clumps around her face. It was past time for her to take a shower, but she couldn't bring herself to move.

She sank back into a doze, her mind fogging.

A noise at the door roused her, but she ignored it. Whoever it was would go away like all the other times.

She pulled the hood of the sweatshirt over her head, burrowing deeper into the couch, sticking her earbuds into her ears to block out the world, letting the strains of Snow Patrol sink her deeper into her sadness.

A hand grabbed her shoulder, and she shrieked, falling from the couch into a heap of tangled blankets.

Panic squeezed her chest as she attempted to fight her way free, her heart pounding. Her door was locked. How did anyone get in? Perry was the only other person who had a key.

Hands reached for her, helping her escape the clutches of the blankets. Once free, she scrambled back against the couch, pressing herself into it, her chest heaving.

Flynn, Gavin, and Dean stood above her, watching her with careful, worried eyes, their mouths moving, but she couldn't hear past the bass thumping in her ears.

She ripped the buds free. "How did you get in here?"

"Perry's key." Gavin winced.

She heaved herself back onto the couch, her pulse finally calming. "Oh. Right. Of course. What are you doing here?"

"You haven't been answering the door or our calls," Flynn said. "We were worried."

"I'm fine."

Gavin raised a brow. "We can see that."

Heat stung her cheeks as she imagined what she looked like, but she shoved the embarrassment away. "I am."

They looked gorgeous. Like always.

Dean stared down at her. "You're coming with us. Pack a few things. Whatever you have to have."

Poppy jerked back against the couch. "What? I'm not going anywhere. Where are you planning on taking me?"

"Home." Gavin squatted in front of her, his gray eyes pained, his hands on her knees.

She shook her head with a furrowed brow, confused. "I am home."

"Our home."

They meant Perry's home.

Her hands shook as she ran them through her snarled hair. "No. I can't go there. I can't."

Gavin's hands tightened on her knees. "You can't be any worse off than you are here. At least you won't be alone."

"But I want to be alone." It was easier this way. She didn't have to pretend she was okay. She didn't have to put on a show.

Flynn picked the blankets up off the floor and folded them. "Maybe you think you do, but you shouldn't be. And we don't want to be either."

"You aren't alone. You three have each other." She didn't want their pity. She didn't want them feeling responsible for their best friend's sister. "You don't have to do this. You aren't responsible for me."

Dean growled. "We don't feel responsible for you because of Perry. We care about you."

Gavin rose to his full height and held out a hand to her. "Enough. We aren't leaving you alone. Come stay at least one night. Get out of this tiny place and try to join the world again."

"The world sucks." She didn't know how to be a part of it without Perry. In her apartment, a small part of her could pretend. Pretend Perry was out with the guys or at the fire station.

Not eight feet deep in the ground.

Gavin kept his hand in her face, waiting patiently for her to take it, for her to come away with them. "It does. But it's a little easier to face all of that when you aren't alone."

They didn't get it. Without Perry, that's exactly how she'd live the rest of my life, as melodramatic as it sounded. The three of them would eventually go back to their lives and without Perry here, they'd slowly disappear.

Their stubborn faces were giving her a headache. "Please just leave me alone to handle this how I want."

"Fine." Dean scowled. "But we're staying here with you."

"That's unnecessary." Why wouldn't they go away?

Gavin shrugged, his hand falling back to his side. "We're doing it anyway. You don't have to entertain us. Do whatever you need to, but we're staying."

She huffed. "Fine."

And now she had to pee.

She winced as she rose, her free hand jerking out to grasp at the arm of the couch when the world swayed and darkened.

Gavin's grip tightened on hers. "Shit. She's going down."

"She doesn't look like she's eaten or slept in weeks."

She hadn't.

Poppy welcomed the dark as it came for her.

GAVIN EASED POPPY BACK onto the couch to keep her from crumpling to the floor, his heart squeezing in his chest, heat prickling the back of his eyes with a harsh burn.

His hands shook as he rubbed at his face, unable to look at the beautiful creature wasting away in front of him.

Dean took charge, like normal. "Let's get food cooked and things cleaned up. One of us should go grab some of our shit from the house."

Gavin shook off the pain and bobbed his head in a brisk nod. "I'll clean up this mess and get a meal going if you two want to handle the rest."

"Flynn, you head home and pack for us. I'll keep an eye on her. I don't want to leave her alone in case she wakes up."

Flynn cast one last dark glance at their unicorn girl before he stomped towards her front door.

Gavin frowned after him. "We need to get him to the gym before he explodes."

Dean sighed and rubbed the back of his neck, tension at the edges of his eyes. "I know."

Flynn had a lot of demons from the way he grew up. His family sucked ass and so did his life until Gavin's mom took him in during high school. Gavin still remembered how skinny and starved he always was. As soon as his mother realized, she'd made sure he always had plenty to eat. Perry and Poppy's mom had done the same. Dean's parents hadn't noticed, and they'd rarely hung out at his house. It was too much like a museum, too cold. Just like Dean's parents.

Sometimes Gavin felt like the only normal one out of the bunch. Flynn still ate like he might not get a chance again, Dean tended to retreat into himself or became the cold leader, and Poppy and Perry were always ready and waiting to be left behind. Perry gathered as many people around him as he could so there would always be backups if someone left and Poppy kept everyone at arm's length, trusting no one but Perry to get too close. Not even them.

Gavin sighed as he placed the last coffee cup into the dish rack to dry. His life hadn't been perfect, but his dad died before he was old enough to remember him and his mother more than made up for it. His dad hadn't abandoned him, he hadn't decided to leave like Perry and Poppy's shitty dad. And with two protective older sisters and his neighborhood best friends who'd turned into his family, he'd never felt alone.

He never wanted them to feel alone either. They'd prove to Poppy that she wasn't alone, that they would not abandon her like everyone else in her life did, whether it was their choice or not.

Chapter 5

Voices filtered through the black lightening to a hazy gray.

"Let her sleep." She recognized Dean's deep voice.

A hand brushed hair back from her face, Gavin's hand. "I don't think she's asleep, so much as unconscious from lack of food and sleep. Fuck, we shouldn't have waited so long after seeing what she looked like at the funeral."

She was still feeling out of it, unable to fully awaken. She wasn't ready to open her eyes and face them.

"Perry would kill us if he was here."

"And we'd deserve it." Flynn sounded so guilty.

Dean cursed. "We need to get food in her. Soon. How'd she lose so much weight so fast?"

"I don't think she touched anything at the wake and there were only dirty coffee cups in her sink. She probably hasn't eaten since she got the call."

Poppy blinked against the light streaming directly into her face from the window. "What's going on? Where am I?"

"You're home, sweetheart. You passed out a few minutes after we got here." Gavin's face was a blur.

"I passed out?" She'd never fainted before in her life. Why were they at her place to witness her weakness? Why had she passed out anyway?

Everything rushed back to her at once, making her gasp and clutch her chest in pain as tears stung her eyes. Perry. He was dead. He was gone.

No.

A hand brushed the tears from her face and she realized her head was in Gavin's lap. When did that happen? He helped her sit up when she squirmed, her head too heavy for her body. Everything felt disconnected and muted.

"Why are you here?" She rubbed at her eyes, trying to clear her vision and brain.

Flynn knelt beside the couch. "We told you we weren't leaving. Did you really expect us to watch you pass out from hunger and exhaustion and leave you unconscious on your couch?"

She huffed as she wiggled into a more comfortable position. "I guess not."

Dean came back into the room and thrust a plate of food at her face. "Here. Eat."

She frowned at the sandwich and pickles, her stomach twisting. "Thanks." She took the plate and stared at the food. She did love pickles.

"You're supposed to eat it." Dean's voice was hard and unbending.

She sighed. It was easier to give in than argue with these guys. They were stubborn as hell.

And she was dizzy and foggy from her lack of appetite. She'd crossed into the space where she was so empty, she was no longer hungry. Was there a word for that like there was for petrichor?

Her throat clogged. Perry would know. And it's something she would have asked him.

Gavin gestured for the others to leave them. "Where's my sandwich?"

Dean rolled his eyes, but he hauled Flynn towards her kitchen.

Gavin adjusted his position on the couch until his leg nudged hers and he faced her. "Everything sucks right now and it will for a long time. Maybe forever for you. But we're here for you and with you. Please eat. You're wasting away and it kills us to see you like this."

Poppy's eyes narrowed, recognizing a manipulative tone when she heard one. She opened her mouth to call him on it, but weariness hit her so hard, she almost swooned like one of those poor women in eighteenth-century novels. But she didn't have the excuse of a corset and sixteen layers of constrictive clothing in the middle of summer without air conditioning and fans.

Gavin's stubborn expression made her realize she didn't have the energy in her to argue or complain.

So she ate the stupid, delicious sandwich, forcing every bite down her throat.

Once her plate was clear, Gavin took the dish from her to set on the coffee table and replace it with a bottle of her favorite pineapple and mint infused water.

Flynn and Dean returned, taking spots on the plush chairs across from them with their owns plates of sandwiches, bringing a third for Gavin. Where did they get the food for the sandwiches? She hardly had any groceries up here.

Poppy shifted in her seat, her belly uncomfortably full, but her head was already a little clearer and she was aware of just how badly she smelled. She scooted away from Gavin, trying to put a little more space between them.

He refused to let her, only spreading out farther so he was still plastered against her, ignoring her scowl.

She sighed. "So, what now?"

Dean frowned at her, a pickle hanging limp in his hand. "Now, you get some sleep."

Flynn sat forward, his sandwich already gone. "I ran home and packed us some stuff. Oh, and by the way, your phone is charging in the kitchen which was dead when we found it in your fridge."

She shrugged, cheeks burning. "It wouldn't stop ringing."

A pained look flashed in Dean's eyes. "Go get some sleep. We can talk more later."

"What are you guys going to do? You should go home. I don't have a lot of room here."

"You've got a guest room and a couch. We'll be fine." Flynn winked. "Two of us can cuddle in the bed."

If they wanted to be uncomfortable and crowded instead of home in their own beds, it was their choice.

They watched her carefully as she stood and headed towards her room. She still wasn't completely back to her usual strength, but the sandwich and water went a long way. She was able to make it all the way down the hall without stumbling.

Poppy slouched against the door of her room, her breath short. This was ridiculous. How had she gotten this bad so fast?

Guilt crawled up her throat as she imagined what Perry would say. He'd be disappointed in her, how she'd given up.

She had to be strong. For him.

After closing the door behind her, she crossed the room to the bed covered in a purple comforter and sat on the edge for a moment, wishing she could curl up beneath the covers, but she could no longer handle the stench of her own self.

She heaved herself to her feet and pulled out a shirt and her leggings with unicorns all over them along with fresh underwear from her dresser and went into her bathroom.

Inside, she avoided looking in the mirror, not wanting to see her brother's face reflected in her own. Fraternal twins or not, they still looked damn similar. Same bright blue eyes, same pale skin, same dusting of freckles across their noses. The only difference was she dyed her hair with four different pastel colors while his was blond.

As she stepped beneath the steaming spray, she tried to figure out why Perry's friends were so adamant at taking care of her. Sure, they were her friends too, and she knew they cared about her. She cared about them as well.

They'd known each other for most of their lives. But she had never really felt like part of their boys club. They were never jerks and pushed her away, letting her play and hang out, but the only time she was around any of them was if Perry was there too. It was weird being here without him.

Poppy didn't expect them to completely disappear from her life quite so soon, but she thought it would take longer than three days before they came knocking.

It was nice, but she wished she was still alone so she didn't have to worry about being clean and presentable and friendly. Maybe it was weak of her, but she had wanted to take the rest of the week off to sink deep into the pit of grief, soaking in it. Then, maybe, she'd be able to pick herself back up and move on.

Losing that time made her feel cheated, unhealthy as it was.

She shut off the shower and climbed out to dry off, enjoying the feeling of clean clothes on a clean body.

She covered it all with Perry's hoodie and padded back into the bedroom.

Where she found Flynn sprawled across her bed.

Chapter 6

"What are you doing in here?" She dropped her dirty clothes in the laundry basket in the corner.

Flynn shot her a lazy grin. "Just checking on you."

"I'm fine." She wrapped her arms around her middle, not moving from her spot in the center of the room, several feet from the bed.

His grin faltered and dropped off his face. "I know. We're all fine. Doesn't mean I can't check on my friend."

"Well, you've checked on me. After guilting me into letting you guys stay."

Flynn rolled from the bed and crossed over to her. "I know everything is hell right now. We just want to make sure you aren't going through it alone. And we don't want to go through it alone either."

She took a step back. "You already have each other. You aren't alone."

He tugged the towel off her head, sending her damp pastel tresses tumbling around her shoulders. "But you're a part of our family. Without you, it's even worse with Perry gone."

Poppy opened her mouth to tell him it was harder for her to be around them because it was a constant reminder Perry was gone, but she snapped it closed. She couldn't bear to add to the pain in his eyes with cruel words.

"I don't want to be the thing you three throw yourselves into so you don't have to face what we lost."

He scowled and threw the towel over to join her dirty clothes. "That's not what this is. At all. Being here with you helps us. Dean made us wait as long as we did. Gavin and I were ready to bust down your door and bring you to our place after the wake. We worry about you when you're locked up here in your apartment and we can't see how you're doing."

Poppy sighed. They weren't going to leave her alone. She was their friend and their best friend's twin. It was easier to just let them have their way. Maybe once she got some sleep, she'd have the energy to fight it.

"All right."

Flynn wrapped her up into a tight, warm hug. She fought the scalding tears burning her sore eyes as she threw her arms around his neck and buried her face in his chest. He smelled good, like clean flannel and leather.

She pulled back, needing the hug to end before she completely lost it. They'd already witnessed her all but trying to crawl into the grave with Perry. If she didn't show them she was okay, they would never leave her alone.

He pressed a kiss in the center of her forehead. "I'll let you get some sleep. You know where we are if you need us."

She cleared the tears from her throat. "I do. I'll see you in a bit after I take a nap. If you get hungry, help yourself."

"We will. We always make ourselves at home here." Flynn squeezed her shoulder. "Which is something we don't want to change now. This has always been our second home. Just like our place is yours."

But didn't it have to change now? Without Perry, eventually the guys would fade away from her life, busy with their own jobs and love lives. None of them had really ever had a serious relationship that lasted longer than a couple months, but they'd find someone one day. She couldn't afford to lean on them when whatever this was would one day disappear. It was better if she learned how to handle life on her own.

"Thank, Flynn."

He nodded and left her alone.

Poppy pulled back the purple comforter and gray sheets, crawling into the bed. She scooted into the center, snuggling under the soft covers. It was barely noon and there was still so much of the day left to get through. Her phone was still in the kitchen and she didn't feel like getting up, so she couldn't watch cute cat videos or scroll through the bullshit everyone kept posting on Perry's feed.

She dug her palms into her eyes. She had so much to handle that she'd been putting off. Another reason she hadn't wanted to leave her apartment. It reminded her of all the things she needed to do. She had to meet with his lawyer, call his insurance company again, she needed to clean out his room, she needed to delete his social media, handle their joint business account, handle his private one, and a hundred other tiny things. She didn't want to think about any of it. She just wanted to pretend none of it existed for a little longer. But now, it was all she could think about. Her mind raced in circles as she mapped out a mental to-do list.

It was all too much.

Poppy rolled over, turning her back to the sun the plum curtains weren't able to block from streaming through the window. She hated how bright and happy the summer was. She preferred cloudy gray skies. It suited her mood. The sun shouldn't shine when things were this dark and sad. She didn't want the world to move on while she was stuck in this darkness. While Perry wasn't here to enjoy the summer with her. It was stupid and selfish to feel this way, but she didn't care.

She pressed her face into the tear-soaked pillow, breathing in the fresh lavender scent.

Poppy checked the clock on the nightstand and turned onto her back with a groan, throwing her arm across her face. She'd been lying here for three hours and she wasn't even close to sleep. How long could a person go without sleep?

A soft knock sounded at the door and Gavin poked his head in. He frowned when he met her open eyes. "You're still awake?"

"Can't sleep." Her voice came out in a croak.

He stepped all the way inside and closed the door behind him, leaning against it. "Have you slept at all since the funeral?"

"Not exactly." She'd dozed.

Gavin pushed off the door and crossed the room to perch on the edge of the bed. "None of us have slept much either. More than you though. But we're all exhausted."

"I can't turn my brain off and I'm scared of waking up." She whispered the admission without meeting his eyes.

Gavin nodded in understanding. "Because when you wake up, you'll have that moment when you forget he's gone."

"Yes."

Gavin shoved down the covers and slid into bed beside her, pulling her in close.

She stiffened in his arms, her pulse speeding up. "What are you doing?"

"I need a nap. So do you. Maybe together we can ward off the nightmares."

She tried to relax with his face too close to hers, a fluttering sensation flapping in her stomach. "I'm sure that's not necessary."

"What does it hurt to try?"

What did it hurt indeed?

Chapter 7

Poppy blinked bleary eyes at the clock, jerking at the time flashing at her in red. How was it ten in the morning? What day was it? How long did she sleep? She needed to get to work; she was late.

And then, she remembered.

She squeezed her eyes shut, but tears still escaped down her face as she choked on a sob, pain radiating through her body. Dammit, she hated this. Hated reliving the loss. But wouldn't it be worse when she didn't have that moment of peace, believing all was right in her world? When the point came when she was so used to his absence, it wasn't something she needed to remember? She didn't ever want to be used to his absence if it meant she'd moved on, leaving him behind.

Their twenty-eighth birthday was in a few months. Perry would never turn twenty-eight. He'd remain stuck at twenty-seven forever while she continued aging and living her life. He'd never get married, have kids, grandkids. She'd never be an aunt, any kids she may one day have would never meet their uncle. All their plans and dreams for the future were ashes.

She tried to curl into a ball, but arms wrapped around her middle kept her trapped. She jerked, panic and confusion ratcheting up her heart rate, distracting her from the despair.

Right. Gavin slept with her. She frowned at the hands pulling her tighter. They were brown, not white. It wasn't Flynn; it was Dean. When did they switch? And why? What were they doing?

She peeled his arms off of her, desperate to pee, and scooted from the bed. He released a soft noise of complaint, but didn't wake, replacing her with one of the pillows. It was rather adorable.

And confusing.

She escaped into the bathroom, taking another shower after relieving herself. She felt better, steadier. Having someone she trusted in bed with her definitely helped her sleep. And sleep hard. Maybe now that she was fully rested, she'd be able to get back into a usual rhythm.

Poppy tilted her face into the hot spray, letting it wash away the signs of her breakdowns. She was so tired of crying all the time, of the ache in her chest, of the burn in her eyes, of the hole in her heart, of the fog in her mind. She needed to be stronger than this.

But she didn't know how to crawl from the pit she'd fallen into as soon as she got the call telling her her twin brother was dead.

After she climbed from the shower and dried off, she realized she'd forgotten to grab a change of clothes with her, and she didn't want to put the clothes she'd slept in for almost an entire day back on. Hopefully, Dean was still asleep and she could sneak in and change before he woke.

She poked her head out the bathroom door, but Dean was no longer in her bed or her room. Excellent. She could calm down and change with no awkwardness.

She followed the scents of coffee back into the main part of her apartment where all three guys sat around her table with mugs and plates of bacon and eggs. They looked up and smiled, waving her over. Flynn hopped up and made another plate, bringing it over to place on the table in front of the seat she took. Dean rose and made her a cup of coffee and handed it to her. It was rather nice, being waited on.

"Thanks. I didn't mean to sleep so long." She sipped her coffee, enjoying the hint of hazelnut. "Uh, why did I go to sleep with one of you and wake up next to another one?"

Gavin grinned over at her. "You were sleeping so long, but we didn't want to leave you alone, so we took turns."

Flynn pouted. "I never got a turn."

"It was the best rest we've gotten in a week. And you're looking a lot more... human." Dean grimaced at his words.

Poppy didn't take offense. She had been looking rough as hell. "I do feel better. You guys should head home."

Flynn snorted. "Nice try. Not happening. We're here till it's time for us all to go back to work."

What did she have to say to convince them she was fine and they should go? "I just want to sleep more and relax. I'm not exactly not up to company or entertaining."

Gavin added more bacon to her plate. "Good. That's all we want too. We are staying and we are feeding you and we are making sure you aren't alone."

"Where are you getting the food?" Poppy asked. "I had nothing in my fridge."

Dean frowned, his lips turned down in disapproval. "No. You didn't. All you had in the kitchen was coffee. Flynn brought some from home and we stole the rest from your shop downstairs."

"Smart." She ate another piece of bacon, glad her stomach was working again. "If I'm sleeping, what are you guys going to do to spend the time?"

The bacon lodged in her throat as she glanced over at the chair Perry usually sat in when he visited to see his reaction and she remembered all over again, he wasn't there. He wasn't with them.

He never would be again.

She forced the bacon down, along with the grief trying to rise. If she broke now, they'd never leave.

Dean pretended he didn't notice the tears shimmering in her eyes. "We need sleep too. None of us have gotten a lot lately either. Maybe download a movie."

She pushed her plate away, no longer able to stomach food with the way her stomach churned. "Fine. But I'm fine, so if you need to leave for any reason, it won't hurt my feelings."

Flynn topped off her coffee and squeezed her shoulder. "Stop trying to kick us out. It will hurt our feelings."

She savored the fresh cup, the one thing that still brought her comfort. "I just don't want you guys feeling like you have to take care of me."

"Have you considered that it's easier for us to be here than at home?" Dean asked, the edges of his lips tense.

She slumped back in her seat, feeling like a piece of crap. "No. I'm sorry. I know this is as hard for you guys as it is for me."

Gavin reached across the table to cover her hand with his. "Not quite as hard, but damn close. It's not a competition though. We're all trying to muddle through this as best we can. Being here with you and for you helps us.

Does having us here help you? Honestly? If it's making it harder, we'll leave. But don't ask us to leave because you think you're a burden or we feel like we have to be here."

She turned her hand in Gavin's to wind their fingers together and sighed. "No. It helps. It's harder in some ways, but ultimately better."

She was more aware of Perry's absence with them there, but they helped her sleep. And they were feeding her. And they fought off the silence.

Dean cleaned up the dishes, pausing to shoot her a smile. "Then stop arguing and stop trying to force us to leave. We're right where we want to be."

Warmth spread through her at their words and reassurance. She didn't really want them to go. She didn't really want to be alone.

"All right. Stay as long as you want." She drained every last precious drop of coffee and stood. "I'm headed back to bed."

"It's my turn. Finally." Flynn chased after her.

DEAN WOKE UP TANGLED up with Poppy, his face buried in the back of her neck. He had pulled her into his arms at some point and tucked her close into his chest.

Again.

He couldn't keep his hands off of her when he was asleep. Thankfully, he had more control when he was conscious. She was going through so much already; he didn't want to add to it with her realizing what he felt for her. What they all felt for her.

His stomach growled and with careful movements, he untangled their legs and scooted back from her. She frowned and buried herself further into the pillows, but she didn't wake as he got out of the bed.

She was still wrapped in Perry's old hoodie, refusing to take it off even as she's changed the clothes beneath it. Seeing her in the thing broke his heart a little.

He wasn't looking forward to going back home to his room right next to Perry's empty one. To the signs of his best friend all over the house in the photos and the throw pillows and his uniform and the couch he picked out.

There were fewer memories of Perry here at Poppy's home for Dean. Perry's ghost wasn't as powerful in a place they had spent little time together.

It had to suck for Poppy. Even worse when right downstairs was the coffee shop they owned and ran together.

Over twenty years all five of them had known each other and barely gone a week without spending at least a couple hours together. Perry's death fractured their family and Dean had no idea how to mend it.

But he'd do whatever it took to get them through this so he didn't lose anyone else.

Flynn and Gavin were awake and seated at Poppy's kitchen table, coffee mugs in front of both of them. The three of them had kept the coffee going for whenever Poppy woke up. They tried to feed her, her appetite still not back to normal, but their girl would never say no to coffee.

They were half convinced coffee ran through her veins instead of blood.

Dean poured himself a cup of the coffee, ignoring the selection of syrups and creamers and flavored sugar. He preferred his black. "She's still asleep. One of you should go in there so she isn't alone."

"I'll go." Gavin stood and placed his mug in the sink before disappearing into Poppy's room.

Dean took Gavin's chair next to Flynn. "How are you holding up?"

"Getting a little stir crazy. We need to get her and ourselves out of here. Go somewhere."

"Go where?" Dean asked.

"No idea. Not our place. Not my bar. That'll be too much for her."

Dean was out of ideas. Everywhere had memories of Perry latched to them. "Let's ask her. We've already pushed her a lot just by us being here. If you need a break though, Gavin and I are fine hanging here. You could hit the gym."

If Flynn didn't make regular visits to the gym, the rage inside him built up. And he had a lot to be angry about right now. Dean didn't want to see his friend lose it.

"I'm fine for now. If she'd rather stay, I'll head out tonight."

"All right." Dean drained half his coffee.

"Do you think she's going to be ready to go back to work tomorrow?"

Dean sighed. "I think she's going to go back whether she's ready or not. Are you ready?"

Flynn snorted. "Nope. But at least we have the holiday weekend coming up soon that we already took off for."

They had asked off for the fourth of July before Perry died. Gavin's mother threw a big party every year and had since they were young.

"Do you think Poppy will still go?" Dean asked.

"I hope so. I hate the thought of her here alone while we're all there having fun."

"Do you actually believe it'll be fun this year?"

They'd never gone without Perry and Poppy. It was going to be hard as hell.

"Probably not. But more fun than us sitting home alone. We won't miss him any more by deciding to be sad and miserable."

Dean didn't love the parties, too many people, too many fake smiles, too many flirtatious comments, and way too many assumptions and jokes about their sexuality. The snide questions about when the four of them were going to stop living together and settle down into real lives. The reminder that they weren't college kids anymore, they were grown men.

If he didn't love Gavin's mother so much, he'd suggest they try something new this year.

"Maybe we should have Gavin's mom call her and make sure she's coming."

"Thinking guilt trip?" Flynn grinned.

"Yeah. The fourth is Poppy's favorite holiday, and she loves going to Stacy's parties." Dean hoped the constant condolences she was sure to suffer through wouldn't ruin the party for her. "We'll need to play defense for her. There will be a ton of people wanted to tell Perry stories and tell her how sorry they are."

Flynn nodded with a small smile of approval. "Agreed. I'll tell Gavin to talk to his mom about that too. Let's try to make this fun for her. And for us."

The problem was every place they could go in this town would have memories of places they all went with Perry. There was no escaping it.

They could only slough through it.

Chapter 8

Flynn was on her bed when Poppy got out of the shower. Again.

"This is becoming a habit for you." She finally dropped Perry's hoodie into the laundry basket. It no longer smelled like him and it didn't smell like her either. It smelled like old tacos and stale coffee.

The time had come for her to let go of the hoodie. It wasn't making her feel any better.

Flynn shrugged. "What? We've all been sharing your bed the past two days."

After so long of getting no sleep, it was nice to catch up and feel rested and human again. She hoped she'd still be able to sleep once the guys weren't in bed with her.

"Yes, but the other two sneak in and out. You're the only one who is so blatant about it and waits for me."

Flynn was completely unapologetic. He made things a little awkward. She didn't know how to respond to him like this.

Flynn sat up and swung his legs off the side of her bed. "Why should I sneak? I'm not ashamed of anything we've done in your bed. Unfortunately."

Her cheeks heated, but she tried to play it off with a laugh. "You will never have cause to be ashamed of anything you do in my bed." Shit. That came out completely wrong.

A Cheshire grin spread across his lips and his green eyes flared. "Oh, muffin. That, I already know. There's nothing we could do in your bed that I'd regret."

She turned her back on him to search for a hair tie on her dresser. "When are you guys leaving again?"

"Later tonight."

"Feel free to make that sooner." Though she'd enjoyed having them here more than she expected.

She wasn't completely looking forward to returning to life in an empty apartment. Even though it was the life she lived before Perry died.

Maybe she should get a cat.

"You should. We can go to a shelter tomorrow and pick one out if you want."

She jerked and spun to face him, almost dropping her hair tie. "What?" Did she say that out loud?

Flynn shot her a wicked grin. "You want a cat, we can get you one. I love pussies."

Apparently, she did say it out loud. Was she losing her mind?

She rolled her eyes at Flynn's pervy joke, but the idea of a cat intrigued her. "I guess that could be fun. It was just a random thought though. Maybe I should wait instead of making any decisions like that so soon."

With Perry gone, she didn't trust herself. She could hear him in her head cautioning her, telling her to hold off.

Whatever poor, innocent cat she might bring home didn't deserve less affection and care with a side of regret because she made a rash decision in the midst of mourning her dead twin.

"Nevermind. It's a bad idea."

Flynn jumped up and strode over to stand in front of her. "Muffin, you've wanted a cat for years. Perry almost got you one multiple times, but never did because he could never find the perfect one."

"I never knew that." She didn't like that, Perry planning and doing things she didn't know about, which she realized was ridiculous and a bit insane and unfair, but she couldn't stop herself.

Perry knew everything about her, even the few things she didn't tell him. But unlike her, Perry had more than one best friend who he confided in.

"Let's at least go look. Holding kittens will lift all our moods."

"All right. I guess we can do that." She didn't have to get one. And she probably wouldn't. It was a big responsibility, and she had enough at the moment.

Flynn pumped his fist. "Awesome. I was hoping we could get out of here today and go do something fun."

"No promises. I'm just looking." It would be nice to have a furry little warm body curled up with her in her bed since she'd no longer have hot firemen beneath her sheets.

They needed to go back home before she let something slip. Or did something foolish, like kiss one of them.

They saw her as a sister, not the love interest in a friends-to-lovers romance novel. She really needed to stop reading that specific trope because it made her hope for things she could never have.

Flynn winked. "Of course. Only get one if you fall in love."

"Even then, I might not." She twisted her hair into a colorful French braid, not feeling like styling it like she usually did.

Flynn scowled at her, strangely upset over her words. "That's dumb. Why would you walk away if you fell in love?"

She searched the room for her phone and purse. "Because it probably isn't the right time. I'm not in the right frame of mind to meet the needs of anything who needs my attention and affection." Though at least a cat wouldn't abandon her like everyone else in her life. Except it could die like Perry. Like her mother.

She couldn't handle another loss and rescued cats so often ended up with major health problems. This was a terrible idea. She should just stay here.

Flynn shook his head, his expression completely serious, like he was trying to make her understand something important. "Finding something or someone to love might help heal the pain you're suffering through. I'm sure the cat would understand when you have your moments of shutting down. Besides that's the good thing about cats. They don't need constant affection and attention like dogs do."

Why did it seem like they were no longer talking about a cat?

"We'll see. Let's just go before I change my mind."

Flynn grinned wide and opened her door, hustling Poppy out of her room. "Hey, douchebags. We're headed to the shelter to cuddle puppies and kittens."

Chapter 9

Poppy was relieved the animal shelter was within walking distance from her place. She couldn't handle riding in a car quite yet. She'd been too lost in grief and pain for the funeral to pay attention to it, but now with her head clearer, she refused to get into a vehicle.

She wasn't ready.

Just the thought of it made her imagine Perry's end. What it was like for him, what he felt, what it looked like, what his last thoughts were.

It was too much.

The guys didn't even suggest driving, seeming to enjoy the fresh air and hot sun.

She hesitated outside the shelter, uncertain if this was actually a good idea. Seeing all these animals who needed homes, who were abandoned and alone might not be the best thing for her in her current frame of mind.

Poppy wasn't completely unaware of the fact that she had some abandonment issues. It was going to take all her control not to adopt every single animal in here so they would no longer be alone.

Dean hung back with her. "Are you all right?"

"This isn't a kill shelter, is it?" Poppy asked.

Dean shook his head. "No. No. They don't do that here."

"Maybe you guys should bring a friend home too. You could get a dog. Oh, a dalmatian and then take him with you to the fire station to be your mascot." She was rambling and couldn't shut up.

Why was she so nervous and scared? She'd been to shelters before and been able to walk back out again.

Flynn joined them, his green eyes bright at the idea. "We should. We've talked about a pet before, but we're all gone at the same time so it doesn't seem fair to the dog to leave them alone so often."

"I'd offer to watch it while you guys were at work, but I can't exactly have an animal in my shop. Health codes."

"We could possibly talk our chief into letting us bring it sometimes into the station."

Dean huffed at Flynn's words. "Good luck with that."

"Or you could hire a dog nanny," Poppy said.

"Is that a thing?" Dean asked.

She shrugged. "Probably. If it's not, it should be. That would be an awesome job."

Flynn grinned. "That's going in my retirement plan when I'm too old to fight fires anymore."

"All right. I'm done stalling."

Dean frowned. "You don't have to do this, Poppy."

"I know. But we came all the way here. Just don't let me make a foolish decision in here."

"We'll try our best." Gavin opened the door.

Not as reassuring as she'd hoped, but she didn't want to turn tail and run home, scared by a bunch of adorable animals.

Her nose wrinkled as she stepped through the doors, the stench almost triggering her gag reflex.

A cute white girl greeted them. "Hello. What can I do for the four of you today?"

"We're here to check out your cats," Gavin said.

She gave them a sunny smile and stood from her desk. "Of course. We have several who need good homes. Follow me."

They trailed behind her as she led them through two doors into a cat prison. Kennel after kennel after kennel of poor, sad cats.

Like she wasn't depressed enough.

This was a truly horrible idea.

The yowling and little cries and mewls hurt her ears and her heart. She wanted to scoop every last one into her arms and run away to take them home with her.

Until her eyes caught on a fluffy gray cat who walked like it was a little drunk before bussing its head against the metal cage.

Like she was caught in a spell, Poppy approached the kennel and squatted in front of the cat.

"That one is blind in one eye. Her name is uh... well, Cyclops." She grimaced. "One of our volunteers named her. A high school boy."

"That is awesome." Flynn chuckled.

Poppy agreed. "Can I go in with her?"

"Sure." The woman opened the cage door for Poppy to slip through, closing it behind her before the cat could make a bid for freedom.

Cyclops didn't startle or dart away from Poppy, instead the adorable thing rubbed up against Poppy's legs, her purr as loud as a kitten's.

Poppy's heart melted as she bent to pick up the furrball. The cat immediately buried her little head in the crook of Poppy's shoulder, her purring almost vibrating through Poppy's bones.

She fell completely, madly, inconceivably in love.

GAVIN HAD TO CLEAR the emotion from his throat as he watched a cat with a jacked up name who looked like she won a terrible fight cuddle into Poppy's arms.

"What's the story with Cyclops?" Dean asked the woman helping them, worry for Poppy tensing the corners of his eyes.

"She came to us about six months ago. She's been here longer than most. Other than her eyesight, she's healthy and up to date on all her shots. She's four years old and usually pretty scared of people. It's amazing that she went right up to your...girlfriend?"

"Just a friend." Gavin swallowed a curse. He should have lied.

The girl's smile brightened. "Really? Can I get your number?"

"Sorry. No." He only had an interest in one person and it had been that way for a very long time.

"Oh. Taken?"

"Something like that." Gavin couldn't tear his attention from the woman with rainbow hair who was smiling wider than he'd seen in weeks.

Dean came over and rescued him. "I think she's going home with that wretched cat and she has no pet supplies for her place."

Gavin could fix that. "Right. You and Flynn can stay here and I'll run to the pet store and grab some stuff."

"How long does this process usually take?" Dean asked the woman.

"Once she makes a final decision, around half an hour for the paperwork. We aren't as stringent here as other organizations."

Perfect. There was a pet store not too far from here. "I'll meet you guys back at her place then."

"Do you have any idea what cats need?" Dean smirked.

Gavin shrugged. "Litter, box, food." What else could the little thing possibly need?

"You might also want to consider food and water dishes too. And a collar and some toys."

For crying out loud. "Do you want to go instead?"

"No." Dean eyed the woman still hovering at Gavin's side. "You need to go."

He did. "Right. Let her know?"

"Will do. And I'll text you if she talks herself out of it."

Gavin looked over at Poppy who still rocked the purring cat in her arms, whispering into its ear. "I don't think that's going to be a problem."

A rare soft smile creased Dean's eyes as he watched her too. "Me either."

He was so far gone on their girl. They all were. But it still wasn't the time.

Gavin took one last look at the happiness and peace on Poppy's face before he left. Even if she brought the raggedy cat home with her that feeling would not last. But hopefully Cyclops would bring it out in her more and more while she was trapped in this hell.

The pet store was only two blocks down on the way back to Poppy's store. The massive size of it overwhelmed him. His family only had dogs when he was growing up. He knew next to nothing about cats other than they were assholes.

A dude who was way too happy to be working here popped up in front of Gavin. "Hi. Welcome to Pet World. Can I help you find anything?"

"Uh, well. A friend of mine is getting a cat at the shelter and needs a few things."

"Oh how fun. Right this way, I'll take you to the cat side of the store."

Cats needed an entire side of this place?

Half an hour later, he was two hundred dollars poorer with four bags of stuff. Apparently, cats needed more than a place to shit and food. They needed toys and a bed and something called a cat tree and matching dishes, a spiked collar and an extra purple one, cat weed, shampoo, and flea medication for just in case. He also had a personalized tag being made with the cat's name and Poppy's number on it.

He might have gone overboard, but he wanted the cat to work for her. And the overly peppy dude was so annoying Gavin just agreed to everything to get him to shut up.

Juggling four bags and a cat tree back to Poppy's wasn't easy or fun. Dean better not have forgotten to text him if she changed her mind.

He'd get a punch right in the dick if he did.

Chapter 10

Poppy cringed at Cyclop's yowling and scratching at the box the entire walk home. She felt awful for the poor thing and hoped Cyclops wouldn't hold it against her.

She still couldn't believe she'd actually adopted a cat. But she was so sad and adorable and had the most kickass name. And no one was going to adopt a half-blind cat. It would have lived its life out in that awful cat jail.

"Gavin really didn't have to go and get the stuff for Cyclops." She felt bad. She hadn't even noticed him leaving.

"He needed an excuse to get out of there," Dean said.

Her brows furrowed. "Why? I know he isn't a cat fan, but he doesn't hate them. Was it the smell?"

Flynn snickered. "The smell of desperation."

Dean elbowed him. "Don't be a dick."

"What are you guys going on about?"

"Just a little too much flirting from the girl helping us for Gavin to stomach."

She ignored the stabbing feeling in her stomach at Flynn's explanation. She had plenty of experience shoving aside jealousy and longing when it came to these three. They were gorgeous firemen, and most women had at least one fantasy about hot firefighters. It was a cliche for a reason.

"She was cute. What was the problem?"

"She's not quite what Gavin is looking for." Dean exchanged a strange glace with Flynn.

"What is he looking for?" She cursed herself for allowing the question to slip out.

Dean shot her a strange look. "You'll have to ask him that."

Poppy shrugged, not really wanting to talk to Gavin about his perfect woman.

"Are you sure you don't want one of us to carry your monster?" Flynn reached for the box.

She hugged it tighter to her chest and glared at him. "She's not a monster. Stop being a dick."

Flynn held his hands up. "Jeez. What is with all the dick accusations? I was trying to be gentlemanly."

Dean shoved Flynn in the shoulder. "Try harder."

Poppy rushed to answer before Flynn did something ridiculous. "I want to carry her. She's not heavy, and she needs to get used to my scent." She had no idea if it was true, but figured it would stop any argument from them.

Besides, they were almost back to her place.

Where Gavin waited right outside with a bunch of overflowing bags.

Was there anything left in the store? "What is all that? And why are you out here?"

"Dean has the extra key. And this crap is evidence of me being a complete sucker when it comes to annoying sales people."

Dean unlocked the door of the shop while Flynn helped Gavin with the bags.

Poppy went to snap a picture to send to Perry before she remembered. There wasn't anyone to receive it.

Dean noticed the look on her face and left the other two to drag a bunch of cat shit upstairs to her apartment. "What is it?"

Her fingers dug into the box. "I keep forgetting he's gone. I turn to look for him or go to call or text him before I remember. I have these moments of peace, hell even almost happiness like I haven't had my heart ripped out and then I remember. For a moment, every time I wake up, he's out there somewhere alive, living his life. And then I remember. And now I've adopted a cat and I don't know if I can be what she needs."

Dean's brown eyes darkened to almost black with shred pain as he reached passed the carrier to grip her shoulders. "Oh, baby. All that cat needs is a comfortable home, food, and the occasional rub and cuddle. She'll be there to curl up next to you when you're sad and lonely. She'll be there to catch your tears. She'll be there to make you laugh when she's high on catnip or bumping into shit because she can't see." He thumbed a stray tear off her cheek. "And the rest you might have to live with for a while. I've caught myself doing the same thing and I've seen the others frowning at their phones so I'm pretty sure they are too. It's okay to find moments of happiness in the middle of all this. It's normal. It's human."

Poppy nodded. It was the same with her mother. She was mostly miserable, but had times where she had fun. She still went to call her after a shitty day or when something exciting happened or just to chat.

Dean released her shoulders. "Come on. Let's get your new friend settled in and see how she likes her new home."

She hauled the still complaining cat up the stairs, her mouth falling open when she opened the door to her home. "How long were we downstairs?"

Dean snorted and took the cardboard cat carrier from her and set it on the floor while she took in her living room.

Gavin and Flynn had put a cat tree right beside the window and placed the cat bed on the floor between her two chairs. A basket of cat toys was under the coffee table and an already filled litter box was in the far corner with a mat beneath it.

"This is amazing."

Flynn and Gavin grinned, looking way too proud of themselves. She bent down to release Cyclops, who shot out of the box like a bullet with a hiss of displeasure. She went straight under the couch and cowered there in absolute terror.

"Well, that's a bit disappointing." Flynn bent his body in half to peek under the couch, jerking back with a curse when Cyclops hissed and swatted at him.

"Give her a minute. She's gone through hell and now everything has changed for her. She's got a new life she doesn't recognize anymore. It's scary."

Dean caught her gaze with his. "I think the two of you are going to get along just fine."

She thought so too. If anyone could understand the cat's fear and confusion, it was Poppy.

Chapter 11

Poppy kept a wide smile on her face as the guys left, needing to get back home so they could prepare for their shift. She didn't want them to put their lives on hold any longer to stay with her. They had their own burdens to face and get through by going back home to a place Perry no longer lived in.

As the door closed behind them, the smile dropped off her face and the first tear fell. She'd been holding them back while the guys were here, trying to focus on sleep and spending time with them.

But now, she was alone, and she could release all the pain and heartache she'd had building in her chest.

She stumbled over to her couch, collapsing onto it sideways, the tears falling faster and faster. The cushions still smelled like the guys. Her bed probably did too. They'd completely taken over her space over the two days while they were here with her. And with them gone, her empty home echoed around her.

Cyclops trotted over and jumped up beside her, butting her head into Poppy's hand, demanding love. It was only the second time she'd come out today since they brought her home. She was terrified of the guys.

Poppy was relieved to finally see her, relieved the cat finally came out of hiding and wanted a little affection.

She readjusted on the couch so Cyclops could find a more comfortable spot, yanking at the throw blanket hanging off the side, fighting to get her tears under control. But they refused to stop, instead they continued leaking down her face, soaking the green throw pillow beneath her head.

Her chest ached and her nose clogged as pain rippled through her so hard she couldn't breathe.

She was scared to live alone, to live without him. Who was she supposed to call when she needed company or when she needed cheering up? Who was she supposed to call when she had a hard decision to make and needed advice?

She didn't want to cry anymore. She didn't want to feel like an empty, broken doll. She didn't want to pretend to be whole and strong in front of the guys and then crumple to the floor every time they left.

Poppy hated this. She wasn't this person. She wasn't a coward who shut herself away from the world and hid her true feelings.

After her mother died, she didn't sink so deep. She still cried, missing her sometimes, but she could keep going, keep moving through her life.

But this loss, Perry's loss, had ruined her.

And she didn't know how to climb out of the pit of despair she was trapped in.

She could hear his voice in her head, telling her it was grief, it was normal.

Well, she hated it. Grief was a scream no one could hear. It was a roaring in your ears, drowning out everything else. It was falling and never hitting bottom.

She wanted to hear his voice for real again. She was desperate for it. With a choked apology to the cat, she squirmed until she got her phone out of her pocket. Cyclops settled as soon as Poppy stilled. She dialed Perry's number and brought the phone up to her ear. It went straight to voicemail since she'd turned it off last week, sick of the notifications.

Poppy held her breath as she listened to his voice in her ear, telling her to leave a message. She hung up and dialed again. And again.

After listening for the seventh time, she spoke, leaving a message for a man who would never hear it. Unless he could somehow hear her from wherever he was.

"Hey Pear Tree. It's Poppyseed. Damn, those nicknames are lame. But I miss hearing you call me that. And I miss your stupid face. We were supposed to do all this together. How could you leave me like everyone else did? I'm alone. Completely. Everyone leaves. Everyone abandons me. Am I cursed? I don't know what to do without you here giving me your usually unasked for opinions. I don't know how to do any of this without you. I love you so much, you jerk." The phone dropped from her hand, clattering to the floor beside the couch as Poppy curled into herself with a sob.

Cyclops shot away from her in alarm, making Poppy cry even harder. Even the cat left her. She clutched the blanket against her face, trying to muffle the wrecked sounds coming out of her.

A strange noise joined her cries, jolting her a little bit out of her grief. It was Cyclops. The cat was crying with her, mourning with her.

Cyclops sat right by the couch, guarding Poppy, raging against their shitty worlds together.

FLYNN WAS GLAD TO BE back at the fire station. Even though Perry had worked there with them too, it wasn't as bad as being at home without him. At the firehouse, they weren't alone; they were busy. The clamor of their team surrounded him and he could finally breathe.

It was quieter than usual tonight since everyone here was missing Perry, but not like their house. The quiet at home suffocated him.

Flynn wished they could talk Poppy into coming and staying with them. He was convinced having her there would help with the loud silence in their home with Perry gone.

Once they left her place, the three of them had gone their separate ways, shutting themselves away. Gavin was usually the one who brought them together, but even he was too lost to put in the effort.

Without Poppy to focus on, they all sank into the darkness clinging to them.

He felt like a dick about it, but Flynn hoped for a massive, angry fire to battle against tonight. He needed the release, the adrenaline, the win.

He needed to save someone.

The way he couldn't save Perry.

He was too late for him.

Maybe tonight, he would be on time. He'd be fast enough.

He wouldn't be partying at his bar while a member of his family died alone.

Fuck.

Flynn's hands curled into fists on his thighs and he swallowed the roar trying to claw up his throat.

Gavin plopped onto the couch next to him. "Have you heard back from Poppy?"

"She said she was busy with work and was fine." Flynn huffed. She always said she was fine. She refused to let them in. It was killing him.

Gavin laid his head back against the couch. "Right."

"Where's Dean?" Flynn hadn't seen him since they got to work.

"Not sure."

"He disappearing on us again?" Flynn's jaw clenched.

Dean disappeared sometimes when things got to be too much for him. When he felt like things were out of his control. He didn't like to be around other people until he settled himself.

Perry had been the one who understood that part of Dean, the one who had been able to pull him out of it.

Gavin rubbed at his eyes, looking exhausted. "He might be. I hope not."

Without Poppy to curl up with, they were back to shitty sleep.

"Shit." Flynn could barely hold himself together. He didn't know how to help Dean. Or Gavin.

"I have an idea for this weekend."

Flynn's brows rose. "What?"

Gavin didn't get the chance to explain before the alarm blared and the lights flashed.

They leapt to their feet and raced for the truck, feet and hearts pounding. Fire.

Chapter 12

The next four days, Poppy spent running around on autopilot. She made drinks, rose early in the morning to bake, she smiled and nodded and wished customer after customer a good day. She answered the steady texts from the guys, assuring them she was fine.

At night, she flopped into her bed with her cat and waited for the comforting presence of unconsciousness to find her.

She still needed to get the books for the shop in order, meet with the lawyer, learn the business side of owning the shop, there were bills to catch up on, insurance forms to fill out, and she should take fresh flowers to Perry's grave and her mother's.

Instead, she kept making coffee and baking pastries, letting Tam and Marie handle most of the rest.

She'd get to it soon. With a holiday coming up, they were busier than usual and it was just better to wait until next week once the celebrations were over and things were back to normal.

Their shop was in historic downtown and the town always put on a big show every Fourth of July. Which was frustrating since they were always closed for the holiday. For every holiday. Perry had argued, but Poppy put her foot down on that. She'd rather take the financial hit than be one of those shitty businesses who made their employees work when they should be enjoying the holidays with their loved ones.

She wished she was open this year, so she'd have an excuse not to go to Stacy's house for the big party. But after a phone call, multiple texts, and two reminder emails from her along with a few mentions from the guys, Poppy couldn't bear to disappoint Gavin's mom.

But returning to her childhood neighborhood was going to kill her.

The bell rang, and she looked up to see the guys walk in.

She plastered on a smile as they approached the counter. "Hey guys. What are you doing here?"

Flynn's eyes widened in innocence. "We used to visit all the time on our days off. We like your coffee."

She held back a sigh. "What can I get you, then?"

They put in their orders and she waved them off to a table while she got to work making them. They didn't pay here. They never had. Especially since they'd helped so much when she and Perry first opened the place.

Once she had their coffees ready and their food arranged on a tray, she brought them over to their table by the window.

Gavin grabbed her wrist. "Sit down with us a minute. We have something we want to run by you."

Poppy set the tray onto the table and looked back over towards the counter, but Tam and Marie were handling it fine.

"All right." She took the remaining seat next to Dean. "What's up?"

"Mom said you're coming to the party."

"I am." She bobbed her head.

"Do you want to ride with us?" Gavin asked.

"Sure." That wasn't exactly a conversation she needed to sit with them for.

"We were wondering if you wanted to come back to our place with us and finish out the weekend there."

Her head jerked up to face Flynn. "Why?"

He gave a half-shrug. "So we can try to have a little fun. Or at least hide away from the world together for a couple days."

Poppy searched for an excuse to say no. "What about Cyclops? I don't want to leave her so soon for so long."

"Bring her to our house," Gavin offered. "We can come pick her up on our way back into town."

"Are you sure that's a good idea?"

"Why?" Flynn asked. "Because she hates us? We don't want her to so it'll give her a chance to get to know her better."

She shook her head. "I don't know if bringing her to a new place is a good plan."

"She'll be fine. It's not like you're leaving her there. She'll have you with her." Dean sipped his black coffee.

True. But was she ready to go back there? Did she want to spend the weekend holed up in her apartment?

"All right. Fine. We can do that." She needed to go through Perry's things at their place anyway.

And she really didn't want to spend a boring, lonely holiday alone.

"Awesome. We'll be here to pick you up in the morning."

POPPY TURNED THE SIGN on the door to closed and went back to the counter to box up the leftover pastries. There weren't many left, it had been a busy day. Marie usually took anything they had left to the women's shelter on her way home every night.

Tam spoke from where she was wiping off the bottles of syrup behind Poppy. "I couldn't help but overhear earlier. You're spending the weekend with your fellas?"

Poppy sighed. "They aren't my fellas. They're my friends. Well, more Perry's friends than mine. But yeah. Gavin's mom throws a big party every year for the fourth."

Marie walked over after finishing sweeping up the floor of the shop. "Are you going to be up for it?"

Poppy snorted. "Not really, no. But she'll be disappointed if I don't show and I guess it's better than spending it alone with my cat."

Tam almost knocked over the line of syrup bottles as she spun to gape at Poppy. "Cat? Since when did you get a cat?"

"Last weekend. She's half blind and her name is Cyclops." And Poppy adored the hell out of her. She was so sweet and feisty and Poppy didn't have an ounce of regret over adopting her.

Tam laughed. "That is the best thing I've ever heard."

Poppy grinned. "I didn't name her, but how could I leave her there with that kickass of a name?"

Tam ran her rag over the counter. "You couldn't. I want to meet this little monster."

Marie clapped her hands. "Yeah. Let's order dinner and meet Cyclops."

Poppy actually liked the idea. "Uh, sure. I think I still have some beer left in the fridge."

Marie beamed. "Excellent. You go upstairs and order whatever you like, we'll finish up here."

Tam winked at her. "Yeah, I bet you need to clean up before we see your messy home."

Tam wasn't wrong. She'd let things go after the guys left. They'd handled all the cleaning while they were there and it hadn't taken long for the mess to pile up in their absence.

Poppy closed the boxes and set them on the counter for Marie to take later. "Just pay the delivery person out of the register and put the receipt in there so I don't forget."

Marie frowned. "You don't have to pay for it."

"I'll write it up as a business expense. We'll make sure we do something business related while we're up there." She could use a little help with that side of things.

Tam chuckled. "I like the way you think."

"I have my moments of brilliance."

Poppy left them to it and hurried upstairs, unable to remember how bad her place actually was. She hadn't been paying attention, the only thing she'd kept up with was the cat litter, not wanting Cyclops to have a gross bathroom.

It wasn't as bad as she feared, mainly just a lot of dirty coffee mugs, overflowing trash, and clothes and shoes scattered around the floor.

She pulled up the app for her favorite delivery on her phone and put in an order. Since she'd spent so much time with Tam and Marie, she knew what they liked.

With the food on the way, she hurried around, shoving the bag of trash onto the fire escape, the mugs in the dishwasher, and she threw her clothes and shoes into her room and closed the door. Good enough.

She sniffed, and it still smelled like trash and litter, so she lit a candle. There. Ready for company.

It wasn't Tam and Marie's first time visiting her place. She'd had them up a few times to get to know them after they started working for her and Perry and it had looked a lot worse. She wasn't the best at domestic chores. Perry was the one who cleaned for her once he couldn't stand it any longer.

Now, she was going to have to learn if she didn't want to live in a dump.

Knuckles tapped at her door and Tam stuck her head in. "Do you need more time to clean or are you ready?"

"Come on in."

"We've got the food. Where's the new baby?" Marie held up a big paper bag.

"I haven't seen her since I came back in." Poppy grimaced. She'd forgotten the cat and had probably terrified Cyclops with all the running around and cleaning.

"Are you sure you really have a cat?" Marie pulled out the boxes from the bag and passed them out.

Poppy grabbed three beers from her fridge and carried them to her table. "I'm sure. She'll come out maybe once no one is moving around in here. She hates the guys though."

Marie laughed. "That's hilarious."

"We will make her love us so we can rub it in their faces." Tam popped open her beer and took a sip.

Poppy chuckled as she dug into her salad.

"So, how are you really doing?" Marie asked.

"I'm fine." Poppy shoved a bite of food into her mouth.

Marie didn't look convinced. "Uh huh. We don't have to talk about it if you don't want to. We can just chat about your guys and your new cat and bond over how much we love coffee. But if you need to talk it out, we can do that too."

Poppy rubbed at her chest. "I can't. I spiral when I think about it too long or try to talk about it."

"Ignoring the elephant in the room it is." Tam raised her beer in the air.

"Thanks. Sorry." Poppy knew they just wanted to be there for her, but she couldn't open up. Not right now.

Marie shook her head. "Don't be. Whatever you need, we're here for."

Poppy sat back, relief filling her. "Hiring the two of you was the best decision I ever made."

"Damn straight." Tam clinked her beer bottle against Poppy's.

Poppy could breathe again when they let the dead brother subject go.

It was selfish and shitty of her, but she wanted a night to hang out with her friends and not sit and rehash her loss. A night to pretend. A night to try to forget that her world was forever damaged.

Marie gasped and stiffened.

"What?" Worry thudded in Poppy's chest.

Marie put a finger to her lips. "Shh. I think I just saw your cat."

Tam sat up higher. "Where?"

"Peeking her head out of the living room. Nobody move. Maybe she'll come to eat."

Poppy sucked her cheeks into her mouth to keep from laughing as Marie and Tam froze. Tam still clutched her beer and Marie had her fork halfway to her mouth.

Little clicking noises came from Poppy's mouth as she tried to call the cat over. Cyclops yowled, but refused to come all the way into the kitchen, eyeing them with suspicion with her head tilted so she could see them out of her good eye.

"Oh my gosh she is so ugly she's the most adorable thing I've ever seen." Marie couldn't keep the squee out of her voice.

Which sent Cyclops racing off towards Poppy's bedroom, knocking over a stack of books on her way.

Tam slumped with a pout. "She hates us. Dammit."

Poppy tried to hide her amusement. She kind of liked being the only one Cyclops trusted. "I think it's just going to take time for her to get used to the new people in her life."

Marie tapped her bottom lip in thought. "You know, instead of taking her with you to the guys' house, we could check up on her for you."

"Are you trying to steal my cat from me?" Poppy narrowed her eyes on her friend. She didn't trust Marie's innocent expression.

"Not steal. But be able to borrow sometimes. My boyfriend is allergic, so I can't have one until I decide to kick him to the curb. And I'm much less noisy and scary than three huge firemen in a new place after barely getting comfortable in this one."

"What if she thinks I abandoned her?" Poppy knew Marie had a point, but she didn't want the cat to feel left behind. She knew exactly how shitty that felt.

Tam snorted. "It's three days, not three months."

Poppy gnawed on her bottom lip. "I should just stay instead of going back to their place."

Marie glared at her. "Don't be stupid. You should go. I'll make sure she's fed, has a clean place to do her little kitty business, has water, and will hang out for a while so she isn't lonely. Tam can come by too if she wants."

Tam shrugged. "I'm more of a dog person, but that thing is going to be my new best friend if it kills me."

"Right. We will call if she seems upset, or she keeps refusing to come out or eat and you can come right home. It's not like you're going to be out of town. Their place is within walking distance."

Poppy blew out a breath. "Okay. That should work."

"Of course it will. We work right downstairs. She needs to get to know us. Besides, if you end up dating one or more of those guys, you might want to have sleepovers. We can take care of her then too." Tam leered.

"I'm not going to be dating any of them. Especially not more than one." That was a dream, a fantasy, she'd left behind long ago.

Tam scowled. "Why the hell not? Have you seen them?"

Poppy chuckled, ignoring her warming face. "Yeah. I knew them back when they had mouths full of braces and pimply faces."

"Did they actually go through an awkward phase or are you making that up?" Tam eyed her with disbelief.

Poppy understood. As gorgeous as they were now it was hard to imagine them gangly and awkward. She'd loved them anyway though. "They really did. I have photographic evidence. But I was awkward at the same time, so they were still hot to me."

"You can't tease us with something like that and not show us."

Poppy rose and ambled into her living room to pull one of her old photo albums off the bookshelf and bring it back to the table.

Marie and Tam pushed the food to the side so Poppy had a clear place to set it down.

She wasn't sure looking through these was a good idea. Perry would be everywhere inside of it. So would her mother.

But maybe it would be good for her.

Marie eyed Poppy, reading the trepidation inside. "You know. We can look at these later."

"No." Poppy shook her head. "Now's fine. If it gets to be too much, I'll have you two here to keep me from going too deep into the dark place."

Tam placed her hand over Poppy's. "You let us know if we need to stop."

"I will. Thanks, you guys. For coming up here today."

Tam's clasp on Poppy's hand tightened. "You've been in a bit of a fog all week. And we were tired of watching you coming up here alone and locking yourself in so early every night."

Marie nodded. "Yeah. We figured we'd lock ourselves in with you."

Poppy smiled in gratitude. "All right. Let's do this then. I might need more beer if we are though."

"On it." Marie jumped up and went to the fridge, bringing the last three beers over.

Poppy took a deep breath as she popped off the lid, drinking deeply before reaching for the cover of the photo album.

"Here we go."

Chapter 13

Poppy woke snuggled in between Tam and Marie. Why were they in bed with her? What the hell happened last night? She needed to stop waking up confused and foggy and with people in her bed.

Right. The photo albums. And the drinks. After the beer ran out, they found a bottle of vodka in the freezer. Tam made up a drinking game -—whenever they came across a photo of Poppy blushing with one of the guys' arms thrown across her shoulder, they drank.

There were a lot of photos of her with a red face. They'd gotten very, very drunk.

It had actually been fun, flipping through old photos of their childhood. Remembering Perry and their life together. Reliving memories of growing up with Perry and the guys -—blanket forts in their house, basketball in the cul-de-sac, birthday parties, holidays, school dances, theme parks, football games. The five of them were together for everything. She'd realized last night she hadn't been on the outside of their group as she thought. Maybe it had just felt that way to her.

It made her rethink everything she thought she knew. Maybe the guys weren't determined to come for her for Perry's sake. Maybe it was for her's. Maybe she could stop fighting against it, fighting against them.

Poppy scooted down her bed, trying not to wake Tam and Marie. The guys would be here to pick her up soon and she still hadn't packed.

Tam groaned and threw her arm across her face. "Sunlight. Bad. Drinking. Bad. Morning. Bad."

"Sorry. Though I remember it being all your idea."

"My ideas. Bad."

Poppy winced against her own headache. "No arguments here." She shoved clothes into a bag, barely paying attention to the outfits she chose. "You and Marie can stay here as long as you want. I'm going to put on some coffee to make for the road and you're welcome to the rest."

Tam groaned again. "Right. Your guys are coming. What time?"

Poppy checked her clock. Shit. "Less than half an hour. I overslept."

"Sorry."

"It wasn't like you used peer pressure against me. You found the bottle, suggested the game, and Marie and I cheered. Literally."

Tam laughed, shaking the bed so hard it roused Marie.

"What the hell. It's a holiday. We should be sleeping." Marie slurred the words and then passed back out, loud snores buzzing from her.

"You should go back to sleep too. Just lock up whenever you guys leave."

"All right, sweetie. Have fun." Tam waved at her before snuggling back with Marie.

"You too. Text me if you need anything. And thank you. For last night."

"Any time."

Poppy finished packing and started a full pot of coffee. She had a thermos to fill to combat the hangover pounding behind her eyes. Though she should spike it if they expected her to ride in a car for half an hour.

Jitters twitched through her, but she breathed through it. The new fear was understandable, but she had to get through it. She couldn't avoid cars forever.

Her phone dinged. The guys were waiting for her downstairs. She double checked Cyclop's food and water, smiling when Cyclops came over to rub against her ankles. Poppy bent to pick her up, cuddling the cat close.

She didn't feel as worried about leaving Cyclops to the care of Tam and Marie after last night. Cyclops had finally emerged, too desperate for food to hide any longer, and Marie and Tam had completely won the distrusting animal over. Cyclops still preferred Poppy, but she accepted the love and affection Tam and Marie had to give.

With one last kiss to the top of Cyclop's head, she set her down and grabbed her stuff.

"Tam and Marie are still here. I'll be back, cutie. Don't hate me."

A soft meow answered her and Poppy almost dropped her bags and stayed behind. But her phone dinged six more times, and she huffed and slipped through the door.

Downstairs, she grabbed the food she'd made for the party and hauled it all outside where Gavin leaned against Dean's car like some gorgeous model from a magazine. He shoved off the car and jogged over to take the bags from her hands and popped them in the trunk.

"Thanks, Gav."

"No problem. You want the front seat or back?"

She wasn't sure. "It doesn't matter."

"Choose. Whichever is easier for you."

She considered it for a moment. Her sight would be more constricted in the back and it might make it easier if she couldn't see the dangers. "I'll sit in the back."

Gavin opened the door for her. "All right. If you need to stop or want to switch, let us know."

"I'll be fine." She slid into the backseat next to Flynn.

Dean glanced over his shoulder at her from the driver's seat. "You really need to delete that word from your vocabulary."

Poppy ignored him as she leaned her head back against the seat, adjusting her huge sunglasses.

"Are you hungover?" Flynn asked, amusement in his tone.

"Maybe a little." She sipped from her thermos, sighing as the elixir of life hit her system.

Dean shook his head as he pulled out into the heavy holiday traffic. "Drinking alone, baby? Should we be worried?"

"No. Tam and Marie were there. Actually, they're still upstairs sleeping it off. Like I should be." Her breath caught as the car moved faster and faster.

"Why don't you lie down on Flynn's lap and try to sleep through the trip. Your coffee will still be hot when we get there." Gavin turned around in the passenger seat, his brows creased.

That was a smart idea. It might make the drive easier on her. She handed her thermos to Gavin and curled up onto the backseat, her head in Flynn's lap. He ran his fingers through her hair, trying to smooth away the headache pounding in her skull.

With her eyes closed, Flynn's fingers in her hair, and the low background noise of soft rock, Poppy could pretend she wasn't in a car. She could sink into a place inside her mind, the place between sleep and awake where everything real seemed like it was trapped behind a wall of fog.

She remained in that place until Flynn nudged her. "We're here."

Poppy sat up and blinked the haze from her eyes, taking in the neighborhood she hadn't seen since last year at the party. Last year, she'd recently lost her mother, and it had almost killed her to be here, but she had Perry there taking on half of the pain.

This time she didn't have him. She'd lost someone else.

A year from now, what more will she have lost? Who would she be? What would her life look like? Would she still be feeling the agony of Perry's loss? Of her mother's?

"You ready for this?" Gavin asked.

"Of course. I'm fine."

Dean huffed at her, but she ignored him again. It was all she knew how to say whether they believed her or not.

Poppy shoved open her door and climbed from the car, turning in a circle to take in the streets she grew up on.

Chapter 14

Hopefully, Stacy had plenty of cocktails because Poppy needed to start drinking as soon as possible to get through this day.

They were the first ones to arrive and as they walked inside Stacy attacked them warm hugs.

"I'm so glad you all made it."

Flynn hugged Stacy back. "Of course. We come every year."

"And we have this conversation every year," Dean muttered under his breath.

Flynn elbowed Dean with a snort. "Which you point out every year."

Stacy saved Poppy for last, their hug lasting longer than the others. Thankfully, Stacy didn't say anything about Perry or her mom, she just let the hug speak for her. Even without words, the warmth and love in Stacy's embrace made tears sting Poppy's eyes.

Stacy released her and they both cleared their throats, their eyes bright with sadness.

"Can I help you with anything?" Poppy asked.

"No, dear. The food you brought is more than enough. I'm almost finished getting everything ready and the other guests will be here in about two hours, so that gives you four time to go to the carnival if you want."

"Carnival?" Gavin's eyes brightened with interest.

Stacy rolled her vacuum into the closet. "It's a new thing the town started this year. It's on the fairgrounds where they set off the fireworks. It runs until around eight tonight, then they shut it down for the show. Your sisters plan to take the kids there later once they're here."

Flynn pumped his fist in the air. "Awesome. We can walk there and check it out if the rest of you are up for it?"

Gavin grinned and shot Poppy a challenging glance. "You in?"

Poppy had never turned down a dare from him. "Hell yeah."

Stacy smiled with fond satisfaction. "You kids have fun. Try to be back by six so you aren't late to eat. And don't ruin your appetites with nasty carnival food."

Poppy chuckled at Stacy talking to them like she used to when they were young. It made her feel like a kid again, like anything was possible, like having fun was the most important thing in the world, like if they raged hard enough maybe their pain would fade or disappear.

Today, she would pretend. She would pretend her only worry was making sure Dean, Flynn, and Gavin didn't discover her feelings for them.

Gavin grabbed her hand and tugged her out the door after Flynn and Dean.

They walked the sidewalks of their old neighborhood, past all the places living on in their memories.

Past the spot Poppy broke her arm after a dare gone wrong with Gavin, the spot where Perry had his first kiss, the spot where Poppy had watched as Flynn kissed one of her friends and then run home in tears, past Dean's old house now owned by a different family, past the park their parents took them to play, past the old basketball court, past the field they played ghost of the graveyard in and camped in and partied in.

So many places swollen with fun and laughter and tears and pain and love and loss.

Memories flickered through her mind like the photos from the album the night before. Memories of dancing with Dean at the prom, butterflies in her stomach as she fantasized about ending the night with a kiss from him. Of cheering the guys on as they played football with the other cheerleaders, wishing she could play with them instead of cheer. Of nights spent around a bonfire playing cards and truth or dare. Of trading pudding cups and apple slices at the park. Of their first time sharing a joint in Dean's backyard while his parents were away on a business trip. Of the night Gavin dared them all to skinny dip and the five of them had each remained in their designated spots, trying to cover their private bits with red faces and embarrassed giggling.

Of trampolines and swings and bike races and fights and secrets and games and lies and parties and dares and spin the bottle and underage drinking and treehouses and falling in love -—impossible love, unrequited love, secret love.

A love she still hadn't gotten over, a secret still burning inside of her. A love still impossible and unrequited.

She'd fallen in love with them when she was young and wild and free. Beneath summer skies dancing with fireflies, shrieks of laughter on her lips.

Then she grew up and buried the feelings. But she never forgot that summer so many years ago. And she'd never been able to shake the feelings off completely.

As hard as she'd tried.

DEAN CAME BACK HERE every year to this neighborhood, but the memories were stronger this time. With Perry's loss still so fresh and painful, everything from their past was closer to the surface today. He hated seeing his old house. It brought back the lonely weeks and the disapproval over his choices and the cold silence.

He barely spoke to his parents now. They exchanged yearly holiday and birthday cards and emails when someone they knew died, got married, or had a kid. His parents liked reminding him of all the other people his age who were married or becoming parents since they hated that he lived with his friends. And that he had squandered a college education by becoming a firefighter and that his desires to be a photographer was a child's fantasy.

What they didn't understand was the family and life he'd created for himself was more important to him than money, his parents' approval, societal expectations, success, or what others considered a normal life.

These people meant everything to him. And his parents hadn't given a single fuck when he'd let them know Perry was dead. They'd replied with a lone sentence expressing their condolences before they'd continued on hinting maybe it was time for him to get his own place.

But fuck them. He didn't care what they thought or wanted. They didn't have time for him when he was a kid; he wouldn't bend himself over backwards to win their support and approval now.

The only people he cared about were right here at his side.

He snapped a picture of Poppy with his phone with the field she stared at with memories in her eyes in the photo's background.

Gavin still had her hand in his, but she didn't seem to notice. She was too lost in remembrance to notice how Gavin wanted her close by. How they all did. They were worried about bringing her back here. They were worried about coming back here themselves, but it wasn't any more painful than living in the same home Perry used to live with them.

Everything sucked right now. For all of them. But focusing on Poppy and making sure she wasn't lost to the fog of grief helped keep them from dwelling too hard on it. Going back home had sucked. Work wasn't much better. Poppy's presence helped. So they were going to make it as fun of a weekend as they could. To keep all of their minds off it.

And Gavin and Poppy together at a carnival was the perfect way. The two of them had always fed off each other when it came to spontaneous adventures where they had a chance to one up the other. Half the trouble they'd gotten into growing up had been because of one of those two and their dares and crazy ideas.

They had seen little evidence of the girl who was always ready for adventure and fun. Since before Perry's death. She disappeared back when her mother first got sick, only peeking out occasionally since then. The new Poppy was darker, sadder, often not completely there with them, lost in thought and memories. The old Poppy lived completely in the moment, giving no care for the past or the future. This Poppy lived almost completely in the past, barely looking up to notice as the present surrounded her.

Sometimes, Dean wanted to shake her and wake her up, remind her she still had a life to lead and adventures to go on. That she had people who loved her and wanted to go on those adventures with her.

Maybe this weekend, they could make her realize it, make her come alive again.

Chapter 15

The music from the carnival reached them first and as soon as the flashing lights and squealing rides came into sight, Gavin rushed forward, dragging her in his wake. She chuckled as she hurried to keep up.

The walk here had been silent and heavy as they spent the time in their own heads. Thankfully, the carnival was new so it wasn't scattered with the ghosts and reminders of Perry and her mother.

For a little while, she could forget.

"Think you can beat me at the ring toss?" Gavin threw the dare at her with a taunting tone and smile.

Oh, he was going down. "Definitely. Loser eats three funnel cakes, then goes on the tilt awhirl."

"Deal." Gavin held out his hand for her to shake.

"You two are insane."

Poppy exchanged an eye roll with Gavin. Dean and Perry always cautioned against their fun while Flynn was usually content to sit back and watch it all unfold.

"If you don't want to play, maybe take a nice boring ride on the Ferris wheel." She pointed at the tallest ride there flashing with welcoming lights.

Dean stepped up close to her and bent to whisper in her ear. "If you join me on the Ferris wheel, it won't be the slightest bit boring."

He stepped back, his expression completely normal, like he hadn't just left her shaken and breathless.

What the hell was that?

Gavin's grip on her hand yanked her out of her fantasies of kissing Dean while the Ferris wheel dipped toward the ground. "Come on, Pop. I've got a bet to win."

She eyed the massive stuffed animals, easily picking out the one she wanted. "I think my prize will be that huge pandicorn when I kick your ass."

"I'll get it for you as a consolation prize when you lose."

The guy running the ring toss booth gave Poppy and Gavin a big smile as they stepped up and handed over money.

Flynn and Dean hung back to watch, Flynn looking amused, Dean looking bored.

They were no fun.

Poppy accepted her rings, ignoring Gavin, not wanting him to distract her. She studied the bottles she needed to land the rings around carefully before she tossed her first one.

Miss.

Shit.

She tossed again.

Miss.

Dammit.

And again.

Yes. Success.

Last one.

Perfect landing.

"And we have a winner." The man pointed at her. "Which prize do you want?"

"The pandicorn, please." She glanced over at Gavin with a gloating face, enjoying his frustrated pout.

She accepted the giant thing, hugging it to her chest. "Time to go order funnel cakes."

Gavin groaned. "I forgot you always win these bets."

It had been a long time since she and Gavin had gone on one of their challenges. It was nice kicking his ass again.

"Come on, buddy. Time to pay up."

Flynn laughed as he plucked the pandicorn from her arms. "I'll carry this monstrosity for you."

"I'm not going on that ride alone. Who's coming with me?" Gavin asked as they headed towards the food trucks.

"After you pound three funnel cakes? Hell no." Dean shook his head.

Poppy shrugged. "I'll go, but you're riding in your own cart. I'm not getting barfed on."

Gavin grumbled as he ordered his funnel cakes while the rest of them grabbed seats at a picnic table, the panda sitting between Poppy and Flynn.

The scent of fried dough and sugar and grilled onions permeated the area, making Poppy's stomach growl, her hangover finally gone.

Gavin dropped the plates onto the table. "We're doing basketball shots next."

"Your funeral." Poppy shrugged, confident. She still shot hoops at the local park when she needed to wind down. "You can choose the stakes this time."

Gavin frowned for a moment as he thought before his face cleared with an arrogant grin. "Loser pays the tab for the rest of the day."

"Deal." Poppy reached across the table to shake Gavin's hand. "But first, you have some fried dough to eat."

He glared at his plate of dessert. "I'm going to have to do so many crunches to burn this off."

"Not if you throw it all up," Flynn said.

"I'd rather do the crunches." Gavin shoved a large piece into his mouth, his lips dusted with powdered sugar.

Poppy handed him a napkin, shoving away the temptation to kiss the sugar off him.

Gavin pursed his sugary lips at her. "You don't want to lick it off? It's quite tasty."

Poppy flushed and clenched her hands in her lap. "I'm good. Stop stalling."

Dean shot her a knowing look and she tore her gaze from his, instead focusing on the carnival sights. It wasn't very busy yet, only a few families there with their kids. It would probably get more crowded closer to time for the fireworks.

Gavin whimpered as he started on the last funnel cake. He never was one for sweets. Flynn would've handled five with no problem. but Gavin liked healthy crap like salads and lean meat. It was the perfect revenge.

Flynn's leg bounced and shook the table. "We're riding some rides after you two finish your next challenge. You guys aren't the only ones here who want to have fun."

"Fine. I don't think Gavin will be able to handle losing anymore after the next one, anyway." She couldn't help herself. She loved teasing Gavin.

Gavin shoved part of the last cake into his mouth, already looking sick. "Oh, there's no way I'm losing again. You're going to pay for this. Literally."

"We'll see."

Gavin pushed himself to his feet, the funnel cakes gone. "All right. Let's do this."

"Dean, are you riding?" Poppy wouldn't mind being trapped between him and Flynn on a tiny ride.

Dean shook his head. "No. I'll stay with your panda. I'm not a big fan of the tilt awhirl."

"Suit yourself." Poppy shoved Gavin in the direction of the ride. "Come on. Time to vomit."

"You're evil."

She snorted. "Like you wouldn't have done the same if I lost?"

Gavin stuck his nose into the air. "I would have been a gentleman and let you bow out gracefully."

She shrugged. "Too bad for you, I'm no gentleman."

He looked down at her with secrets in his eyes. "That's definitely not something any of us find unfortunate."

She hated when they got flirtatious and made comments like this. It always confused her and made it even harder to ignore her feelings for them. Perry always used to interrupted those kinds of comments, which annoyed her too, but at the moment she was missing it.

They paid for the ride and Poppy and Flynn climbed into one of the cars. Far away from Gavin's.

The worker in charge of the ride took her sweet time in checking everyone's doors and buckles.

"Gavin still plays basketball pretty often. How sure are you that you can beat him?" Flynn asked.

She gripped at the bar to keep from sliding her weight all the way into him, their car already tilted and gravity working against her. "I play pickup games and shoot hoops at the park at least once a week. And hopefully he'll still be shaky from a sugar overload."

Flynn laughed. "I missed this."

"What? Me humiliating Gavin?"

He peeled her fingers off the bar and tugged her down the seat into his side, throwing an arm across her shoulders. "Yes, but not just that. Watching you two go head to head is always hilarious. I'd been worried you had grown out of it."

Poppy sobered. "Not so much grown out of it as much as life kept getting in the way."

Flynn squeezed her arm. "It's still nice to see you laugh again and enjoy yourself. You've been strained around us for a while now."

She didn't know what to say in response. She could blame it on all the adulting she'd been swamped with or the loss of her mother or general busyness, but it had begun long before any of that.

Years and years before that. And it had gotten harder and harder to hide. What could she say to him? That it hurt being around them when she still hadn't been able to get over her crushes on all three of them? They'd be horrified. Especially since it wasn't just one. It was all three.

All. Three.

Even though they lived together and worked together and shared basically everything, it didn't mean they wanted to share a girlfriend.

The ride lurched to a start, saving her from having to come up with something to say in response.

It started slow, but was quick to pick up speed and Poppy's heart did as well as excitement coursed through her. She loved fast rides, loved the sensation of her belly dropping, loved the speed.

Her laughter rang out and her face ached from the wide smile on her face, all her concerns and awkwardness whipped away by the air rushing past them.

This was bliss. Utter bliss.

GAVIN COULDN'T STOP grinning as they walked back to his mom's house. He'd lost every single challenge to Poppy, but seeing her smile and triumph made it all worth it. He hadn't seen her so happy and carefree in a very long time. And he hadn't had such fun in a long time either.

Even Dean had defrosted enough to shout and laugh on the rides and Flynn hadn't subsided into an angry brooding once.

They had needed this.

His mom had promised she would be more selective of who she invited to the party this year so it would be less stressful on all of them. His sisters and their families and a few close friends from her church and book club instead of basically everyone she knew like most years.

He didn't want Poppy or Flynn and Dean to have to deal with the comments and the questions and the sympathy.

Not this year.

Poppy didn't need to go through that and neither did they. Especially not after having such a fun afternoon.

Flynn and Poppy walked side by side, chatting about something while Flynn still carried around that panda unicorn hybrid thing. The other prizes she'd won, she'd gifted to a few children at the carnival, but refused to give away the pandicorn.

"You still feeling sick?" Dean asked from his spot next to Gavin.

"No. That passed a while ago." Gavin was just glad he hadn't ended up with his face in a trash can. He'd felt awful after the ride, but it passed pretty quickly.

"Today was fun."

Gavin smiled. "It was. She seems better today."

"Hope it lasts." Dean yanked on his ear.

"Me too. Sorry you didn't get a chance to make a move on the Ferris wheel." Gavin smirked at his friend.

She had ended up on the ride with Flynn. Who also hadn't made a move.

"We decided we'd wait." Dean sounded like he regretted the decision.

Gavin did too. "I know. But it was harder today than it usually is."

None of them had been able to keep from teasing her with flirtatious comments and little touches.

"Yeah. It was."

Because today was like things used to be other than Perry's glaring absence. And this was the place where they all fell for her, so those feelings were stronger here.

Gavin wanted to kiss her beneath the fireworks, but he couldn't. She needed more time to get over Perry's loss. And so did they. They were all raw and messed up, so now wasn't the time for romancing the woman they adored.

Now wasn't the time to find out if she didn't want any of them. Or worse, only wanted one.

Chapter 16

Poppy still rode the high of winning as she followed the guys back inside Gavin's childhood home. Flynn put her pandicorn in the backseat of Dean's car to keep it safe before jogging over to join them.

Stacy smiled at their entrance. "Just in time. We're about to eat."

Flynn patted his belly. "Good. I'm starving."

A fond expression crossed Stacy's face. "Of course you are."

Flynn's face softened with love and appreciation for the woman who took better care of them than his own parents. "I miss your food, Mama Stacy."

"I have a couple lasagnas in the fridge for you to take back with you."

Flynn kissed Stacy's cheek. "I love you."

"Love you too, dear."

The other guests surrounded them with hugs and hellos and introductions. Poppy breathed out a sigh of relief when she realized it was a much smaller crowd this year and she liked everyone here.

Stacy usually invited all who wanted to come, but this year she had cut the guest list in half, which Poppy appreciated. She wasn't in the mood to deal with the gossiping hags from the neighborhood.

Two women shoved through the crowd and Poppy was thrilled to see who threw their arms around her, smooshing her between them. Brittany and Michelle, Gavin's sisters.

"We're so happy to see you." They left unspoken that they'd seen her at the funeral.

Poppy vaguely remembered them being there, but wasn't sure if they spoke. That day was all a blur.

"I'm happy to see you guys too. It sucks that you live so far away."

They lived less than an hour away, but with adult responsibilities and four kids between them, it took a lot to have the chance to see them.

Michelle sighed. "We talk about moving back all the time, but somehow it's never the right time."

"One day. Now where are those little rugrats?" Poppy looked around for them, wanting hugs from the kids who were growing up way too fast.

"They're in the backyard. Mom set up a slip and slide so they're having the time of their lives getting covered in wet grass."

Stacy overheard and harrumphed. "A little lawn clippings never hurt anybody. And it was your brother's idea."

"Of course it was." Brittany rolled her eyes.

Gavin slung an arm over his mother's shoulders. "My nieces and nephews deserve to have a good time when their mothers can't ruin their fun."

Brittany glared at her brother. "Right. Because that's our job in life. To be the ruiners of fun."

Gavin grinned back, unrepentant. "That's how I remember it. Prove me wrong and go slip and slide with your children."

Michelle groaned. "Oh no. Have the two of you been making bets again?"

"Maybe." Poppy avoided their eyes, kicking at the floor.

"And he lost again?" Brittany laughed.

"Every single time." Gavin didn't sound too bothered over it.

He had always been a good loser. Poppy was not.

Michelle poked her brother in the chest. "So he's trying to recover his manhood and win a challenge with us."

Brittany sighed and shook her head. "Just like when we were kids."

Michelle grabbed Poppy's arm. "Sorry, bro. You're going to have to lose this one too. Poppy, come on. You got him all riled up, you're sliding with us. I have a bathing suit you can borrow."

Poppy laughed and let them tug her towards the stairs. "You didn't need to guilt me into it. I love slip and slides."

Michelle glanced over her shoulder at Poppy with a smile playing at the edges of her lips. "Of course you do. I swear you are perfect for those three idiots. Especially our brother."

"All three?"

Brittany opened the door of Gavin's old room. "Of course. Everyone else expects them to find three women to settle down with, but that's never going to happen. They're never going to leave each other. And you're the only person who gets that."

"They don't see me like that. They never have." Poppy hadn't realized Gavin's sisters had noticed the way she pined after them when they were all teenagers. "I outgrew all of that."

"Right." Michelle drew out the word with a skeptical brow raised as she handed Poppy a tiny black bikini.

The three of them stripped and yanked on the bathing suits.

"Maybe try paying attention to their expressions when they see you in that bathing suit." Michelle pointed at Poppy.

Poppy blushed and tried to cover herself a little better with the tiny scraps of fabric. "That won't necessarily mean anything. I have an overabundance of boob showing."

Michelle snorted. "You always have an overabundance of boob showing, babe. You're basically all boob and ass."

"I know." Poppy sighed and frowned at her chest. Stupid things.

Brittany elbowed her. "It's a good thing, dummy. You're hot."

"Oh, I know."

Michelle grinned. "There she is."

Brittany opened the door. "Let's go show Gavin he will never win against any of us."

"Poor guy." Poppy felt a little bad for him, but not much. His sisters loved giving him a hard time. It was hilarious.

"He'll be fine. We taught him how to lose to girls very early in life."

"I remember." Poppy was certain they were the reason he'd never gotten butthurt over how often she beat him at their games.

Michelle threaded their arms together. "Damn, I've missed you. We have to make more of an effort to get together."

"We do. I don't have kids so it should be easier for me to come visit you guys." Guilt plagued her. She should have been making more of an effort.

Brittany waved a careless hand through the air. "You own and run a business that's open six days a week. I'd say you have plenty keeping you here."

"You both work too."

Michelle shrugged. "Yeah, but we have the whole weekend off. But then the kids have sports and recitals and plays. Ugh."

"We'll figure it out. Once a year for Independence Day isn't enough."

"Agreed."

Poppy had forgotten how close the two of them were. They weren't twins, but they were so close in age, they might as well have been. They'd even moved their families into the same neighborhood and their husbands worked together.

It made the ache in her chest grow as she watched them finish each other's thoughts. Just like her and Perry.

But the pain faded as four little wet bodies collided with her. "Aunt Poppy!"

FLYNN MADE A STRANGLED noise when Poppy came outside with Gavin's sisters dressed in a tiny black bikini barely keeping her tits covered. Dean stiffened next to him, sucking in a sharp breath. Flynn didn't need to look at his friend to know they had matching expressions of shock and want on their faces.

Wherever Gavin had disappeared to, he probably looked the same.

Fuck.

Her rainbow hair tumbled around her shoulders and her blue eyes were bright with happiness as the kids crowded around her, demanding hugs and kisses.

Poppy hated black, but she looked deadly in the color. Flynn shifted on his feet, peeling his eyes away from her body he wanted to sink his teeth into. He searched for Gavin in the crowd of people in the backyard and spotted him looking like someone had punched him in the throat.

She had no idea. No idea how wrecked they were for her.

The kids led her and their mothers towards the slip and slide, almost vibrating with excitement that the adults were joining them.

Poppy's bathing suit was almost indecent and Flynn wasn't sure if he hoped or feared that she'd spill out of her top when she took her turn.

Michelle and Brittany's suits didn't cover any more than Poppy's, but Flynn barely noticed. He only had eyes for one. Only one of his best friend's sisters had ever gotten to him.

Stupid bro code had stopped them when they were younger, but as the years passed and their feelings didn't fade, bro code started to itch.

A few months ago, they'd sat Perry down at one of their family meetings and talked about it. They'd explained how they felt, what they wanted, how they thought it would work. Perry wasn't thrilled, but he wasn't as against the idea as he once was. Maybe because Poppy had never found happiness with anyone else and neither had they.

Even after all this time.

But then Perry died and left them all reeling and unmoored. And as much as Flynn wanted to lose himself in Poppy's curves, everything was on hold for now.

With a smirk at Gavin, who had recovered control over his face, Poppy went first. She took a running start and then sailed through the water with a shriek of laughter, moving so fast she slid completely past the end and into the mud.

Oh hell. Now she looked like one of those women mud wrestlers.

Flynn turned his back on it all and stomped over to the table covered in food. If he wanted to get through the day without a raging hard-on, he couldn't watch that.

Dean joined him, then Gavin, the three of them exchanging strained glances.

That woman had always and would always be the end of them.

Chapter 17

Poppy chuckled as Stacy fussed and rinsed her, Brit, and Michelle off, the grass and mud sliding from their skin.

The kids still played, but the three of them were sore and rug burned. Slip and slides were a lot easier on the body when you were young.

After ringing the water from her hair, Poppy wrapped herself in the fluffy blue towel Stacy handed her. She was starving, but she wanted to get dressed before she ate. She looked around for the guys and found them clumped together chatting quietly. They hadn't stayed to watch or join the fun, instead they'd disappeared soon after she came out.

Dry enough she wouldn't mess up Stacy's house, Poppy slipped inside and back upstairs to Gavin's old room. She hadn't really paid attention when she changed in here before.

It looked nothing like it used to, Stacy had turned it into a guest room after he finished college. It was still weird being in here. She'd never spent much time in here when they were kids, they'd hung out in the den or backyard. Though she'd had daydreams of being in here with Gavin.

Dirty ones.

She'd barely gotten her sundress over her head when someone knocked on the door and pushed it open a crack.

"Poppy? You decent?"

"Yeah. Come on in." She smoothed the skirt of her dress, making sure it wasn't tucked into her underwear and showing her ass.

Gavin pushed inside. "My sisters and their families are planning to head to the carnival and then watch the show from there. Everyone else is going to meet them there later. Do you want to stay here or go with them?"

"I'm fine either way."

"The guys and I thought about staying here to watch. We should have a decent view from the backyard."

"Works for me." She preferred their idea to the crowds.

A yawn overtook her. She never had finished her coffee. That was a first for her.

"You know if you're tired, you can take a nap in my bed."

A nap sounded nice, but she'd rather eat. "Right now, I'm just hungry. Besides, Michelle probably needs to get in here to change and get the kids cleaned up since she's staying in here tonight."

"Well, come on and eat. There is plenty of food left."

Poppy fluffed her hair and checked one last time that she was put back together before she followed Gavin back to the party outside.

Dean handed her a plate of food with a small smile. "Here."

"Thanks."

He tossed his empty beer bottle into the trash bag set out by the table. "Figured you'd be hungry after playing so long and hard with the kids."

"It was fun. You guys should have joined us." She would have liked to see them shirtless and wet.

Shit. She needed to stop those thoughts. They'd been creeping in more and more all day.

"No extra swimsuits."

"I'm surprised that stopped Flynn. And it didn't stop Gavin." Eventually. He'd disappeared at first, but had come around once Michelle and Brittany started talking smack, reminding him of the challenge.

He hadn't lasted long though, claiming his food was getting cold.

Dean handed her a beer. "I hate wet clothes. So does Flynn. And with children present, it wouldn't have been appropriate to strip down to our boxers."

Poppy almost choked on her beer at the picture Dean's words splashed in her head. She fought to collect herself. "Even in your boxers, you guys would have been more covered than I was."

Hunger flashed in Dean's eyes, but she blinked and it was gone. It was probably her imagination.

Poppy carried her beer and her plate over to the pile of blankets Gavin and Flynn were stretched out on, Dean grabbing more beer before joining them.

The four of them finished out the evening in the backyard watching the sunset while they ate, chatted, drank, and dozed while everyone else from the party trickled off to the carnival and fairgrounds after Stacy cleaned up, refusing to let anyone help.

As night finally fell, the twinkly lights Stacy decorated the backyard with flickered and winked around them.

They moved around on the blankets until Poppy was sprawled in between Gavin and Dean with Flynn leaning back on his hands behind her, her head in his lap while they waited for the show to start.

She had a mild buzz from the beer going, completely relaxed and drowsy, glad Gavin was the DD for the trip home. He'd only had a couple beers earlier in the day, so he was plenty sober for the drive.

She broke the comfortable quiet when a stray thought hit her. "I forgot to tell you guys, Cyclops is staying at my place."

"Are you sure?" Gavin looked down at her with confusion on his face.

"Yeah. Tam and Marie are going to check in on her. They won her over last night."

Flynn jerked beneath her. "What? Your little demon came out for them?"

"Yep." Poppy grinned as she imagined Tam's triumph at Flynn's reaction.

"Does she hate men?" Flynn sounded hopeful, like there was an excuse why Cyclops preferred her friends to him.

"Maybe." It was possible. Poppy didn't know much of Cyclops's history.

Flynn shifted, pulling her closer to him. "We should still bring her to our place. It'll give her a chance to get to know us."

"If I'd had her longer, I would, but I don't want to uproot her again after only a week." She'd text them tomorrow and make sure Cyclops was still all right.

Poppy could always go back home. She didn't have to spend the whole weekend with the guys.

A shrill whistle interrupted them and then green and blue exploded in the sky. Poppy felt the boom in her chest.

Her breath caught and her mouth curved in delight as colors flashed and sparkled in the sky. Her favorites were the white crackling ones.

Flynn played with the edges of her hair as he tilted his head to watch the fireworks.

Gavin and Dean's hands slid into both of hers and her smile grew as she clasped them back. She liked being here, in the center of the guys.

She liked it too much.

She gasped as the finale began, echoing in her chest, whistling in her ears, lighting up the entire area in flashing colors. She sat up, breathing in the smell of black powder, wanting a closer look.

Her grip tightened on Dean and Gavin's hand as Flynn helped prop her up, tucking her between his legs.

One last boom and explosion of red, white, and blue and it was over.

She and the guys sat in silence for a moment, caught in the magic of the night and the show. Fireworks never failed to fill her with awe and hope. She wasn't sure why, but it was one of her favorite things. She was glad she came, glad the guys were here with her, even while most of her ached at Perry's absence.

He loved them too.

A familiar scent teased her nose and she jumped up. "Petrichor. It's about to rain.

The words were barely out of her mouth before the sky opened up and poured all over them.

Flynn laughed. "This will help battle all the fires that always happen on this holiday."

This was the first time it had rained since Perry's funeral. The scent made her think of the day she watched her brother lowered into the ground.

Was this some kind of sign? But a sign for what?

She arched her back and held her arms spread wide at her sides as she tilted her head back to greet the rain beating down on her, laughter bubbling up her throat, joining the grief burning the back of her eyes.

Flynn grabbed her hand and spun her in a dance, laughing with her. After a moment of stunned disbelief, Gavin and Dean joined them and they all danced in the rain, letting it wash their pain away for the moment.

Chapter 18

Her breath left her lungs as Poppy stepped inside their house. It was her first time back here since weeks before Perry's death. Damn, this was harder than she expected. All the fun and relaxation she'd experienced all day disappeared.

"Do you need anything or would you rather go right to bed?"

She winced at the reminder of the now empty room where Perry used to live. "I'm not sleeping in his room."

Dean shook his head and took her bag from her. "You know we have an extra one. We've always considered it yours since you're the only one who's ever slept there."

It had been a while since she stayed over. "I didn't realize you still had it set up as a guest room."

"What else would it be?" Flynn scowled like she'd personally offended him somehow.

"I dunno. Game room? At-home-gym?" It's not like she needed her own room here.

They lived almost within easy walking distance from her home and shop. She'd only spent the night a handful of times when she'd had too much to drink and didn't feel like calling for a ride or the occasional holiday.

"Nope. It's always been your room and it's going to stay that way. Forever." Flynn was still scowling.

Poppy was too tired to try and figure out what his problem was. "Okay. Then I'm going to bed. I'm exhausted."

Dean carried her bag upstairs and she trailed behind him, looking over her shoulder when Flynn and Gavin didn't follow. They headed for the kitchen, apparently needing a late night snack.

Poppy ignored Perry's closed door and the lump in her throat. She could tackle that tomorrow.

Her room was at the very end of the hall on the other side of Gavin's and across the hall from Dean's. He pushed the door open and gestured for her to walk inside.

They had decorated it in her favorite colors, purple and gray and there was even a couple unicorn knick knacks scattered around. She'd told Perry and the rest of them it wasn't necessary, but they'd insisted on her having her own room. She'd never been able to consider it hers though. Even though it was Perry's idea, at least she thought it was, he'd never really acted like he wanted her to stay over. He'd always called cars for her or offered to drive her back. It was never him suggesting she stay except on holidays. It had always been that way with her and those three. He didn't leave her out exactly, but there was always a barrier. A barrier she was comfortable with and didn't really have any interest in knocking down.

It had kept her interest in them in check. Perry's friends were gorgeous and sweet and dangerous and they ruined other men for her. The few they didn't run off. Most of the guys she dated couldn't handle her friendship with them.

"Take a shower if you want or not. Make yourself at home. Do you...uh...need one of us to sleep with?" Dean rubbed the back of his neck.

She was tempted, but it was a bad idea. "No. I've been sleeping okay on my own the last week."

She must have imagined the disappointment flashing across his face.

"Sleep as long as you want. See you tomorrow."

"Good night, Dean. Thank you. For today. And this weekend."

"Trust me. We have selfish reasons for it." With that last cryptic remark, Dean left, closing the door softly behind him.

Poppy blew out a long breath and dug through her bag, snorting at the strange choices she'd packed for herself in her hungover state. Two of her fancier dresses along with her oversized soft shirts and a few pairs of leggings. She'd also added some of her sexier underwear which made her flush. What was she thinking? Did she unconsciously hope one of the guys would get a chance to see it?

No. She couldn't go there. It would ruin everything.

Too tired to shower, she changed into something more comfortable and climbed into the bed.

Poppy woke the next morning after a restless night of weird and twisted dreams, alone with the covers tangled around her legs. She should have taken Dean up on company in the bed. With Perry's room right down the hall, it was haunting her.

Since she was already here, she might as well get started on Perry's room and the rest of his stuff littered throughout the house. She didn't care about the furniture or major stuff, but the guys probably didn't want to leave all his clothes and other stuff sitting in his room like it was just waiting for Perry to return there. She couldn't bear the thought of his room sitting like that, growing stale and being covered in dust.

She'd take care of his room, one thing crossed of her list, and then go back home, out of the guys' hair. She didn't think she could handle staying here the whole weekend.

Since she'd be sorting through Perry's stuff, Poppy chose another pair of leggings and off-the-shoulder shirt with a purramid of kittens. Her throat closed as she read the sparkly letters. She'd picked it with Perry in mind since he loved puns, thinking it would make him laugh.

It had.

Showered and dressed, she headed downstairs where the guys were drinking chatting over coffee.

"Morning, muffin." Flynn smiled at her.

"Good morning." She grabbed a mug from the cabinet and poured herself a cup.

"Sleep okay?" Gavin asked.

She stirred the caramel creamer into her coffee. "Not really, no." She was still too tired to be convincing. Especially considering the dark circles ringing her eyes.

"None of us did either. Maybe we should all pile up together in one bed so we can finally get some damn rest." Flynn rubbed at his eyes, looking as crappy as she felt.

"I actually thought since I was already here, I could get started on sorting through Perry's room so you three don't have to deal with it yourself." Though they were more familiar with what was in there than she was.

Dean shrugged and sipped his coffee. "We don't mind. We wouldn't get rid of anything we think you might want, but you don't need to put yourself through that."

She didn't want to put herself through it either, but she had to start somewhere and she was already here. "I think it might help me. It's better if I stay busy and get started on all the things I need to handle with him being gone."

Dean blew out a breath, looking worried. "If you insist, how about we all do it? But tomorrow."

She set down her cup with a furrowed brow. "Tomorrow? I'm already here."

"Yes, and today we are having a lazy, movie day." Gavin pointed to the living room. "We already set up the blanket fort."

Poppy turned to see what he was pointing at and gasped at the sight of the tent made of blankets and pillows and even fairy lights filling most of the living room. It was beautiful. Her breath hiccuped.

She used to make those with Perry all the time. They'd cover the whole house in them with separate rooms connected by tunnels and then Gavin, Flynn, and Dean would come over and play inside, usually ending in a pillow war that demolished their fort.

She blinked hard and sniffed, trying to hold back the emotions welling in her chest. "Why do all this?"

"Is it too much?" Flynn asked. "We wanted a way to kind of honor him and our time together. We agreed those days at your house with blanket forts and pillow wars were one of our favorite memories. It's not going to be the same, but we thought it might help us and maybe help you too."

Her heart swelled like the stupid Grinch's at their thoughtfulness and effort. How could she possibly say no and insist instead they all put themselves through the torture of clearing our Perry's rooms instead?

"It's not too much. I think that sounds like a much better way to say goodbye to him than a dumb wake."

Flynn made a sound of distaste. "Wakes are stupid. Why did we do one again?"

Gavin grimaced. "The funeral director talked us into it. We just kept agreeing to everything he suggested so we could get it over with."

A ghost of a smile crossed Poppy's lips at Gavin's words. "He was incredibly pushy. Probably shouldn't have chosen the first one I found when I searched for them."

Gavin snorted. "They probably get eighty percent of their business just by being the first one listed."

"You think they pay to make sure it stays that way?" Flynn asked.

"Is that even possible?" Poppy curled her hands around her mug as she leaned against the counter.

Gavin shrugged before setting his mug in the sink. "No idea. I'm not a computer person. None of us are."

"Hey, I do just fine with computers." Flynn shoved his friend.

Gavin shoved him back. "Weren't you the one who threw yours out the window last year? The second story one?"

"That was the computer's fault. Not my skills."

"Right."

Flynn rolled his eyes. "Assholes." He clapped his hands. "All right. You guys get the movies set up, I'll grab the snacks I ran out for early this morning. We are not leaving that fort except to use the bathroom."

Chapter 19

Flynn bought a ridiculous amount of food. He brought two tote bags overflowing with snacks into the fort. Poppy crawled inside behind him, staring in awe at the lights they'd strung up.

"Did you raid the Christmas decorations for this?" Poppy asked.

Gavin grinned. "Of course. They should get used more than just for one holiday. I'm starting to think we should make this a regular thing."

Dean shook his head and wrapped his hands around her feet, giving them a squeeze. "Maybe a once a year thing. It's a lot to clean up."

Flynn blew a raspberry at Dean. "Such a killjoy."

Dean shot Flynn his middle finger.

Gavin flopped closer to Poppy, almost in her lap. "I don't plan to move until I have to. I'm still tired."

Flynn huffed. "I call dib now. I'm pretty sure it was my turn to sleep with Poppy next."

Poppy wasn't sure what to think about them invading her bed again. At first just to get her back into a sleeping rhythm was one thing, but again? She needed to be able to sleep alone. She couldn't move in here and have them take turns sleeping with her.

"Are we watching a movie or TV show?" Poppy needed the subject changed before she thought too long about them in her bed.

"Let's binge something. Poppy, anything you've been wanting to watch, but haven't had time to get into?" Flynn asked.

She didn't watch much TV, but there was something she'd been wanting to try. "I've actually never had the chance to watch *Psych*. I keep hearing it's awesome and hilarious."

Flynn gaped at her, the fairy lights flickering in his green eyes. "It is. You definitely need to watch it. I can't believe you haven't watched. It's not a new show."

She ripped her gaze from his, not liking the tingly feelings he created in her belly. "We can find something none of us has seen."

Gavin shook his head. "Nope. Definitely *Psych*. You'll love it and we could probably all use the laughs."

Dean's hold on her feet tightened at Gavin's reminder of why they needed humor instead of something emotional or sad. And Flynn was right. Watching anything other than something funny would shatter her. Maybe watching a comedy would take her mind off things for a little while. And take their minds off it too. They could use the break from grief and darkness. Yesterday wasn't enough. They needed more. A chance to pretend all was normal for another day before they had to dive right back into reality.

Once Flynn started the first episode, the four of them settled into more comfortable positions. They adjusted her until her feet were in Gavin's lap and her head in Dean's. Flynn snuggled up right next to her, his feet digging beneath Gavin's legs and his head propped up on his hand right by Dean's thigh. They were one big puppy pile, snuggling close, giving comfort, reminding each other they weren't as alone as it felt.

It somehow made her miss Perry more and less all at the same time. She wished he was there with them, but it almost felt like he was. For the first time since she found out he was gone, she could almost feel his presence. Maybe it was because the memories of him were so strong, or the way it felt to have the guys wrapped around her, almost like they were guarding her, protecting her.

For a little while, she'd allow herself the comfort. Especially as it hit home even harder that she wasn't the only one with a broken heart and a missing piece.

She didn't have to go through this alone.

Perry wouldn't have wanted her to shut herself off from their friends. So, she'd soak up this comfort while she had it and be strong later because this felt too good to leave.

Gavin's fingers brushed through her hair, stroking through the strands still damp from her shower. She bussed into him like a cat, almost purring at the sensation. Nothing relaxed her like hands in her hair. Something they all seemed to know and take advantage of.

Flynn stroked along her arm, snuggling closer, and with Dean still massaging her feet, she melted completely, barely able to keep her attention on the show playing on the TV peeking through the opening of the fort.

She fought against the other feeling building inside her. A forbidden feeling, a dangerous one. Something she'd ignored for over a decade. She couldn't crush on her brother's best friends. She couldn't lust after them. Especially since she didn't favor one of them over the other. She adored them all. She wanted them all. Perry had guessed a few years ago, so he'd helped by keeping them all separated more often. Which was fine with her. It was easier when she didn't see them, smell them, touch them.

And they'd never seen her that way. She was Perry's sister. Their buddy who played in blanket forts and climbed trees and raced them on bikes through the neighborhood. Their friend who fed them cupcakes and cookies, experimenting with different tastes and almost poisoned them a few times.

They had never seen her as someone more than a friend. And most of the time, she was fine with it. But her confusing thoughts and feelings for them was the one secret she'd tried to keep from Perry, the one thing they never discussed out loud, even when she could tell he'd figured it out. It was too awkward and weird. She didn't want him to have divided loyalties or mess with their friendship, so she kept her distance and Perry helped her.

But with him gone, the guys seemed determined to cross the line she had drawn between them and she didn't have the strength to lay it back down. She didn't really want to. But she had to remember they were treating her like one of them. The four guys had always been cuddly and close with each other, so none of this meant anything.

Poppy focused back on the show, startling when it coaxed a hoarse laugh out of her. Guilt trickled into her belly. She shouldn't be laughing. She shouldn't be happy, even for a moment. It was too soon.

Flynn threw his arm over her middle and held her tighter, pressing his lips close to her ear. "It's okay to laugh and find little moments of peace even in the middle of all this. It isn't a betrayal to him. Especially when he wouldn't want you to stop living along with him. The pain will still be there when we crawl out of this blanket fort. In here, just try to let it go as much as you can. Let your mind take you away into the world of this show. Tomorrow is soon enough to slog back through the pain and responsibilities." He kissed the spot under her ear and backed off a little, but kept his arm around her.

She shivered, trying to stop herself from leaning back into him, craving more of his touch and wise words. Instead, she did what he suggested and threw herself into the ridiculous show. Flynn was right. The pain wasn't going anywhere. She could take a moment to disconnect herself from it.

A few times throughout the day, the guys changed positions, but she was always in someone's lap, they were all always touching her and each other. They stuffed themselves on candy and chips and cookies, not a single healthy thing allowed in the blanket fort according to Flynn. Gavin bitched, but even he munched on some of it.

DEAN TRIED TO FOCUS on the show, but it was almost impossible with Poppy curled up against him, on top of him, around him. Her coffee and cupcakes and burnt sugar scent had imprinted onto his clothes and it was all he could smell. She somehow even smelled like a damn unicorn. He'd always wondered if she tasted like one too. So many times over the years he'd almost given into the temptation to find out.

Guilt stabbed him and he clenched his jaw. She'd just lost her fucking twin, her favorite person in the world, the last piece of her family and he was sitting here fighting an erection.

One of his best friends was dead and he was fantasizing about tasting his sister.

What the fuck was wrong with him?

It wasn't anywhere near the time to bring up anything like that with her. If the time ever came. Perry had been almost violently against it for a long time, so everything with her had remained platonic for all these years.

Right now, she just needed to know she wasn't alone in the world. She needed to know people cared about her.

He looked down at her when she laughed at something happening on the screen and his chest tightened at the sight. This was what she needed. Companionship, some laughs, food, and rest. She didn't need him to fuck her until she screamed. As much as he wanted to bury himself in her so he could forget his own pain and loss for a little while, it wasn't what she needed.

And he wanted to be what she needed because she was who he needed. Who they all did. She just didn't know it yet.

She was the gasoline to their fire and he wanted to burn. They all did.

Chapter 20

They finished the first season by dinner time.

Flynn stretched, his shirt riding up and showing the precise cut of his abs. "I can't keep eating this shit. I need real food. I can't believe I didn't buy at least some jerky or something. I need meat. I'm going to go grab some bacon cheeseburgers. Anyone want anything?"

Dean's fingers paused in her hair. "Fish sandwiches for me."

Flynn made a disgusted face. "Gross, but okay. Poppy? Gavin?"

"I'll take some kind of salad. Whatever they have," Gavin said.

Poppy's stomach rumbled. She hadn't eaten much of the snacks they'd brought into the fort and what she had eaten, hadn't really satisfied. "I could go for a bacon cheeseburger. And a milkshake. And fries."

Flynn grinned wide. "A woman after my own heart. Too bad you said milkshake instead of pie."

A small smile tugged at her lips. "I eat pie all the time since I sell them."

Flynn winked at her. "I know. And yours are my favorite."

She knew. Perry used to bring any leftover pie home every week for Flynn since it along with bacon cheeseburgers were his favorite food. She had no idea how he stayed in such perfect shape when he ate like a teenage boy. Or a kid who didn't know when he'd get his next meal.

Anger at his parents swelled inside her. She still hated them so much for the neglect they'd put him through.

"All right. No one move and don't start the next season without me. I'll be back in twenty minutes."

Gavin flicked him off. "You've already seen it all. We aren't waiting for your hungry ass."

"Fine. But don't watch the episode after the next one. It's my favorite."

Flynn crawled out, almost kicking Gavin in the face, who punched him in the ass in retaliation. A small giggle fell from Poppy's mouth and Gavin grinned over at her.

The blanket fort suddenly seemed too small, like she couldn't get enough air in here. "I'm going to use the bathroom before we start. Be right back." Her voice came out high and squeaky, and she scrambled from the blankets trapping her.

Her breaths eased once she was free and she all but ran to the downstairs bathroom, leaning against the closed door with eyes shut so hard she saw stars. How long was she going to be like this? Fine one moment, and a panicked mess the next? Yesterday, at the party, she'd been fine. But today she was struggling again. How was she supposed to run a business and handle all the things left for her to do to wrap up Perry's affairs if she couldn't get through a single day without a breakdown?

Poppy slid down the door to the floor, burying her face in her knees, trying to piece herself back together. She didn't want the guys to know. She didn't want them worried about her and trying to fix it. No matter how sweet and amazing the blanket fort day idea was, they couldn't fix this for her. They couldn't fix *her*. She didn't know if anything ever could. But especially not three guys who were as shattered as she was.

They needed this day too. They needed to forget for a while. To wallow. To ignore. She didn't want to be the one who dragged everyone back down into the pit of despair.

She sucked in a sharp breath and stood, crossing to the sink to splash cold water on her heated eyes and cheeks. She'd enjoy the rest of the day, keep holding it all in. A few more hours and she could release everything crashing inside her into her pillow. As long as Flynn didn't actually attempt to sleep in her bed tonight.

Flynn's voice came from the other room. He was back already? She'd spent way too long in the bathroom. Shit.

Poppy hurried from the bathroom with a forced calm expression. Back inside the fort, the guys glanced at her with concern, but they didn't ask her if she was okay or mention how long she was gone.

"You waited for me?" Flynn's lips spread in a triumphant grin.

Gavin rolled his eyes. "We did. We all needed a break to piss and stretch."

"Awesome." Flynn passed out food to everyone and Dean restarted the show.

Poppy stared down at the food in her lap, no longer hungry for any of it. The smell of the greasy burger turned her stomach, but she took a bite anyway. And by the third, her hunger returned with a roar and she devoured everything but the milkshake before the theme song was over.

The peaceful feeling returned too.

Maybe she'd be a little crazy for while. Maybe for the rest of her life. Maybe this was her new normal. She didn't know. But she needed to accept the peaceful moments when they came.

As the night turned into the next day, Gavin shut off the show. "I think it's time to call it."

An evil smirk crossed Flynn's face. "Agreed." Then, he ripped the pillow from under his head and smashed it right into Gavin's face.

Gavin growled and returned the favor.

A laugh burst from Poppy as she scrambled for her own weapon, nailing Dean in the back of the head before he had a chance to hit her. The four of them crashed together with laughter and shrieks and grunts until feathers burst from the pillows and floated around them and the blanket fort collapsed right on top.

Poppy could barely breathe from laughing so hard. She flopped onto her back beneath the mountain of blankets, letting the guys handle digging them all out of the mess.

And then she was crying too, tears joining the laughter until she wasn't sure what she was feeling other than guilty and confused and sad and grateful. How many times had their blanket fort days ended just like this when they were kids? Dammit, she missed him so much. He should be here with them, laughing and playing, tangled in Christmas lights with feathers stuck in his hair.

Not her.

The blankets lifted off her and Dean's worried face hovered above hers.

"He should be here. Not me. I can't replace him for you. And you can't replace him for me." Her words came out on a sob.

Dean's expression crumpled and he wrapped her in a hug. "Oh, baby. No. That's not what we're doing. We're not trying to replace him for you and we aren't trying to replace him with you. You were always there when we did this. You were already a part of it." He lifted her into his arms and whispered something to the other guys, who abandoned the mess and hurried upstairs.

Dean carried her over to the couch, keeping her in his lap as he sat down, letting her cry into his chest. "I'm sorry. This was too much, too soon. We're forcing it with all our plans for the weekend."

She hid her face in his chest and behind her hands. "No. It's not that. It's just me. I don't know."

"There's no right way to grieve. There's no time table." His arms tightened around her, grounding her.

"Today was amazing. It really was." She sniffed, trying to clear her head and her emotions. She needed to be stronger than this.

Dean's chest rose in a deep sigh. "It was good for us too. But sometimes, the memory and the pain can pop up out of nowhere and send you to your knees. We understand. You're here with people who are fighting the same battle you are. You don't have to hide it from us."

They kept saying all the right things, the perfect things, but she wasn't able to really let go. She was a private person and didn't want an audience for her breakdowns.

Flynn reappeared beside them. "It's ready."

Dean stood and carried her bride-style up the stairs to the bathroom where Flynn and Gavin had transformed the bathroom into a spa-like setting. They'd run her a bubble bath and scattered lit candles across the edge and the countertops, a book, a glass of wine, and a towel folded up to act as a pillow waited for her.

Dean set her down in the middle of the bathroom floor. "Thought you could relax for a bit. We noticed you wincing from sore muscles after lying in the fort all day."

Heat stung her eyes and she swallowed the lump in her throat. "Thanks. This is really sweet."

Flynn cupped her cheek and brushed away the remaining tears with his thumb. "Take your time, muffin."

They filed out, leaving her alone with the scents of lavender and vanilla swirling around her. Which one of them liked bubble baths? Or did they get it specially for her? Either way, the thoughtfulness of the gesture almost had her swooning.

She peeled off her clothes and slid into the scalding water, hissing at the heat. A blush stained her cheeks as she noticed the book they'd chosen for her to read. It was one of her bodice rippers that she usually kept hidden in the dusty corners of her bookshelves. How did they know about those? How did they find them? Did they steal it to read when they stayed with her? Scoundrels.

Poppy settled into the water, leaning back with closed eyes, trying to breathe out and release the tension coiled tight inside her. She tugged the tray closer and lost herself in wine and words until the water cooled.

She smiled at the large gray robe hanging on the back of the door and wrapped herself in the plush fabric after drying off. Unsure what to do with the bath tray, she lifted it from the tub, rinsed out the wine glass, and left it sitting on the counter.

Back in the guest room, Flynn already dozed in her bed.

Chapter 21

Flynn's eyes popped open and he grinned. "Told you it was my turn."

Poppy shook her head. "I'm too relaxed to bother arguing." And she was afraid all the bad feelings and memories would return if she was alone.

"Good. Come on. It's late." Flynn patted the bed.

She hesitated, not wanting to strip from the robe and change in front of him. With a shrug, she left the robe on and climbed into the bed beside Flynn. The robe was more comfortable than her pajamas or t-shirts and leggings anyway.

Flynn flopped over to face her with his head propped up on his palm. "I like seeing you in my robe."

"It's yours?" Her eyes widened in surprise.

"Yeah. We didn't want to rustle through your things, so I figured you could use something more comfortable than a towel to wrap up in."

"My robe is nowhere near as comfortable as this." Her lips thinned at the small talk they scrambled for.

Clearly, she wasn't the only one feeling a little awkward with this situation. It should have reassured her, but instead it made her more nervous.

Flynn reached out and stroked the collar of the robe, rubbing the fabric between his fingers, his skin brushing against hers, branding her with heat.

Poppy cleared her throat, trying to calm her racing pulse. "So, who's the bath taker?"

He huffed out a short laugh, his hand falling away from her. "Dean. He likes to soak in bubbles when he gets stuck on inspiration for his photography."

That was so freaking hot and adorable.

"Do you think he'd be willing to photograph some of my drinks and food for my website? I've been meaning to get Perry to ask him, but I kept forgetting."

"Of course. He did it last time. Ask him tomorrow."

"I will." A fair amount of their success was the pictures Dean had taken and the web design he'd been able to create to bring in more traffic to her coffee shop. In return, they'd let him cover the walls of their shop with his work, not that it was a hardship at all. It made their place look gorgeous and artsy.

He refused to call it anything more than a hobby, but he was talented as hell. They'd all tried to get him to send his work into magazines or even set up a gallery, but he refused.

"Do you need any help with the business side of things? I know...uh...Perry took care of that part."

"I'll figure it out." She wasn't sure how yet and hadn't even begun, but it was on her list of things to do.

"Let me know. I have a really good accountant and I can teach you how to handle the boring stuff." Flynn owned his own bar a couple streets over from her shop. A very successful one.

Though it was more pub than bar, soccer and rugby and boxing always playing on the screens instead of football, baseball, and Nascar. It was a quiet place instead of a bass thumping dance club. He always said it was a place for grownups to get together and drink and chat. Poppy wasn't much for the nightlife, but his place was one of the few she didn't mind hanging out in for an evening.

"I will." She was glad he offered to teach her how instead of offering to just take over completely for her. As tempting as it was to hand it all over to someone else, that was why she was in the mess to begin with. She'd never tried to get Perry to explain things and show her how to handle it. She'd just let him.

Granted, he never learned how to make delicious pastries or even a fancy latte either. They stuck to their strengths, never expecting to end up in this situation, expecting to work together and grow their business for years and years to come.

Flynn tilted her head up with a bent finger beneath her chin so she'd meet his eyes. "You're brilliant, muffin. You always have been. You'll be able to handle it."

She swallowed, hoping he was right, terrified he wasn't. "Maybe."

"Definitely." He leaned over and pressed a kiss to her cheek, really close to the corner of her lips.

Heat rushed through her, pooling low in her belly and a small gasp escaped her.

"You okay?"

She hesitated, but decided to leap. "I just want to feel something. Something good. I want to forget. Just for a little while."

It didn't have to mean anything. But she needed more than a bubble bath and a funny TV show. "Don't you want the same thing?"

Heat flickered in his eyes, causing the green to darken. "Are you sure that's what you want?"

"I am. It doesn't mean anything, so don't worry about that. I know there's no possibility of more. But please." She wasn't above begging to get what she needed.

And what she needed was anything that could penetrate the numb fog surrounding her, no matter how bad of an idea it was.

A shadow crossed his face at her words, something like hurt, but he blinked and it was gone. It was probably her imagination. She'd been imagining a lot of things about them lately. She wanted it to mean something more, but knew it couldn't. And it was reckless and stupid, but right then, she didn't care if she'd regret it in the morning. Right then, she just needed.

"You never have to beg me, muffin. But I like it when you do."

She shuddered as he gripped the front lapels of the robe and yanked her half on top of him, slamming her mouth onto his. *Yes.* This was what she wanted, what she needed. No emotions, no strings, just mind-numbing pleasure. And based on the way Flynn's tongue danced with hers and the way his fingers teased, he knew exactly what he was doing.

Poppy sucked his bottom lip into her mouth and Flynn's restraint broke with a groan. He tossed her onto her back and ripped open the robe, his heated eyes raking over every inch of her naked flesh, making goosebumps race across her skin and her nipples harden to sharp points, begging for his touch, his tongue.

"Fuck, I've wanted to see you like this for a long damn time, muffin. You're gorgeous."

She didn't want him saying stuff like that. Nothing sweet or tender or hinting of more than a foolish night of grief and bad decisions.

Poppy grabbed the back of Flynn's neck and pulled him down to nibble at his lips to shut him up. Flynn groaned again and slid his fingers, calloused from guitar playing across her skin. She arched into his touch and buried her fingers into his hair as he dragged his lips down her belly and right to her core. She spread her legs and cried out as he teased and tasted her, his fingers plucking at her nipples.

Poppy's mind blanked and she felt nothing but desire and pleasure as lust fogged her brain.

She yanked at his clothes, wanting his naked skin against hers, wanting to explore the hard body he had from firefighting training.

But he caught her wrists in a gentle clasp and trapped them above her head. "Let me make you feel good, muffin. Let me help you forget."

She kept her hands in place when he let go and gave herself over to the pleasure each one of his kisses, licks, and touches brought out in her. He didn't leave a single inch of her body unexplored, taking his time getting to know each dip and curve and freckle, bringing her higher and higher as she trembled with need and bliss.

He touched with a surprising gentleness, like she was precious, something to be treasured, worshiped. It was something she'd imagined from Dean in her fantasies. He was always so quiet and careful. With Flynn, she'd expected teasing and something light-hearted before he fucked her brains out. With Gavin, she'd thought he would be the dangerous one, the adventurous one.

Flynn knelt between her spread thighs and bent to taste her, his tongue light and exploratory before he fell on her with a groan, his careful control snapped just a little bit. She wanted to see it shatter completely.

She opened her legs wider, giving him better access as he teased and licked and nipped at her sensitive flesh. His hands reached up to play with her nipples, sending electric heat shooting straight to her center, making her gasp and buck into his mouth.

His satisfied growl vibrated through her and she cried out as warmth washed through her, dragging her off on a tide of bliss.

Flynn threw himself on his back beside her, their chests heaving as they tried to catch their breaths. He curled her up next to him, pressing a gentle kiss on her forehead. She'd wanted him inside her, but she was so relaxed and pliant she couldn't find it in herself to question it or feel guilty that he was still dressed and hard. Poppy refused to allow the worries, doubts, or second thoughts in. There would be time enough for that in the morning.

Chapter 22

This time, when she woke, Poppy remembered Perry was gone, but it took her a moment to remember her foolish decision to jump Flynn's bones the night before. She winced and glanced over at him, still asleep, thankfully this time only his hand rested on her hip instead of her trapped in his arms. She was still naked, but he was fully dressed in pajamas.

She scooted inch by inch from the bed until she was free, scooping the robe from the floor and grabbing her bag as she rushed from the room and into the bathroom across the hall. She still smelled like him.

Once she was cleaned up and dressed, she tiptoed into the hall, listening for signs of life from the guys, but everything was silent and still. It was really early, especially since they were up so late. She needed a little time to get herself together before she saw any of them. Especially Flynn. She didn't want him to think she expected anything from him. And she didn't want the others to get pissed or weird about it. Or think he took advantage. If anything, she did.

She halted at Perry's bedroom door, one of her hands curled into a fist and pressed against her chest as she tried to gather the courage to enter. She had to get this done. It wasn't fair to leave it all to the guys to deal with alone. After sucking in a deep breath, Poppy pushed open the door and walked inside, her heart beating too fast, her head heavy.

Gavin sat on the end of Perry's bed, his head in his hands, his shoulder slumped.

"Gavin?"

His head jerked up and he turned to face her, tear tracks and devastation on his face.

Poppy's eyes closed as her heart clenched and her throat clogged. "Sorry. I'll come back later."

"No. I just wanted to sit here before we..." Gavin trailed off, his voice hoarse.

Before they stripped it of everything that made the room Perry's.

This was a terrible idea. It was too soon. "We don't have to do this today. I can come back in a few weeks or something."

He shook his head. "We'll stick to the plan. I guess I was just saying goodbye. Part of me hates to do anything other than leave it just like it is, but it's worse imagining it all still in here, like it's just waiting for him to come back."

"Yeah. He always made fun of shrines." He'd barely waited until the funeral before going through their mother's things after her death.

A slight smile twitched at the edges of Gavin's lips. "That's right. I'd forgotten."

She was trying so hard to remember everything, not wanting to forget a second she had with Perry. She was terrified of the day he became a cloudy memory in her mind.

"Fuck, this sucks." She crossed the room towards the bed, leaving the door open behind her.

"Understatement."

"It still smells like him in here." She picked up his pillow and pressed it to her face, her composure shattering as she fell to her knees with a whimper.

Gavin knelt in front of Poppy and wrapped his arms around her, pillow and all. They huddled there on their knees, shaking as they poured out their grief on each other's shoulders.

Flynn and Dean were suddenly there and joined them in their embrace and moment of mourning, on their knees beside them. Poppy could barely breathe between her own tears and the tight grips they all had on her, but she loved it.

She welcomed the pain and reminder she wasn't in this alone as the sorrow swept her away, crashing over her in waves until she didn't know which way was up or down. They kept her from completely sinking to the bottom.

Eventually, they calmed and squirmed around until they leaned against the side of the bed on the floor in a line side by side.

"Fuck."

The rest of them snorted at Flynn's groan, lightening the mood a bit.

Poppy's entire body ached as she got to her feet with winces and grimaces like an old lady. All the crying and tension was wearing on her, leaving her sore and exhausted even though she was finally sleeping better. She was too wrecked to even feel awkward with Flynn at the moment.

She stared around Perry's room, unsure where to even begin. "Do you guys want any of his clothes?"

"We'll probably keep a couple things. Do you want any of them?" Dean asked.

"I already have his hoodie and I'm keeping it. Maybe I'll steal a couple of his funny shirts." She didn't like the idea of his favorites wasting away in a thrift store."

Gavin took a step towards Perry's dresser. "Does that mean you want to start with clothes?"

"It's mostly what's in here, so yeah, seems like a good place as any." Now that the time had come, she found herself hesitant and filled with dread.

But it needed to be done.

FLYNN WAS A FUCKING idiot. He should never have let it get so far last night. He shouldn't have let it go anywhere. She was vulnerable and sad and he was a complete asshole for staying and enjoying the way she writhed beneath him.

At least he'd held back from actually fucking her. But that had more to do with the lack of a condom than any decency inside of him.

And here they were in Perry's room, going through his things, smothering beneath the weight of misery and loss and guilt. Perry would kill him if he knew what he did. Gavin and Dean might when he had a chance to tell them. They'd already talked about this, planning to hold off and be her friends, her family while they got through this hell.

They'd waited this long for her, they could wait a little longer.

But he screwed all that up by tasting her.

And now that he'd had a taste, he wasn't sure if he could stay away. He'd woken up hard with the scent of her surrounding him, still on his skin and clothes.

She'd been so gorgeous with her unicorn hair spread around her, her sadness replaced with ecstasy as he explored her.

It took all his control not to drag her from the room and press her against the wall to finish what they started.

His eyes caught Perry's photo of the four of them on his dresser and his throat closed. Dammit, he missed the fucker. How were they supposed to go on with life when such an integral piece was missing?

The four of them had lived together and worked together for so long. They'd rarely spent more than a few days apart since they were mud covered kids in elementary school.

Were they even whole without him?

Chapter 23

It took them the rest of the day to sort through all of Perry's things, the time broken up with shared memories and tears and laughter. Perry's entire life was boxed and bagged up, everything they decided not to keep piled on his stripped mattress. She wasn't concerned about the things scattered throughout the rest of the house like throw pillows and curtains and kitchen supplies and furniture. She considered all of it belonging to the house, to the guys.

Dean scowled at the covered bed. "I'll cart all this stuff off to the thrift stores and clothing drops tomorrow."

"Thanks."

"This is depressing as hell. I need to get out of here. I need a drink." Flynn turned and stomped from the room.

Poppy stared after him in concern, her cheeks flushing as she worried part of his mood was due to what they did the night before. He hadn't mentioned it or even alluded to it the entire day, all of them focused on sorting and packing. Should she follow him? Make him understand it was no big deal, they were just sad and lonely and looking for comfort in all the wrong places? She didn't want him to feel guilty, like she thought he took advantage. Especially since she was the one who took advantage.

Maybe she should apologize to him for it.

Without a word to the others, she chased after Flynn, finding him in the kitchen nursing a beer.

"Want one?" he asked.

She gaped for a moment, thrown. "Actually, yeah."

He opened the fridge and pulled one out, tossing it to her. She plucked it from the air and twisted the top off, drinking deeply, needing the courage found inside the bottle.

Finally, she just blurted out awkward words. "Are you okay? I mean, with what happened last night?"

"Are you?"

"Yes. I mean, no. I mean, ugh." She shook her head, frustrated she couldn't find her words. "I wanted to know if I needed to apologize for taking advantage?" She winced. She was making it worse.

A strange light gleamed in Flynn's eyes. "Isn't that usually the guy's line?"

She refused to let him sidetrack her. "I've known you a long time, Flynn. Don't pretend to be a douchebag misogynist."

He took another pull of his beer. "No, you don't need to apologize for anything. I don't regret last night at all and I hope you don't either."

"I don't. Not unless I made things awkward between us." She honestly didn't. She wished things were different and it could mean more to him and to her, but she'd long wanted to know what a night with one of them would be like.

He hadn't disappointed at all.

He huffed and raked his hand through his brown hair. "You didn't fucking molest me. I was a willing participant. It's just as much my fault that things are weird right now. Well, maybe a little more your fault since you followed me in here to apologize for having your way with me."

Poppy winced. "You seemed upset earlier and I just wanted to make sure it wasn't because of what we did."

"It's not."

"Okay. Good."

Something in his expression kept her from believing him fully. There was a rawness in his eyes, a searching in his gaze, but she couldn't quite read him.

Hopefully, things between them would go back to normal soon.

He set his beer on the counter. "I need to get out of this house for a while. Want to grab the guys and go to my place?"

It took her a moment to realize he was talking about his bar. She really didn't want to, but she wasn't too keen on hanging around with Perry's bare room next to the one she was staying in either. She had to face the rest of the world soon.

Gavin and Dean joined them and Flynn smiled. "We're going out."

Dean raised a brow. "We are?"

"Yes. To my place. Have a couple drinks, see people, listen to some good music."

Gavin groaned. "Shit. It's Saturday."

"So?" What did that matter?

Dean looked a little pained. "So, it's classic rock night at Flynn's. That's why he wants to go."

Poppy snickered. She'd forgotten about his theme Saturdays. It was also the only night people danced there. Classic rock wasn't her favorite, but she didn't mind it. Especially when Flynn sang it. His voice was....well, panty-melting.

"Are you singing tonight?" She hoped not. She didn't think she could handle it.

Flynn shook his head. "Not tonight."

He hadn't brought his guitar to Stacy's either like he usually did. And he hadn't played at Perry's funeral. She couldn't remember the last time she saw him play. Had he stopped?

"I'll go change." Poppy ran upstairs and searched through the clothes she packed.

She changed into the galaxy dress with sparkling stars and planets scattered across the fabric and pulled her hair into a artfully messy ponytail on the top of her head, deciding not to bother with makeup since she had so little control of her emotions and didn't want black streaks on her face.

She shrugged at her drawn and pale reflection and stuck her feet into her purple flats. She hadn't brought her purse, only her wallet and phone, so she shoved her ID and some cash into her bra and since her dress was awesome and had pockets, her phone would be fine in one of them.

She went back downstairs and the guys were gone. They must have been changing too. Her beer still sat on the counter, so she picked it up to finish it, needing a headstart on the drinking tonight.

By the time her beer was drained, the guys trooped back downstairs and raked their eyes over her where she stood with her hip leaning against the counter. Slow matching grins spread across their lips as they took her in.

She barely noticed since she was giving them the same treatment. Flynn wore faded jeans, a tight black undershirt, and a green flannel shirt the same shade as his eyes with asskicker boots. Gavin wore strategically ripped jeans, his motorcycle boots, and a graphic tee with Wonder Woman stamped across the front. Dean was smoking in a black tee, red scarf, tight jeans, and white high-top sneakers.

She was tempted to snap a photo of them, standing there like freaking models, but the image was stamped in her mind and it was a sight she doubted she'd ever forget.

"You look gorgeous, Corny."

She glared at Gavin for calling her by her childhood nickname. She'd always hated it when they called her the shortened version of unicorn just because she had a mild obsession with them and had before it was cool. Now, everyone was obsessed with them, which annoyed her because it had become almost cliche. Which sucked, because unicorns were awesome.

But she didn't want a shitty nickname because of her love of them. Though, she supposed Corny was better than Horny.

"Ready to go?" Flynn asked.

She eyed the front door, a little wary of going out among happy, drunk people who weren't in the middle of a tragedy, who were still living their lives like it couldn't end in a single moment.

"I called a car. None of us are driving."

She shot Dean a grateful smile. They didn't know if the hit and run driver who killed Perry was drunk or not, but the cops seemed to think so based on the skid marks. She'd always thought drunk drivers were shitbags, but now she hated them even more.

She'd barely handled the car rides yesterday, but hoped she could tonight. She almost opened her mouth to ask that they walked instead, but she shook off the tendrils of alarm sticking to her as Dean's phone dinged, letting them know the driver was out front.

She had to get used to them again sometime. She couldn't spend the rest of her life walking everywhere.

Chapter 24

Flynn sat up front with the driver while Gavin and Dean squeezed her between them, both clutching her hands for the entire drive to Flynn's bar. She was grateful for the anchor, keeping her steady in the storm of panic in her stomach. She couldn't stop imagining what it was like for Perry as he drove to Flynn's bar. Did he take this exact route? Did he notice the other driver run the red light? Did everything turn to slow motion or was he suddenly spinning and bleeding and dying?

Her grip on the guys' hands tightened so hard it had to hurt them, but they didn't say a thing, only squeezing them back, trying to pour comfort into her. Her breaths shortened and her vision blurred as the lights of the town flickered around them, lighting up the streets. This was a bad idea. She should have told them she wanted to walk. She should have told them she wanted to go home. She should have locked herself up and stayed out of the public eye, not wanting anyone to witness her like this.

She didn't want to be this weak, scared, tense, sad, broken person. She wanted to be strong and brave and face this horror like a grownup, with at least a little grace and dignity.

But there was no dignity or grace in grief. It ripped through you, dragged you through muck and pain. It overwhelmed and froze you, leaving you helpless to keep moving forward, stuck, stuck in the disbelief and agony. It drowned you and cut off your air until you choked and gasped for air. It ate away at you, at your soul, your heart, your mind, until it left a husk of who you used to be.

She'd never be a whole person again. But she had to learn how to be who she was now and live with it.

The car finally stopped at the front of Flynn's bar, and Poppy all but shoved Gavin through the door so she could escape. With the summer air wafting in her face, warming the chill wrapped around her spine, she was able to find her calm.

Dean pressed a warm hand on her back and led her towards the door behind Flynn, Gavin bringing up the rear. She blew out a loud breath and looked up at Dean with an apologetic grimace.

He leaned down and dropped a kiss in the center of her forehead. "Any time you want to go, you tell us. And we'll definitely walk home tonight. That drive sucked."

She felt sorry for Flynn. He had to make this drive all the time.

Though she had to work in the shop she and her brother owned and worked in together, and all the guys had to live in the same house Perry had made his home, so it all sucked for all of them.

Determined to rally, she shrugged. "Let's drink, dance, and forget."

Dean nodded. "Sounds unhealthy, but good."

They pushed inside, the music spilling into the street as soon as the door opened, a piano cover version of a Metallica song playing. The mournful tone of the song called to her. To the missing piece, the hole inside her. What sort of pain did the musicians go through to make such powerful and heart-wrenching sounds? She wished she could sing and play an instrument so she could release the scream constantly caught in her chest.

Flynn led them over to his table near the stage. No one was performing tonight, the music pumped through the speakers. Usually, on Saturday nights, Flynn would give a special performance of a cover, but tonight he was here to relax.

"Is it weird to be here not working?" Poppy asked as she sat in a seat facing away from the dance floor. She didn't want to watch happy couples and friends celebrate the weekend.

Flynn sat across from her. "What do you mean?"

She shrugged. "It would be weird for me to go order a coffee and sit on one of the couches at my shop."

"I guess, a little. But lots of nights, I sit here and let my employees run things and they only come to me if there's an issue. My manager is awesome and I'm big on delegation. Something you could stand to learn." Since half his time was spent at the fire station, he didn't really have a choice.

She snorted. "It wasn't me who was the micromanager. It was Perry. I finally talked him into letting me hire on extra help."

Gavin chuckled from his spot next to her. "He was such a stubborn shit, wasn't he? Never could get him to relax."

She smiled in fond memory. "Even as a kid, we had to play our games a certain way or it would send him off the deep end."

Flynn let out a loud laugh. "Dude. Remember the time he dated that girl who turned out to be a hoarder? He showered like fifteen times in a row when he got home and swore he saw a rat and a cockroach fighting."

Gavin snorted in amusement. "Then he refused to date for like six months, too scarred from that experience to try again. He also for a while had that weird distrust of hot women."

Poppy's sides hurt from laughing so hard. She remembered it all. He'd smelled like bleach for a week after. He wasn't OCD really, but he never did like mess. He was big on order and despised any kind of chaos.

The clothes they'd sorted through proved that. Everything meticulously folded and color coordinated. He hadn't even left any dirty laundry or ratty clothes.

She couldn't be more different. She was always a mess. Not hoarder level, but she was not tidy or organized. It had always driven Perry crazy. He would still sneak into her apartment and clean up after her like some sneaky maid.

They quieted as they each sank into thoughts of Perry. It wasn't a depressing quiet though for once. It was peaceful and fond.

Flynn's chair scraped the floor as he stood. "I'm gonna grab drinks. What does everyone want? Except you, Poppy. I have a surprise drink for you. New bartender and he's awesome."

"Should I be worried?" She was a bit picky when it came to alcohol. She liked beer and wine and the very occasional cocktail.

"Nope. I asked him to create something with you in mind and he came through perfectly. I hired him on the spot." A pleased smile teased across his lips.

Lips she'd kissed. Lips that had touched her most intimate of places. She shook off her dirty thoughts and focused on the here and now.

Poppy didn't understand. Why would he create a drink for her? Why would that be part of his hiring technique? He made no sense.

Gavin smoothed a hand over his mouth like he was trying to scrub away a grin. "Don't fight it. He's been waiting to surprise you with this for weeks."

Weeks?

"Was that why Perry tried to get me to come out that night?" Normally, he didn't invite her that often. Only when she seemed extra lonely. He knew she preferred going home alone and relaxing with Netflix or books.

Most of what she considered fun was theme parks and rock climbing and other outdoor adventures. Not bars or restaurants or plays. She'd rather just go home.

Dean shook his head. "No. Honestly. And don't go there. He asked you that night because he said you'd been a bit down that week. Seemed overworked. He felt guilty for waiting so long to agree to hire extra people especially since he was at the fire station half the time, leaving you to handle it alone. It had nothing to do with Flynn."

Gavin scoffed. "Of course it had nothing to do with Flynn. Perry was pissed he made her a drink."

Poppy jerked to face Gavin. "Why?"

Dean glared at Gavin, who grimaced, but shrugged.

"Why?" Poppy asked again.

"Look, Perry loved us and he loved you. And he was the best fucking friend. But he had a problem with you hanging with us too much. He was worried something like what happened last night would happen."

Flynn told them? What did they think of her? Did they think she was pathetic? That she wanted only Flynn? That she was trying to steal him from them?

Dean growled. "Dammit, Gavin. Shut the fuck up."

Gavin scowled at his friend. "No, man. I'm not going to lie to her. She knew him as well or better than us. She knew how he was when it came to his love of the spotlight and jealousy issues. He didn't like to share."

"He didn't. I always thought it was because he had to so much growing up with me as his twin. We shared everything. While I loved it, he could sometimes resent it." Okay, not sometimes. All the time. "So, you know what happened last night?"

Gavin winced. "The walls are kind of...well, they aren't sound proof."

She covered her burning face with her hands. Crap. This was going to make a mess of everything.

Dean shook his head, frustration tensing his shoulders. "Shit. You are such a fucker."

Gavin shrugged, completely unrepentant. "We've started now, might as well finish."

"You mean *you've* started." Dean sneered the words.

What the hell were they talking about? Her eyes bounced back and forth between them as they argued.

Gavin's hand curled into a fist on top of the table. "Whatever. I told you guys I wasn't willing to wait forever."

"Yeah, but we agreed to wait longer than this." Dean jerked at his scarf like it was strangling him.

"Why should we? Flynn certainly didn't."

She'd had enough. "Guys. Shut up."

They both slammed their mouths closed and looked at her.

She had to try and fix this before it turned into something bigger than it was. "What the hell are you two going on about? Are you upset about Flynn and I? Because it didn't mean anything. Honestly, if it had been either one of you, I would have tried the same thing."

The words were completely true. She'd never favored one of them over the other.

"What if it was someone other than us?" Gavin asked.

Her brow wrinkled. "What do you mean?"

"I mean, what if it was that hot new bartender of Flynn's?" Gavin pointed towards the bar.

"I..." Poppy paused, considering it. She was tempted to lie, but she never wanted to do that to them. "No. Only you three."

Something like relief flickered in Gavin's eyes. "Then no, we aren't upset."

"Then why are you arguing?" This made no sense.

Dean cursed. "Because we want things you are ready for and we don't want to push you or even bring it up yet. It's all too soon. Can we please drop it for now? I swear we'll explain it all soon, but can we just have a good time tonight?"

She wanted to demand or shake the answers from them, but something in their expressions and their argument made her afraid to hear what they had to say. "Yeah. We can do that."

Gavin sighed, looking annoyed, but he dropped it. But that was Gavin, fearless and ready to jump headfirst into any situation, regardless of the hazard. Dean was the one who was calmer, more thoughtful and observant, in touch with his emotions and the emotions of others. If he said she wasn't ready, she believed him.

Flynn returned with a tray of booze and glanced between the three of them with a concerned expression. "Do I want to know?"

Dean shook his head. "Nope."

"All right then." He passed out drinks to the guys first. A margarita for Gavin, a scotch for the brooding artist, a beer for himself. Then he turned to Poppy with a flourish and handed over a purple and blue and pink layered frozen drink, a stick of rock candy poking out of it. "A unicorn daiquiri for you."

Poppy's jaw dropped as she took in the frozen work of alcoholic art. "What? How? This is the best thing I've ever seen."

Flynn grinned and sat down. "The real test is the taste. Try it."

She sipped at it from the swirly straw stuck into it and her eyes widened as the flavors of cotton candy and marshmallows and blue raspberries exploded on her tongue.

"Well, what do you think?" Flynn asked.

"I think I want to marry your bartender."

All three guys scowled at her joke, not finding it nearly as amusing as she did. She shrugged and pulled more through the straw, closing her eyes and moaning at the taste. She wasn't sure she was actually joking.

Chapter 25

By the third unicorn daiquiri, Poppy was really feeling it, relaxed back in her chair, her feet propped in Gavin's lap as she watched the dance floor through half-lidded eyes.

Gavin eased her feet to the ground and held out his hand for her to take. "Dance with me. I need to burn out some of this booze."

She took his hand and let him pull her to her feet and over to the area cleared out for dancing. The floor was already packed with mostly tipsy couples in different stages of embrace. Classic rock brought out a rather interesting crowd.

Bohemian Rhapsody came on once she and Gavin joined the dancers and the crowd immediately joined in. What was it about that song? She couldn't help but shout out the lyrics either, melding her voice with theirs as she and Gavin hopped in time with the rest of them, their fists pumping in the air.

Something strong and powerful swept through her as the entire bar screamed out the chorus of the song, completely in harmony. Her hand reached out for Gavin's and she clutched his hard. He pulled her into his side, grinning down at her, his eyes dancing with excitement. Dean and Flynn watched them from their table, both of them mouthing along. They each shot her winks as she smiled at them over her shoulder.

Bohemian Rhapsody ended and a slow song she didn't recognize replaced it. Gavin twirled her into his chest and they swayed to the beat, their bodies pressed close.

Poppy avoided his eyes, instead focusing on the other couples over his shoulder, not wanting to give away any of the confusing feelings swelling inside her. His body so close to hers made it hard for her to concentrate, his spicy scent and the heat radiating from him overwhelming everything else. Which was extra awkward and uncomfortable considering what she and Flynn did the night before.

What was wrong with her? Sure, she'd always had a crush on all of them, had been attracted to them, but since they had stayed over at her apartment, something was different. And she didn't think it was Perry's death. She hoped not. But maybe it was his absence. He wasn't there frowning or interrupting every time one of them touched or flirted with her. And it had her all kind of mixed up.

She needed to keep distance between them, because regardless of what she did with Flynn, she refused to choose one of them over the others. It's why she'd never called Perry out on his admittedly possessive behavior. It was better not to rock the boat and capsize a twenty year friendship. Which had probably been Perry's concern as well.

As soon as the song ended and another one began, Dean appeared next to them and swept her away from Gavin. "My turn."

"But I want to keep dancing."

"It's why I brought Flynn. He'll dance with you." Dean twirled her away from their pouting friend.

"There are plenty of women here, why doesn't he ask one of them?" Poppy asked.

"He has his reasons."

Poppy's brow furrowed in confusion, but she shrugged, accepting Dean's answer for now. He was really bringing out the brooding, mysterious artist side of him lately.

She liked it. Too much.

The song they danced to was a fast one, so their hips rolled to the beat, almost grinding against one another. He kept a respectable distance between them, not taking advantage, but a few times his pelvis brushed against hers, shooting lightning crackling through her veins.

His eyes caught hers and she lost herself in the coffee color of his gaze as they spun and danced to a song not really meant to be danced to. She wasn't completely sure how Flynn's classic rock dance nights were so popular. Most of the music he loved so much was older than him.

"Having fun?" Dean asked.

She nodded, tempted to lay her head on his shoulder. "I am."

"Good." A pleased smile spread across his lips.

"Are you?"

"Always when I'm with you."

She frowned a little at his sweet words. "I'm really confused."

Dean winced. "I know and I'm sorry. Let's get you and us through all this hell first and let things kind of settle and then we'll all have a conversation."

"Why does there need to be some big talk? We're old friends. Last night doesn't change that. It doesn't mean there needs to be a family meeting." Perry always joked about the meetings the four of them would have whenever something needed to be decided or changed or discussed.

She'd never been to one since she didn't live with them. And she didn't now. She was just taking a small break from her life.

"Oh, but there does need to be one. Just definitely not drunk on unicorn drinks."

"I'm the only one drunk on those. Other than Flynn, you guys were too macho to try it."

"Not macho. We just want to keep our teeth."

She grinned, already craving another. "Worth it."

Dean shuddered and twirled her. "If you say so."

She stumbled into his chest when he tugged her back, laughing up at him, breathless. He missed a step as he stared back down at her, his amusement disappearing from his face. Her body reacted to his, her belly tightening, her chest fluttering, her pulse racing. Her eyes widened when his hand raised to cup the back of her neck, his palm warm against her skin.

Another Queen song came on, a slow one, but she couldn't remember the name. The tone of their dance changed, turning sensual and teasing. He refused to release the stare he trapped her in until she believed she'd drown in his coffee eyes. Coffee was her very favorite thing and his eyes had always made her think of the drink.

She licked her lips and he followed the movement with his coffee eyes, his throat bobbing. His fingers flexed against her hips, so tight it rode the edge of pain and she played with the edges of his hair behind his neck. All thoughts fled her mind, leaving nothing but need and want. Those damn unicorn drinks packed an evil punch when mixed with grief, because she didn't have a single hesitation or inhibition left and she hoped his scotch had done the same for him because she needed his lips against hers.

"Kiss me."

He didn't question or argue or even hesitate. Before she could blink, he was kissing her, lifting her onto her toes by his grip on her hips, teasing the seam of her mouth with his tongue, and she was opening for him, wordlessly begging him to take it deeper.

He tasted like desperation and relief and pain. She could become addicted to his taste. He tasted like she felt and she wanted more. The music swelled around them like the emotional manipulation in the soundtracks of movies and TV shows. And it worked on her now just like it did in the movies.

Ozzy Osbourne scream startled her, making her jerk back as *Crazy Train* pumped from the speakers. She and Dean stared at each other, shock on both their faces.

What had she done? She was scared to look around to find out if Flynn saw. There was no telling what he would think. She didn't know what to think either. Almost fucking one of them, then kissing another the next night? Was she going to give Gavin a blow job tomorrow? Unfortunately, the idea didn't horrify her as much as it should.

She stumbled away from him, losing herself in the dancers and retreated towards the bathroom.

Dean grabbed her before she could escape. "I'm sorry. I shouldn't have done that."

"I asked for it. You don't have to apologize. I just..." Poppy trailed off, unable to explain the mess of confusion twisted and snarled in her head.

He nodded like he heard her unspoken words. "Too much, too soon. I get it. Just forget anything happened and let's go have another drink."

"I think I'm going to stick to water the rest of the night." She didn't need to make any more inebriated decisions.

"Fair enough. We can go, if you want."

She shook her head. "The guys look like they're still having fun, I don't want to cut their night short."

"They won't care. Trust me. About leaving or about what just happened."

Somehow, that was worse. She was a horrible person. She didn't want to hurt any of them, but at the same time a part of her wanted them to care if she was kissing or sleeping with one of them instead of the others. It was time for her to get out of this entire situation and find some space and perspective.

"I think I'm going to head back alone. I need a little while to myself."

Dean didn't look like he was anywhere near okay with that. "Are you sure that's a good idea?"

"I'll get a ride, don't worry. No way I'm walking alone still half-drunk." She wasn't so messed up she'd do that.

"I can go with you and then give you your space once we're back. Or we all can."

She patted his arm, touched at his worry, even though it was completely unnecessary. "I've been going home alone for years now, often much drunker than this. I'll be fine."

Dean played with the edges of his scarf. "Sorry. I'm hovering. I don't usually hover."

"I get it." She wasn't exactly thinking straight or making the best decisions lately. "Explain to the guys for me?"

"Sure. But listen. We all really need to talk tomorrow. Explain things we should have admitted a long time ago. But also explain things we planned to wait for. I'm worried if we don't, you'll ghost on us, thinking the worst. So promise me you won't take off until we talk. Please." His eyes begged her to agree.

Nerves fluttered in her belly like a flock of crows taking off at a loud noise. "Should I stay so we can have the conversation now? You're starting to freak me out about it now."

"Tomorrow is good. We'll all be sober and rested."

She snorted. "You mean hungover and exhausted."

"Drink a lot of water when you get back and we'll have plenty of coffee ready in the morning."

"Fine. I promise." She turned to leave.

He stopped her with a hand on her arm. "One more thing."

She almost screamed, desperate to escape the sweltering club and pounding music. "What?"

"Text us when you get back so we know you're safe? We'll give you at least a couple hours so you can have some space."

She relaxed a little. "I can do that."

"Thanks."

She smiled in response and turned away, rushing outside, refusing to look back.

DEAN WATCHED THE WOMAN he loved run away from him after kissing him like he was all she ever wanted in this world.

Fuck.

They were all making such a disaster out of this. First Flynn made her scream with pleasure, then Gavin spilled half the beans, and now he'd kissed her.

Idiots, the lot of them.

Perry's death had snapped the hold that had kept them away from her all these years. Not because they didn't need to worry about Perry's permission or blessing or whatever the hell they'd hoped for. But because they were all desperate to remember they were alive even if one of their favorite people wasn't anymore. They were all struggling with misery and grief, so their decision making skills were shit at the moment.

Dean slumped back over to their table, not looking forward to explaining where their girl went.

Gavin and Flynn looked up from their conversation when Dean sank into the chair Poppy had been using.

"She left."

Flynn jerked back. "What? Then why the hell are we still here?"

"She needed a little space from us."

"Why?" Gavin asked.

Dean groaned and pinched the bridge of his nose. "Because I'm as big of an idiot as the two of you."

"What did you do?" Gavin's eyes narrowed into slits.

"Kissed her." Dean was half-hard still after the kiss and having her in his arms for their too few dances.

A man he vaguely recognized sat across the bar, staring at them. When Dean met his eyes, the guy looked away. Dean couldn't pinpoint where he knew him from, but he had bigger things to worry about at the moment.

Gavin swore and drained his drink. "Bit of a hypocrite, aren't you?"

"Yeah. She asked me to. What the hell was I supposed to do?" Dean was incapable of denying her when she looked at him with such want and need.

"Shit. What the hell are we doing?" Flynn rubbed his face.

Dean ran his finger though the drops of water on the table, drawing designs with the condensation. "I told her we'd explain everything in the morning."

A sad smile twisted Gavin's lips. "Family meeting?"

Dean cleared the pain from his throat. "Yeah."

Flynn groaned. "She's going to run."

Dean had the same dread. "If she does, we're going to have to let her. She's in no condition to make decisions like this and neither are we. But I'm afraid if we don't explain, we'll lose her completely."

"We may either way." Gavin stared glumly into his empty glass.

Which was the exact fear that had held them back for so long. And a respect for Perry, since he was so adamantly against it even though he'd recently started coming around. They'd planned to wear him down over time. It felt wrong, like they were doing it behind his back now that he was no longer here to disapprove.

Chapter 26

Poppy hovered at the bottom of the steps, listening to the guys murmur and putter around their kitchen. She'd actually slept the whole night through by herself, not needing one of them with her. She didn't know if it was the booze or emotional exhaustion or she was actually healing a little bit, but she was grateful. She'd been terrified she'd return to her apartment and back to sleepless nights.

Spending some of the worst days following the news of Perry's death with the guys was helping. It kept her mind from dwelling on it constantly and kept her from hiding alone and trying to wish herself into the grave with Perry.

She nibbled at her bottom lip, hesitating at actually joining them. She had no idea what they wanted to discuss with her, but she was fairly certain whatever it was would make things even more complicated than she'd already made it.

The lure of coffee to ease the ache pounding the back of her head finally got her hauling up her big girl panties and sweeping into the kitchen like she didn't have a care in the world. She would face this the way she'd been facing a lot of things lately. With utter denial.

She smiled at them in good morning and headed straight for the coffee pot. They grunted at her, bent over the counter, clutching mugs in their hands.

"How much more did you guys drink after I left?" Poppy fought a smile.

"Not too much." Flynn circled the edge of the mug with his finger.

She arched a skeptical brow. "Oh, really?"

"In comparison to some of the others there, sure."

She perched on the stool across from them. "Do you need more time to recover before we have whatever conversation you want to have with me?"

Gavin smirked. "We're good. Just don't take offense at any wincing or groaning we might do."

"Fair enough." Poppy shrugged.

Flynn glared at her with suspicion. "Why are you fine? You may have left sooner, but you still had a lot of those unicorn monstrosities."

"I hydrated. And apparently can handle my liquor better."

Dean shook his head. "You always have. You and Perry both."

"I always wondered if it was a twin thing." Gavin tapped his bottom lip with his index finger.

Amusement almost made her choke on her sip of coffee. "Nope. I think it's genetics. We're Irish."

Gavin frowned. "I thought that was just a myth."

"Maybe. I'm not Google." She sipped her coffee. "Let's get this over with, then. What is it you have to tell me?" A sudden, horrible thought occurred to her. "You're not selling the house, are you?"

Dean's head jerked up. "What? Of course not."

She sighed out in relief. "Well, you guys need to tell me now because I'm starting to imagine odd and horrible things."

Flynn rubbed his temples. "It's a little awkward. And talking about it sober was a horrible idea."

Dean cleared his throat. "We don't want you to get the wrong idea after what's happened between some of us this weekend."

Ah. It was *that* talk. "I don't have any wrong ideas. I know none of it meant anything. Just sadness and booze mixing together into a cocktail of bad choices."

Dean's grip tightened on his coffee mug. "Right. Okay. You have exactly the wrong idea."

"What are you talking about?" Poppy asked.

Dean's eyes speared through her. "It meant more to us than meaningless fun. A lot more."

Flynn looked almost wounded. "Did it really mean nothing to you?"

She gaped for a moment before she was able to stutter out words. "I...well, not exactly. But I didn't expect anything to come from it."

"Do you want something to come from it?" Gavin asked.

She leaned back, holding her mug like a shield between them. "This is starting to feel like a trap. Or a meeting with a therapist. I'm going to need you to be very clear what you three are saying."

The three of them shared a glance and sipped their coffee almost completely in sync to sort out their thoughts.

Gavin finally blurted it out. "We've been in love with you for years."

What? Her mug clattered onto the counter, the precious coffee ignored and forgotten for the moment. "I don't understand."

Flynn elbowed Gavin. "Dude. Why the hell did you throw it out there like that?"

"Because it's the truth and if we keep pussy footing around it, she'll think she means nothing to us. She's already expecting to basically never see each us again once regular life starts to pick up again."

She didn't remember mentioning those thoughts to him. Was she talking in her sleep again? She hadn't done that since she was little and her dad left.

"Can we bring the focus back around, please?" She needed more information. Her brain whirled with chaotic thoughts and fears and disbelief.

Gavin shook himself. "Right. Sorry."

"Guys, seriously. What the hell are you saying?" She squished the hope trying to rise inside her.

Dean looked straight at her, his expression grave. "We're saying we want to be with you."

"All of you?" The question squeaked out of her.

"Yes." The trio said the word at the same time.

She wanted to bury her face in her hands. She wanted to run and never look back. She wanted to leap across the counter and kiss each one of them. "I don't understand."

Dean rubbed his bottom lip. "We've actually discussed this for years. But you never seemed interested and Perry was wildly against it."

"I think he was worried I'd choose one of you and ruin everything."

"Why choose?" Flynn asked.

She picked her coffee back up, desperate for caffeine to continue this conversation. "I never could."

"You don't have to."

"And how exactly would that even work?" Sure, the four of them, three now, shared everything, but wasn't sharing a lover a little far?

"We'd figure it out together, but we needed you to know this was something we wanted," Dean said. "The timing of it sucks, but since two of us moved faster with you than we meant to sooner than we meant to, we didn't want you going home thinking it was a mistake or it meant nothing."

"I don't know what to say." More than anything she wanted to say yes, but she wasn't completely reckless.

Not all the time. Not with romantic relationships. Actually, not with any kind of relationships. She didn't make connections easily. Never had. That was Perry's domain.

Gavin reached across the counter to squeeze her hand. "You don't have to say anything. You can think about it as long as you need to. Or if you'd prefer we never bring it up again, that's fine too. It's your decision."

Flynn's green eyes caught hers. "We love you, Poppy. We have for a long time. But out of respect to Perry, we kept our distance, waiting for you to make the first move. We're a family and you've always been a part of it. Just not as a sister."

Could she really have this? Have everything she'd ever wanted? The only three men who had ever made her feel anything stronger than a mild interest and attraction?

How could she make any decisions this important right now? How could they drop something so huge on her barely over a week after her brother's funeral? How could her brother keep so fucking much from her? Something that meant so much to her? And to his best friends?

Fury washed over her in red waves and she tried to fight it back, hold it down. She wasn't even sure why she was suddenly so angry. She should have been ecstatic. But all she could see were the four most important men in her life keeping secrets from her and them being more worried about respecting Perry's wishes than trying to find out what hers were.

She wasn't Perry's property. She wasn't his to give out permission to court her like this was last century. He had no right to act like he had any say over her love life and they had no right to abide by his wishes. Not if she was family and as important as they claimed she was.

This was bullshit.

She hadn't spent her life waiting for them like some sort of virgin bride. And as pissed as she was at them now, she might actually finally be able to move on because whatever it was they wanted from her, she didn't think she could give it. They were asking for something verging on crazy. Society wasn't ready for a relationship like theirs. She couldn't even legally marry all of them. Instead, society would brand her a slut and it was highly likely their families may disown them all.

She had no family left to offend, but they did. Had they really thought this through or was it some kind of fantasy they never expected to last? She didn't want to agree and once it started getting tough, they backed out and broke her heart and she really lost everything.

No.

She had to leave.

She had to go home.

She had to get the hell out of there before the burning rage inside her made her say something awful she wouldn't be able to take back.

"I think I'm going to go back to my place a day early."

Chapter 27

The guys let her go without too many questions and objections. Their pained and worried expressions haunted her as she walked home. She needed the fresh air, the ride alone back to their place the night before still left her raw. Leaving them behind left a hollow feeling in her chest that grew with each step she took away from them.

Their words played over and over again in her head, but they still weren't any clearer. The rage searing through her chest ran out of control, she couldn't wrangle it, making her feel insane.

Poppy reached her shop and breathed out a sigh of relief as she unlocked and opened the door, the warm scents of coffee and muffins embracing her.

Tam and Marie must have been in here recently working since the smells were still fresh instead of old and stale. She was grateful for their help, they'd basically handled everything around the shop for her since she got the call.

She let out a whining groan as she remembered everything she needed to handle. The last couple of days were nice, pretending the real world didn't exist, pretending her responsibilities could wait, pretending her brother wasn't dead. She'd enjoyed it while it lasted, but now she needed to get to work even if it was the last thing she wanted to do.

She dropped her bag onto one of the tables and pushed into the kitchen. There needed to be fresh pastries and muffins ready for the morning crowd the next day. She hooked her phone up to the speakers she kept in there and blasted angry girl rock through the room, the screaming lyrics and pounding drums the perfect match to her mood.

She whipped ingredients and punched dough to the heavy beat of the music, lost in her head as she made lavender and vanilla bean scones and fresh bread for the mini paninis they served for the lunch crowd. Focusing on what she loved helped settle her mind and push away the confusion and worries over the guys.

With Perry gone she was doing stupid things, crazy things. And considering stupid things, crazy things. His loss made her reckless and wild, even more so than her usual. She had to get herself under control. Which meant staying away from the guys for a while. She needed space until she got her head on straight since she couldn't make proper decisions in this frame of mind.

They loved her? How had they hidden it for so long? She'd never had the slightest inkling. And they'd discussed it with each other, deciding to share her. All without taking what she wanted into account. It didn't matter that they were right. She didn't want just one. But they made all the decisions and plans behind her back.

If Perry hadn't died, would they have kept it a secret forever? She didn't want to start a relationship that would have been impossible with her brother alive. She didn't want to take advantage of his death and find some sort of twisted silver lining. No. If she couldn't have them with Perry in her life, then she didn't want them with him gone.

She couldn't.

A pounding banged against the door of her shop right as she slammed the oven door closed on a pan of strawberry vanilla granola. With a sigh, she wiped her hands off on a towel and went to probably explain to someone why she was closed. If she wanted to compete with the coffee chain who must not be named, she had to be open at least six days a week. Even though that place's coffee was shitty and bitter.

Her heart thudded in her chest when she recognized the man at her door. Did he finally have answers for her?

She threw the door open. "Officer Maxwell. Come in."

He stepped inside and gave her a respectful nod. "Ms. O'Sullivan. Thank you."

"Did you find the driver?" She almost crossed her fingers, desperate for answers, for justice.

He grimaced. "No. I'm sorry. We still don't know anything other than a blue sedan was the vehicle in question."

Her shoulders slumped as the hope vanished. "Right. Which doesn't exactly narrow it down."

"Exactly."

"Then why are you here?" Poppy asked.

He cleared his throat. "This is the first time I've been able to catch you since before the funeral."

"Yes. Well, I've been a bit busy. You could have called." She struggled to keep the bitter sarcasm out of her voice.

"I felt this was better handled in person."

Her stomach dropped and she sucked in a sharp breath. "What was?"

"Your brother...I got the autopsy report. He wasn't wearing his seatbelt. We thought as much after seeing the scene, but the coroner confirmed it."

Her eyes closed and she stumbled back a step to grip the edge of the counter as a silent scream rang through her head. That fucking moron. How could he be so careless?

She reopened her eyes and forced herself to remain calm and steady. "What does that mean exactly? For me, I mean."

"It won't change any of his insurance affairs other than you might have issues with the vehicle insurance."

"It was totalled and I have no plans to fix it. Why couldn't this be handled with a phone call?" Her eyes narrowed.

"I did try to call, but never got through to you and it didn't feel right leaving this information on a voicemail."

Right. She hadn't been answering her phone. "Was there anything else?"

He shook his head. "No. We're still investigating, but there were no cameras aimed at the street at the scene. No witnesses have come forward. I should warn you, it's highly likely whoever did it will get away with the crime. You should prepare yourself for that."

"I'll keep that in mind. Thank you." She didn't let on how much his words destroyed her. One of the main things keeping her going was discovering who took her twin from her.

He eyed her with concern. "Is there anyone I can call for you?"

He'd asked the same thing when she'd met him at the morgue to identify her brother's body. She gave him the same answer she'd given him then.

"No. I'm fine."

He stepped towards the door, clearly ready to get on with his day. "I'll keep you updated as we learn more. I am sorry for your loss."

"Thank you."

Numb, Poppy watched the officer turn and leave, his responsibility finished. If the cop investigating her brother's death, his *murder*, had no hope he'd find the killer, then how could she?

A burning smell pulled her out of the despair and fury. With a curse, she raced for the kitchen and yanked the blackened granola from the oven, slamming it on top of the stove.

She ran a trembling hand through her hair, wincing at the tangles pulling at her scalp. She tried to slow her breathing, calm herself, but it only made her lightheaded. A sweat broke out across her body as she overheated with out of control rage.

She couldn't believe her careful and precise brother didn't wear his seat belt. What was he thinking? Was he upset about something and forgot? Distracted? He was always the one who reminded her to buckle up. What sort of sick, cosmic joke was this? The one time he didn't wear it, some probably drunk asshole crashed him into a tree and killed him.

With a scream, she threw the entire pan of burnt granola across the kitchen, sending it crashing into the wall, granola raining down on her and the room. Her chest heaved and eyes stung as she stared at the mess around her.

Poppy's shoulders slumped and she swallowed around the pain swelling her throat. This was unbearable. Loving someone so much, so completely was agony. There was no moving on from this loss. Not this one. Not Perry.

This was her life now.

Chapter 28

Poppy bit back a curse when Flynn walked through the door of her shop the next afternoon. It had barely been twenty-four hours since she saw them. Was this all the time they were willing to give her?

She closed the register with more force than necessary and plastered on a strained smile to the woman who just bought a coffee. "Thank you. Have a nice day."

The woman gave her a strange look as she turned to leave. Hopefully she hadn't just driven a new customer away for good. She'd struggled all day to keep a leash on her temper, but the demanding customers and the constant jangle of the bell above the door wore on her frayed nerves. She'd already snapped at Tam and Marie several times and really needed to apologize.

Flynn got in the back of the line and waited patiently as she rang up the customers in front of him. It was the time between lunch and dinner, and people mostly wanted coffee for the afternoon pick me up instead of food, so the line moved too fast. No one came in behind Flynn, so she was trapped with him, no excuse to rush him through.

"Can you take a break for a few?" Flynn asked.

Tam leaned over Poppy's shoulder. "Yes. She can. We've got this. You haven't taken five minutes since we opened."

Poppy sighed and her shoulders drooped a little. "Fine." She gestured to an open table near the back that would give them privacy and Flynn nodded, following her over to it.

She sat with her back to the wall so she could see the whole shop and Flynn took the seat across from her, cupping his coffee between his hands.

"What are you doing here?" It was hard to look him in the eyes, so she stared at the spot past his shoulder.

"Checking on you. I know you want space, but unless you tell us in no uncertain terms to fuck off, we're not going to completely disappear."

She wasn't ready to tell them to fuck off yet. She didn't know what she wanted which was the problem. Part of it, anyway. "I'm not great, but I'm getting through the day. It's easier having the job to focus on."

He nodded. "I'm looking forward to going back to work tonight too. The time off was nice, especially the weekend, but I like my job and I need to keep busy."

She winced. "I'm sorry. I feel like I've made it all about me when you guys miss him as much as I do."

"We do, but he was your twin. It's different for you. Harder. And we have each other. We live together and are constantly around one another. You don't have that to the extent we do. And we've been trying to make sure you have us too. It's easier on all of us when we know you're as okay as you can be. It's easier on us when we have you to take care of. We like feeling useful. And before you get your back up, don't. You took care of us too, even if it didn't feel like it. Just by being there, hanging and playing, it was you taking care of us too."

"If you say so." She wanted to believe him and Flynn had never lied to her. None of them had. Kept secrets, yes, but so had she.

"I do say so."

"Okay."

"Now Marie might have mentioned you've been a bit on edge today. Want to talk about it?"

Poppy raised a brow. "Did she say on edge or did she say bitchy?"

Flynn's lips quirked. "Pissy, actually. What's going on?"

Word vomit began spewing from her mouth and she couldn't stop it. "What's going on is my brother is dead, our childhood friends suddenly spill an apparently long kept secret about their feelings for me at basically the worst possible time they could bring it up. I'm confused and furious even though I have no idea why.

"I have a million things to handle I've been putting off, half of which I have no idea how to do even though I'm a twenty-seven-year old adult woman because I let my brother take care of it like the good little woman who couldn't be bothered to worry her pretty head about business."

She sucked in a breath before she continued. "The piece of human garbage who killed my brother is still out there somewhere living their life, free even though their actions have completely ruined me." She fought the sob trying to crawl up her throat. "My emotions are all over the place and I feel like I'm losing my mind all while I'm trying to pretend everything is fine and go about my life because that's what I'm supposed to do, right? He wasn't my husband or child. He was my brother. You don't get a lot of time off for grief when it's just your brother even though he was my whole fucking world, my best fucking friend. He was everything to me. Now, I'm alone. My family is gone. I'm the last one standing and it fucking sucks and I don't know how to pretend it doesn't." She panted wildly once she ran out of words, her whole body flushing with humiliation at her word vomit.

Everything she'd been holding in since the officer came the day before and her sleepless night tore away her filters.

Flynn's eyes shimmered with tears and pain. "You are not alone. Dammit, muffin. You have us. We are your family. You aren't the last one standing. You just have to let us in. And I'm not talking romantically. We can just be your friends if that's what you want or need. It's enough for us. It always has been. You are enough for us."

"Was I?"

He nodded with a confused look. "Yes. Of course."

"Then why wait so long to say something to me? Why wait until he was gone?" She held up her hand and pushed back from the table. "You know what? I can't talk about this right now. I'm fine. I'll be fine. I need to get back to work. And you need to get ready to do the same. I'll talk to you about all this later." Before he could argue, she jumped from her seat and hurried back behind the counter, trying desperately to keep her face calm.

Flynn shot her a sad look, but he nodded and left and she was finally able to breathe again.

Tam and Marie exchanged worried glances, but she ignored them. She was fine. She had to be. She had gotten through her mother's death. She'd get through Perry's too.

Somehow.

Poppy threw herself into her work, refusing to think about the guys any more that day. She'd channel Scarlett and think about it tomorrow. If she could just focus on the here and now, maybe she could get through this hellish day and finally enjoy the bliss of being alone to break down however she needed with only her cat as witness.

Until then, she fought every emotion off churning inside of her and went through the motions, forcing herself to remain pleasant even when she wanted to scream at indecisive and rude customers. Even when Tam spilled coffee all over the floor. Even when she looked for Perry to share a commiserating glance and she remembered all over again that he wasn't there.

Closing time finally neared, and she sighed as the bell clanged again ten minutes before they flipped the sign. There was always a straggler on Mondays. Always.

She looked up, fake smile in place, but it melted from her face as she took in the man waltzing through the door like he had any right. Even after all this time, she recognized him.

Her father.

Chapter 29

Poppy clenched the edge of the counter with numb fingers as the man who abandoned her and Perry approached her, a woman and two teens, a boy and a girl, trailing behind.

"Poppy. It's been a long time."

"Yeah. Twenty years." She jerked her head towards Tam and Marie, signaling them to give her some privacy.

They hurried to the kitchen, muttering about cleaning things up. There wasn't much point. She was about to spend the rest of the night baking more, but she didn't want an audience for this. Or, more of an audience than the people with her father. She had a bad feeling she knew exactly who they were.

His replacement family.

"You look good." He pointed to the woman and kids behind him. "This is Callie, my wife and Blake and Tiffany, our children."

He did. He brought his fucking replacement family

She ignored the introduction. "What are you doing here?"

He ignored her glare and unfriendly tone. "I came to pay my respects to your brother. I'm sorry for missing the funeral. I was in the middle of an important job and didn't find out about his loss in time to make it."

Of course he was too busy. Of course his job was more important than his fucking dead son or grieving daughter. "Why did you bother?"

He had the balls to actually look offended. "My son was killed, of course I came."

Poppy bit back hysterical laughter. "You haven't given a shit about him or me for twenty years while Perry was still alive. Or when our mother was dying from cancer. Why do you suddenly care now?"

His wife and kids hovered in the background, looking incredibly uncomfortable. She almost felt sorry for them, but not enough to make her be polite or reconciliatory. Fuck him and them for coming here and putting her through another level of hell.

Could she just have a small break? One day of no drama, revelations, or stupid choices?

"Of course I care. I always have." Her sperm donor was losing patience, his voice irritated.

Good.

"Right. Well, if that's all, I need to close up here." She gestured to the door, hoping he'd take the hint and vanish like he did twenty years ago.

"Well, I was hoping to catch up with you while I'm still here in town. I'll be here another week." He barely acknowledged the family at his back, like they didn't matter.

Why the hell did he bring them here? And why was he acting like she was an old college roommate he wanted to reconnect with instead of a daughter he'd spent more time ignoring than living with.

She shook her head and gave him an easy out. Whatever it was that brought him here wasn't worry for her or wanting to get to know her. "I'm a little busy right now handling the business alone and wrapping up Perry's affairs. I'm afraid I won't have time."

He checked his watch before looking back at her with stupid blue eyes that were too familiar. "I heard the two of you owned this little place. Are you sure you can run it on your own? Maybe you should sell the place. I could put you in touch with someone to take care of it for you. It can't be making you much money with two of the most popular coffee chains in the country right around the corner. Owning your own business is a big responsibility. If you dye your hair back to a normal color and dress more like a grownup, I'm sure you could find an excellent job that won't be so risky for you."

What an utter son of a bitch.

She laid both her hands flat on the countertop to try and keep from swinging a punch directly at his smug, conceited, jackass of a face. "We're in no danger of having to close the doors anytime soon. Thanks for your concern. Have a safe flight home." She scribbled a few words on the back of a take home menu and slid it across the counter. "Here's the address to the grave site if you still wish to pay your respects. As I said, I need to close up."

He sniffed and took the paper. "I'll come back when you're not so busy."

"That's not necessary."

The woman tried to smile, but it only trembled a moment on her lips before it fell away. The two kids glared at all of them, clearly pissed at being there. Poppy had no idea what his family knew about her father's past and didn't care. She just wanted them gone. She couldn't bear to look at the kids with their blue eyes just like hers, just like Perry's, just like their bastard father's.

Her father's jaw clenched and he spun on his heel and stalked to the door, expecting his family to fall in line and follow. Which they did. Poppy watched, her stomach churning with bile at the thought of two siblings she never knew she had. Two siblings Perry never got to find out about, never got to meet.

Blake looked so much like him, it was liking getting a glimpse of the past, like seeing a ghost.

Her hands shook so hard, she couldn't get her apron untied and a rush of heat exploded through her as she fought to pull air into her lungs. Her vision blurred as she yanked at the ties imprisoning her inside the apron, and little whimpering gasps fell from her lips. She couldn't breathe, she couldn't get out. She was trapped.

Tam and Marie were suddenly there, freeing her from the apron, sinking to the floor with her, holding her hands, reminding her how to breathe. They sounded like they were yelling at her from underwater and she couldn't understand them, but their touch and company helped.

Tears splashed down her cheeks and onto her chest as she fought to get herself under control.

Someone else joined them on the floor behind the counter, pushing between Tam and Marie to cup Poppy's cheeks. Dean. A choked sob ripped from her as Dean's thumbs brushed the tears from her face, his expression pained and empathetic and worried.

The surprise of his arrival helped snap her out of the panic controlling her.

"What the hell happened?" Dean asked, a growl in his voice.

Tam held her hands out in a helpless gesture. "We aren't sure. Someone stopped by who she seemed to know and didn't want to see. We went to the kitchen to give her privacy and when we came back out we found her like this."

Dean nodded, never moving his hands away from Poppy's face or taking his eyes off hers. "Thanks for texting. You guys can go. I've got her."

Marie patted his shoulder. "We'll open in the morning. Make her sleep in."

"I'll try." He looked like he planned to more than try. He looked like he planned to demand it.

Tam stood finally. "We'll come in early and bake too. She needs to take it easy. It's what she hired us for."

"Thanks, you two."

"Just take care of our girl."

"Always."

Dean gathered her closer to his chest, cuddling her into him and dropping a kiss on the top of her head as he rocked her back and forth. "I'm here, baby. You're not alone. You're never alone and you never fucking will be if I have any say in it."

Poppy closed her eyes and focused on the feel of him wrapped around her, the smell. His presence helped ground her, bringing her back to the present. In Dean's arms, she found safety and peace.

The bell on her door rang out again and she stiffened, but Dean shushed her and brushed the hair back from her face. "It's the guys. They got the same text I did from your friends."

She relaxed again, her heart calming once she realized it wasn't her father back to tell her all the things wrong with her. The bastard. How dare her come here after so long, acting like a concerned father with all sort of opinions. Like she gave a shit what he thought.

Gavin and Flynn came around the counter and rushed over at the sight of her curled up on Dean's lap on the floor.

"What's going on?" Flynn squatted next to them.

Poppy struggled out of Dean's hold and to her feet. "What happened was my bastard of a father just showed back up."

"Are you fucking kidding me?" Flynn shot to his feet, his question almost a roar.

"After twenty years?" Gavin scoffed with a disgusted twist to his lips.

"What a prick." Flynn looked ready to track down her father and beat the shit out of him.

Poppy had the same temptation.

She nodded and stepped away from them. "I...I can't be in here right now. Can you lock up when you leave? I just...uh...I need...yeah." She shook her head and pushed past the still-gaping and furious guys, hurrying up to her apartment before the banked rage flared back to life.

Her heart pounded in her ears in time with her steps as she slammed into her home, stomping back and forth in her living room with her hands curled into fists at her side.

She could not believe the nerve of that man. To come over a week after the funeral of the son he abandoned and expect to just get to be back in her life. And to tell her handling the business she and Perry had worked themselves to the bone over was too much for her to handle alone. It's not like she didn't already know that. She was more than aware of her shortcomings as a business person. But he sure as hell didn't know that. He was assuming it for whatever reason.

Because she was female or liked pretty clothing or had rainbow hair or something he remembered about her personality when she was seven which was the last time he saw her.

And the worst part? He brought his new family. The one he had after his first wasn't good enough. At least he'd had the decency to wait around three years, before he started over. At least his kids weren't twins. She might have bashed him in the head with the cash register if he'd brought in twins.

She grabbed a throw pillow from the couch and buried her face in it to let out a scream. Once her throat ached and the pillow started to smother her, she ripped it away from her face and pelted it across the room where it smashed into the side table filled with framed photos of Perry and her mother. The pictures crashed to the ground, glass splintering and cracking, scattered across her floor.

Fuck.

Her door burst open, and three angry and worried firemen fell into her home, searching for the threat. But what could they do when the threat was inside her? When she couldn't keep it locked down deep any longer?

Gavin approached her carefully like she was a wild animal he needed to tame.

It was too much. It was all too much. She couldn't take anymore. No more horrors, no more surprises, no more confusing revelations. And no more pain.

It wasn't worth it. It wasn't worth the pain. She didn't want to love anyone so much, so hard ever again. She'd already lost too much, she couldn't handle another loss.

Gavin wrapped his arms around her, but she fought him off. He kept coming, determined to console her even as she pushed and shoved and hit his chest with her fists.

"Let it out, sugar. Just let it out."

A screaming sob ripped from her ragged throat and she let him hold her, clutching at his shirt to remain upright as she lost it. "I didn't get to say goodbye. He died alone in the middle of the street, bleeding out while I was here, safe and comfortable. I should have been with him. It should have been me. Why the fuck did this happen?"

"I don't know." Gavin's voice came out choked in pain and rage, matching the tornado inside her. "It's bullshit and we all hate it. But not a single one of us wishes it was you instead. And you know damn well Perry wouldn't have either."

She didn't give a shit what Perry would have wanted. He was careless with his own life, refusing to wear a seatbelt, clearly not caring what it would do to her and to them if he died.

It had always been all about him. Death hadn't changed that either.

How could she hate and love and miss someone so much? "I can't get past this."

His tears soaked the shoulder of her shirt. "I know. Neither can we. But we will eventually. Together."

FLYNN AND DEAN CLUTCHED at each other while they watched Poppy break down in Gavin's arms and Gavin break down a little right along with her. Flynn needed to punch something, break something. Anything to release the pressure in his chest, behind his eyes. Her prick of a father would be an excellent target.

Her pain and fury so perfectly matched his it almost sent him to his knees.

"We need to call in to work. Or at least one of us does. She's not staying here alone tonight." Dean kept his voice low so Poppy wouldn't overhear.

Not that she was in the condition to be at aware of anything other than the pain ripping her apart.

Flynn nodded. "I need to work. You or Gavin should stay."

"I think Gavin is best for her tonight. I'll call in for him."

Flynn wanted to stay here with her, protecting her from any more horrors that might come for her, but he had his own demons he needed to expel if he wanted to be able to be there for her.

Dean needed the same thing. He needed to recover his control and work was the best place for both of them. Gavin was steady enough to handle her heartbreak and roll with any punches. Literal and figural.

He hadn't even flinched and Poppy had hit him hundreds of times over the years. She wasn't weak and she didn't pull her punches.

Flynn brushed away the few tears that had escaped. "I know you want to give her space, dude, but I don't know if that's the right idea."

Dean leaned his head back against the wall holding the two of them up. "We have fucked this up so much I don't know if it is either. But I don't think any of us can leave her alone. She needs to know we aren't going anywhere regardless of what she decides."

"I can't believe that shithead is back." Flynn's jaw clenched as violent fantasies played out in his mind.

"Me either. Hopefully Gavin will get the story out of her."

"Yeah. We need to know if we need to handle it for her."

Dean shook his head. "She won't thank us for that."

"Right now, I don't give a shit." Flynn trembled so hard he made the pictures on the wall shudder in response.

"Let's go. You need to hit the gym."

"Yeah."

With a few gestures and mouthed words, they let Gavin know what was going on and left the two to grieve alone.

A part of Flynn stayed behind with them, but he kept walking with Dean.

Chapter 30

Poppy spent the entire next day on edge, her head jerking up to check the entrance every time the bell rang, terrified her father would walk through the door. She felt brittle, wavering between anger and agony. Tam and Marie had shuffled her off to man the coffee machine since she kept screwing up orders and those bloody men refused to leave her be. Even though Dean and Flynn were on shift, they'd both come in twice already. And Gavin had refused to go anywhere. He was over in the corner with a coffee and a book. He probably expected to stay the night again.

But that wasn't going to happen.

Last night, she was just too vulnerable and needy to fight it after the shock of her father showing up. Even with Gavin there, she'd barely slept, too pissed off to relax. She was furious all the time, she couldn't get passed it, she couldn't muzzle it. Anger was a rare emotion for her, one she usually didn't struggle with.

And yeah, she knew all about the stages of grief and what they were and knew it was probably the reason, but she hated the thought of following some schedule or phase like once she made it through the stages, it would be over and she'd be fine. There was comfort in the thought of an end, but she didn't believe this was something she'd ever be over. She went through something similar with her mother, but she still wasn't the slightest bit over her death and that was over a year ago.

And this was worse.

She fanned her face, irritated at the sweat coating her skin. Even with the AC blasting so hard it felt like winter in here, she couldn't cool off. She was trapped in some sort of hellish cycle. The angrier she grew, the hotter she was. The hotter she was, the angrier she grew. And on and on it went.

As she handed a customer an iced coffee, she was tempted to pour it right over her own head.

She needed a minute. One minute to stand in the freezer and maybe she could calm down, control herself. "Tam? Can you take over here for a few?"

Tam nodded. "Of course."

"Thanks." Poppy tried to smile back, but it felt more like a twisted grimace on her face.

Based on the pity in Tam's eyes, a twisted grimace was exactly what Poppy pulled off. Oh well. They understood and even if they didn't, she was their boss and if they wanted to keep their jobs, they'd deal with her insanity.

Poppy avoided Gavin's eyes as she fled the shop and through the kitchen doors to the back where they'd installed a walk-in freezer they barely used. It was Perry's idea. And it was a terrible one. They weren't a restaurant, the space wasn't necessary.

But at the moment, she was grateful as the frigid air dried the sweat dotting her skin. In here, she could breathe. She leaned against the cold metal shelves and closed her eyes. Maybe she should try yoga again. Before when she'd taken some classes, they'd bored her. But she'd read yoga was good for mental health, which was something she needed help with lately.

The door opened and Poppy's eyes popped wide as Gavin entered. "What are you doing in here?"

"Trying to cool down."

He nodded, like she made complete sense even though she didn't. She didn't know whether she was grateful or annoyed over his non reaction. She wanted a fight, so she settled on annoyed.

He closed the freezer door and stepped deeper inside until he was right in front of her. "I have to get back to the shift in a couple hours, so I have to leave soon."

"That's fine. I didn't ask you to guard me today or the others to keep checking in." She crossed her arms.

"We know. But we wanted to. And it's not guarding you. It's just hanging out."

She snorted. "Right. Hanging out on the few breaks you have and you calling into work after taking so much time off."

"None of us feel much in the mood for regular life right now. And we've always spent a lot of our breaks here, so it's not that strange."

It was since Perry was no longer here to entertain them. He was the one they always came to see, not her. Or they tagged along when he came to check on her and the shop.

She wasn't exactly exciting company compared to him. Especially lately. She thought if she'd disappeared along with Perry, no one would notice. She'd always been second best, second choice when Perry was around. Usually, she hadn't minded, content to let him shine, to let him have control while she did her own thing, found her own fun.

But sometimes she wanted to fucking sparkle like the unicorns she loved so much. Unfortunately now, sparkling made her feel like an asshole. And being around the guys made her feel anything but dull. She felt seen and appreciated and desired and nothing had ever scared her so much.

"You guys don't need to babysit me. Last night was just a...well, I would've reacted that way at his sudden appearance regardless of the current situation. It's over and if he comes again, I'll handle it. I don't need your pity. Perry didn't freaking leave me to you to take care of."

"How is it possible you see yourself the way you do?" Gavin threw his hands into the air, completely exasperated with her.

She scowled at him. "What are you talking about? I'm not some self-conscious sad sack. I know I'm hot and amazing."

"I'm not talking about your looks. Though, yes. You really fucking are. So much, I'm hard half the time I'm around you. It gets uncomfortable sometimes. But you act like you're Perry's replacement to us. You have always been your own separate person from him. The two of you couldn't be more different. It's actually hard to believe you're related, much less twins. You're brilliant and kind and hilarious and generous and a little mean and original and determined and independent except when it came to him. He's the only one you ever allowed yourself to rely on. And part of that is his fault. He liked you that way. He craved being needed and depended on."

She held out her hands like they'd protect her from the words he threw at her like throwing stars. "Stop."

Gavin moved closer, so close the warmth from his body made a strange contrast between him and the freezer shelves she leaned against. "No. I'm not going to stop. I loved that bastard so much and I'm pissed as hell he left all of us behind. But I wasn't blind to his faults. None of us were. And he wasn't blind to ours. We've been friends most of our lives. We're family. We love each other anyway. And our biggest issue with him was always the way he treated you."

"You're acting like he treated me badly. He didn't. He loved me."

Gavin's gray eyes were wintry with icy anger. "Of course he did. He loved you more than anything else in this world. Us included. And no, he didn't mistreat you, but he also wanted you in his shadow and made sure you stayed there. This shop was your idea, your dream. You could have handled it on your own, but he flew in, determined to be involved and run it, leaving the hardest part to you. Hell, he hired accountants and financial advisors to handle a lot of it in the beginning."

She shoved him away from her. "Stop. Enough. I have to get back to work."

He slumped a little, some of the anger trickling away, the ice in his eyes melting. "I'm not trying to bad mouth him to you."

"Then what are you trying to do?"

He rubbed his face. "I don't know. I think I'm trying to process all this myself and it's laughable that I think I can help you when I can't help myself. I'm so pissed at him right now. Which then makes me feel like a piece of shit for being angry at a dead man. Which only pisses me off more. I'm sorry, Poppy. We're all a mess right now, just trying to get through each hellish day together."

Her own frustration floated away, leaving her exhausted. "I know. I'm angry too. It's taken over everything."

"It'll pass. Hopefully. Flynn is struggling with it too."

"What about Dean?" Even after all this time, he was still a bit of a mystery to her, so closed off most of the time, always in control.

Flynn gave her whiplash sometimes with his extreme emotions, but she never had to guess what he was thinking or feeling. Gavin was usually the steady one, the one who was the least damaged from their shitty childhoods.

"I'm not sure. He's been more brooding artist than usual, but he doesn't seem angry. Just quiet and withdrawn. I'm a little worried about him actually. Both of them, but more Dean. He's not as decisive as he usually is the last couple days."

The last couple days. He meant since she ran out on them and then they found her having a panic attack on the floor when they were supposed to be heading to work.

Guilt rode her hard. "I'll try to talk to him tomorrow, see if he'll let me in a little."

"If anyone can get him to open up, it's you. We get done with our shift later tonight. And he'll be here at some point in the morning. Flynn's coming by tonight."

Poppy rolled her eyes. "You guys really need to stop taking turns here."

"Let us have one more day, then we'll try to back off. Knowing your father is here makes us a little nervous."

She shuddered and rubbed her arms. "Me too. But I can handle him. And I've filled Tam and Marie in, so they're here as backup if I need it."

"Fine. We'll back off a little. But we're not disappearing on you. We miss you when we don't get to see and talk to you."

"I just need time to figure out everything you guys said the other day." It was a lot. Too much.

Gavin rubbed his arms. "Right. I am sorry that you found out like that. We should have waited."

She scowled at him. "No. You should have mentioned it years ago."

A small sign of sardonic amusement quirked his lips. "Mom said the same thing when I talked to her about all this last night."

"Stacy knows?" Poppy gasped. What must Stacy think about that? She had to be horrified.

"Of course. She's known since we were kids."

She gaped at him. What? "And she doesn't find it...crazy?"

"No. You know Mom. Love is love is love."

"Right. I still remember the rant she left on my voicemail after she read some shitty article bitching about the sanctity of marriage."

A fond smile spread across his mouth. "Sounds like dear old mom."

Poppy chuckled. "Remember when she used to terrify me and I refused to ever come over to your house?"

His smile grew into a grin. "She terrified all of us. Hell, she still terrifies me sometimes."

"Now, she's my hero. I want to be her when I grow up." Stacy was the best. She was strong and kind and refused to let anyone give her any shit.

Gavin winced. "And that thought is even more terrifying considering...uh...well, my interest in you."

She laughed. "Maybe you should rethink that interest now that you know my goal in life."

He shook his head, his gray eyes glinting like quicksilver. "Never. Still worth it."

Poppy cleared her throat. "Well, I need to get back to work and you need to go get ready for your shift. Be careful out there, okay?"

"I will. I need to stay later to make up for calling in so I won't be by until later tomorrow."

Poppy tried to hide her worry as they exited the freezer. Their jobs as firefighters never really worried her before, she just found it hot. But now that she'd lost Perry, Gavin's adrenaline junkie personality scared her. He craved adventure and danger. Between his weekends rock climbing, motorcycle riding, skydiving, and working on getting his pilot's license, he was always thrusting himself into life-threatening situations.

She ignored Perry's voice in her head reminding her she used to do all of those things with him or even on her own.

The other guys were firefighters too, but he was more reckless and it worried her.

And yet, her careful, precise brother was killed driving to his friend's bar. The world made no sense.

Chapter 31

After closing and sending Tam and Marie home, Poppy trudged upstairs. She'd gotten enough baking done for the next day during the last couple hours of the day she didn't need to remain downstairs.

Flynn had never shown up for his shift guarding her after Gavin left and Poppy tried not to worry over it. She was already concerned over what Gavin mentioned about Dean. She couldn't worry about Flynn too. She could barely handle herself.

Her apartment door was unlocked and she muttered a curse. Gavin must have forgotten to lock up when he left this morning. It didn't really matter since the only way to this door was through the shop and the kitchen and the door in the kitchen leading to the stairs was locked.

She pushed inside and made sure to lock up behind her, half expecting one or all of the guys to show up any minute demanding to stay the night. Not Gavin, since he'd be spending the night at the fire station, but the other two. Maybe they were finally listening and giving her some space to figure everything out.

She flipped on the light and turned to face her living room and jumped with an embarrassing squeak. Or not. Flynn sprawled on her couch.

"What are you doing here? How did you get here?"

She dropped her phone and keys onto the little table she kept by the door, trying to convince her heart it should remain in her chest.

"Shouldn't you be at your bar?"

It didn't close for several more hours. Since he hadn't shown up downstairs, she'd thought he decided he needed to check in at his bar. This week was supposed to be back to regular life, shitty as it now was.

He didn't move his arm from across his face. "I'm letting my employees handle it. My presence isn't really necessary for it to run smooth."

"Okay." She drew the word out. "It still doesn't answer why you're here."

"Gavin is at the station and Dean is holed up in his room, so I went to work out. Then I ended up here."

"How did you get in?" She shifted from foot to foot, his dark tone making her nervous.

"We still have that key."

She really needed to get it back from them. "I know, but I would have noticed you sneaking through."

"I have my ways."

Poppy rounded around the edge of the couch, coming to stand in front of him. He moved his arm and raised his head to look at her and she almost took a step back at the banked rage in his eyes. Her eyes roved across his body and her brow furrowed at the sight of his red, swollen, split knuckles on his hands.

"What the hell is that?" She pointed at his injuries.

He shrugged. "I told you I went to the gym."

"And you decided to forgo wrapping your hands before you beat the shit out of a heavy bag." She fisted her hands on her hips, making her disapproval clear.

"I wrapped them."

She shook her head in disgust and frustration. "What are you doing here, Flynn?"

"Do you want me to leave?" he asked.

"Would you if I asked you to? I've told all of you to leave me alone for the past couple of days and none of you are listening."

He sat up to face her fully. "Do you really want us to disappear?"

She gulped. "I want to know what the hell is going on. What you want from me. You can't keep barging into my life like this, acting like you know what's best for me. You can't replace Perry for me and I can't replace him for you. I have to learn to stand on my own and not expect you three to hold me up."

Flynn shot to his feet, his face flushing with anger. "Why? Where the fuck does it say after you experience a horrible loss that you have to do it alone? When your mother died, you moved in with us for weeks. Why is it so different now? Why do you insist on not letting us in? We've told you over and over again you help us as much as we want to help you."

She clutched at her hair, completely at her wit's end. "I'm not in the right frame of mind for this. I'm too twisted and fucked up inside to be what you guys want or need.:

He circled around the couch, eyeing her like a predator. "We just want you. Why are you being such a stubborn ass about this?"

"Because I can't choose one of you."

"Why choose? We haven't asked you to."

She stepped back, needing space between them. "I don't know if you've noticed, Flynn, but me shacking up with three men isn't normal."

"So what?"

"So what? So what?" Poppy spluttered and threw her hands into the air. "I don't understand how it will work. What if there's jealousy or hurt feelings or eventually you do want me to choose and I can't? I'll lose all of you."

Flynn raked a bruised hand through his hair, making the brown strands stick up. "Look, I don't have the answers for all of that. It's something we need to discuss and figure out together. But muffin, we have wanted this for years. That's not going to change anytime soon. I doubt it ever will."

"I don't see what kind of future we can have. Why would we start something like this when it's only going to end in pain?" She couldn't handle any more loss or pain. She was already overflowing with it.

"Why the fuck can't we have a future? It may not be a normal future with one man, one woman, and a couple of kids with a house in the suburbs, but who decided that was normal? Who decided that nightmare was something to aim for? We make our rules and our own futures, fuck what anyone else thinks or says."

"As lovely as that speech is, there are logistical things that have to be considered. And I don't want to make any decisions right now in my current frame of mind." She sounded like Perry, preaching logic and patience.

Usually she jumped into new experiences without a thought. But that girl was gone. She was buried right along with Perry.

He leaned his hip against the edge of the couch. "We aren't asking you to. We just want to be there for you and want you there for us. This isn't us feeling sorry for you. We don't want to spend this time of grief alone either. We can get this through together."

"But you guys want more than that."

"Not right now. We had planned to wait to bring this up, but certain events caused us to spew it out sooner." He groaned. "Look, are your feelings for us new?"

She really didn't want to do this now. She didn't want to admit things she'd been hiding for so many years. But she didn't want to lie to him or the others either. "No. I've been half in love with all of you since we were like twelve."

A little of the fury and fire in his eyes died down at her admission. "Then who cares what finally brought us to this? It's not your grief telling you you're attracted to us, but maybe it's finally giving us all the permission and excuse to give in to what we want. What we've always wanted."

Her mouth opened and closed, and opened and closed again. He said all the right things, but he looked so pissed while he said them, sounded furious with her for all the questioning she'd put them through.

Her own rage rose up to meet his. "You've been talking about this for years without saying a single word to me about it. I can't help it that it's a lot for me to take in and figure out."

Flynn growled at her. A literal growl. She wished she didn't find it so sexy. "Stop acting like fucking Perry. You were always the brave one, ready to jump right into things. Just because he's not here to talk you out of it, doesn't mean you should make yourself small in his absence."

She clutched her chest, trying to smother the ache. "What is with you guys slamming him lately?"

"We're furious with him. I want to beat the shit out of him for dying. And I want to beat the shit out of myself because if it wasn't for me, he'd probably still be alive."

Her hands fell to her sides as she gaped at him. "What are you talking about?"

Flynn stared daggers at her floor. "He didn't really want to come out that night, but I pushed since Gavin was off at his mom's and Dean was locked in his darkroom."

Oh. Oh, Flynn. No. "You jackass, that's bullshit."

His head jerked up so he could frown at her. "What?"

"How many times had he made the drive to your bar? How many times did you push him into coming and he got there completely safely? There are only two people I blame for his death. The asshole who crashed into him after running a red light and Perry for not wearing a seatbelt."

Flynn fisted his hands and fresh blood welled on his knuckles, but he didn't seem to notice or feel it. "But if I'd just left him alone, he'd still be here."

"Maybe. He asked me to go too, you know. After he talked to you. But I said no. He would've taken a different route if he had to pick me up and I'd have made sure he had his seat belt on. You aren't the only one with guilt. And you aren't the only one pissed off at him and the universe and everything else. So, don't come to me with that bullshit."

Flynn's eyes flashed as he approached her with his predatory gait. Poppy stumbled back a few steps until her back hit the wall. Time slowed as he stalked her with anger still smoldering in his eyes.

Her own anger was a match to his and she stepped forward, refusing to back down. A smirk curled the edge of his lips and he stopped right before her, only a breath separating them. Desire pulsed through her body as they stared at each other. Her lips tingled in anticipation of feeling his lips on hers, remembering what he tasted like, what he felt like.

But he stood, trapping her in his gaze, and didn't move. He waited for her to make the first move.

So, she pounced.

Chapter 32

The crashed together with teeth and nails, nipping and ripping at each other's clothes, desperation and need fueling them. They took their rage out on each other as their mouths fought for dominance and their tongues danced and teased.

Their clothes fell in tatters to the floor, leaving them bare and aching for each other.

Flynn growled into her mouth when she raked her nails down his back, sinking his teeth into the flesh between her neck and shoulder in retaliation. There was no gentle lovemaking here tonight. It was pure furious need.

He shoved her against the wall and trapped her hands above her head as he trailed his hot mouth down her chest with bites and harsh sucks, marking her. She shivered at the primal sounds coming from both of them. They were more animal than human at the moment as they snarled and snapped at each other.

She snaked a leg around his waist and he raised his thigh to press against her mound, pressing it hard and grinding it against her. She writhed against him with a whimper as he sucked her nipple into his mouth, swirling his tongue around the tip, his free hand digging into her ass with bruising strength. She reveled in each rough touch, wanting more, wanting him to brand her, wanting to brand him in return. She wanted to forget everything but the shockwaves exploding through her, leaving her breathless and excited and more turned on than she'd ever been.

She'd never seen this side of Flynn before and she like it. She wanted more. She wanted to feel anything to break through the numbness constantly invading her. And sweetness wasn't going to do it.

She caught his earlobe in her mouth and bit down, making him jerk against her with a curse and a groan. "You like it rough, muffin?" He replaced his thigh with three fingers shoved deep inside her.

She moaned in answer.

"Can you take more?"

"Can you?"

A dark chuckle vibrated against her lips as he crushed his mouth against hers in an unyielding kiss. He ripped away from her, leaving her gasping and light-headed. Before she could jerk him back to her, he spun her around and trapped her back against the wall. The cool air of her apartment brushed across her back as he held her there by a possessive grip at the back of her neck and one at her waist.

She bit back a moan, not wanting to give him the upper hand, instead she remained still and silent, biding her time. Goosebumps raced across her skin and her nipples sharpened to points, brushing against the wall with each breath, sending bolts of pleasure straight through her.

A stinging smack landed on the left cheek of her ass, making her startle, Heat spread from the spot he hit, growing as his hand slid between her legs to pluck and pinch at her clit.

She pressed her ass out, silently begging for more, for harder, deeper, rougher. She wanted whatever he had to give and hoped he could take it too.

His grip on the back of her neck tightened and her pussy clenched in response, a moan escaping before she could stop it. He drew one of his nails right over the center of her and she hissed in pleasure, spreading her legs wider. Another strike to her ass and back to torturing her clit, never enough to give her what she needed, but just enough to keep her hovering at the edge.

She shoved away from the wall, knocking him off her and spun, leaping at him. He caught her and they tumbled to the ground, him taking most of the impact with a grunt and a surprised smirk. Poppy adjusted until she straddled his erection with her wet heat, teasing him with it as she bent over his chest and sank her teeth into the spot right above his nipple.

He lurched up into her with a curse, grabbing her hips and flipping them until she was sprawled beneath his hard, beautiful body. His eyes were hard and heated as they roved up and down her heaving form covered with his markings. A possessive sound rumbled in his chest. She couldn't look away from the teeth marks embedded in his chest, swollen from her touch. A similar feeling rose up in her.

She wanted to give him more. She'd never felt like this during sex before, never wanted anything almost violent in its passion.

She never wanted it to end. "I want to fuck like this until we can't stand."

His cock nudged her entrance, making her breath catch as her legs spread wider. "Oh, muffin. We are. I'm going to fuck you until you can't speak from screaming my name."

"Do your worst. You can't hurt me."

"Right back at you, baby."

Her blood surged with molten heat as he shoved inside of her, her hips rising to meet him. Her arms slid across his back and her fingers curled into claws she scratched along his skin.

His eyes closed and he plowed into her harder.

"Don't look away from me."

His green eyes popped open at her demand, smoldering at her, the green so deep and dark like the sky before a hurricane. A hurricane he swept her up in, sending her spinning and smashing until she had no idea which way was up or down.

They took each other in a punishing, bruising pace, their pelvises slamming together over and over, their eyes tangled and pulsing with every single sensation they felt, both of them bared wide open, hiding nothing.

He bent down to kiss her with his red, swollen lips. Lips she'd bitten and licked. She surged against him with a cry he drank down like the sound was the most delicious cup of coffee he'd ever tasted, their eyes never closing as bliss combusted inside her, leaving her jerking and bucking against him. He snarled and yanked out of her with a hiss, spilling onto her heaving breasts and belly, searing her skin with one final brand.

She'd never experienced anything so depraved or carnal before and wasn't sure what to think of herself or of Flynn as she slumped back against the floor.

"I'm nowhere near done with you yet, muffin." Flynn's words were a dark promise reigniting the spark still fluttering inside.

"Good." This time, she was going to spank him.

Chapter 33

Poppy woke the next morning before Flynn who was passed out in her bed, one of his arms thrown across her waist, cuddled into her back, his breath and constant five o'clock shadow tickling the middle of her back.

She searched inside of herself for any feelings of horror or regret like last time, but only found an achy satisfaction. She'd needed the furious and chaotic release with Flynn and even though she had no idea what it meant for them going forward, she had no regrets.

After peeking over her shoulder at Flynn, his expression peaceful, she eased away from him and off the bed. Most of her body still ached from the exquisite torture Flynn put her through the night before. Remembering some of the things they did brought heat to her cheeks.

And to other places.

She grabbed her robe from the chair in the corner and wrapped it around herself, padding into the kitchen to start coffee. She still had a few hours before she needed to be downstairs since Tam and Marie insisted on taking the morning shifts for the rest of the week. It was nice, being able to relax at the start of the day, instead of hustle through a quick breakfast and shower after staying up half the night baking. It was time for her to hire new help. Once she returned all the phone calls she'd ignored from the insurance company and lawyer, she'd start looking into that.

A soft tap came from her front door. She clutched her mug of coffee to her and went to open it with a sigh. It was probably one of the others and if she didn't answer, they'd use the key to come in anyway. She knew they had more than one copy at this point, there was no way they were passing it around.

She opened the door and scowled at Dean and Gavin. "What are the two of you doing here so early?"

Gavin held up a canvas bag full of groceries. "We came to make you breakfast. It was supposed to be a surprise since we thought you'd still be asleep."

"All right, stalkers. Come on in."

Gavin stepped through the doorway. "Where's Flynn? Dean said he never came back last night."

Her cheeks heated. "He's…uh…asleep."

Gavin grinned as he set the bag of groceries on the kitchen counter. "You two have a sleepover?"

"Something like that." She cleared her throat and looked away from the amusement in Gavin's eyes.

Dean advanced on her, his eyes narrowed on her chest. She froze, her heart picking up speed. What was he doing? Was he planning to take her right here in the kitchen in front of Gavin?

Why wasn't she more horrified at the idea?

He reached out for the opening of her robe and peeled it back just a bit. But enough to bare some of the marks scattered across her chest. She couldn't move. She didn't want to. She let him look his fill, part of her hoping he'd search out the rest, find every single bite and hickey Flynn left on her.

"Looks like the two of you had a good time last night." Dean's pointer finger brushed against a mark high on her breast, making her shiver, making her nipples poke through her robe.

She cleared the lust from her throat. "You should see the other guy."

His coffee eyes darkened to a mocha color and his tongue ran across his bottom lip. "I look forward to it."

"Here's your chance." Flynn sauntered in, shirtless in only his jeans riding low on his hips, spinning so everyone could take in what she'd done to him.

Poppy gasped at the sight of scratch marks across his back and arms, the bites on his chest and neck. He had almost as many as she did. Heat flooded her at the satisfied and cocky smirk on his face.

She shook it off and focused on Dean and Gavin, searching for any hint of jealousy or upset. They both just looked turned on, like they wanted to add their marks to Flynn's. Like they wanted her brand on them too.

They had distracted her with their sexiness so much, she'd forgotten about her coffee sitting on the table, now cold. She never let a cup get cold.

Ever.

What had they done to her?

Poppy turned her back on all of them and made herself a fresh mug of coffee with shaking hands, trying to pull herself together. Flynn crowded behind her, dropping a kiss on the side of her neck, right over one of the hickeys he left on her.

Poppy's breath caught and she pressed back into him, unable to resist his touch.

He broke something free inside of her last night and she didn't think she'd be able to bury it again. She didn't think she wanted to. She'd expected to feel uncomfortable, showing PDA in front of the others. But for some strange reason, it felt right. Almost normal.

Flynn squeezed her hip and reached around her to make his own cup of coffee, making sure to brush against her as much as possible. As soon as he pulled away, Gavin stepped forward and put her through the same treatment. Then Dean.

Her entire body tingled and she had to curl her fingers into her palms to keep from reaching for them and having them take her right there on her kitchen table.

"I'm going to go get dressed while you three do whatever you're planning on doing with that food." She needed to put on something with a little less access.

Three matching, cocky grins and twinkling eyes were the response to her words. She escaped before they made her melt, leaning against the closed door of her bedroom and breathing hard with closed eyes.

Poppy shook it off and unpeeled herself from the door to sort through her closet for something that would hide Flynn's marks on her. It was way too hot for a scarf and would be incredibly obvious what she was hiding.

She found the perfect blouse-—bright pink with a stand-up collar. It cupped the back of her neck perfectly and would hide any evidence of her night with Flynn. She paired it with black skinny jeans and matching pink flats with sparkling unicorns stamped across the fabric.

After brushing her teeth and smoothing on a little makeup, she followed the scent of bacon back into her kitchen. The guys were making spinach omelettes with bacon and fried tomatoes. Her mouth watered at the sight and smell. And not just of the food. All three had borrowed her aprons and were chopping and cooking wrapped in pastels and sparkles.

She had never witnessed anything so arousing.

Could this be her life? Their lives?

Them cooking for her, teasing her, making her scream with ecstasy? Days spent lazy in a blanket fort, nights dancing at Flynn's club. Was this sort of life possible? Could it actually last?

Or would it end in heartbreak and tears, happiness ripped from her grasp just like with Perry.

Could she take the chance? Could she walk away after getting the taste?

Before she could decide, someone knocked at her door. She crossed the living room to answer it, frowning at Marie's presence. "Everything okay downstairs?"

Marie nibbled on her bottom lip. "Yes. it's just...you have a visitor who refuses to leave until he speaks to you."

Poppy's stomach lurched. "Who?"

"Uh, your father."

Chapter 34

Poppy's jaw clenched as Marie's words slammed into her. "Right. I'll handle it. Thanks."

Marie grimaced and patted Poppy's shoulder with a sympathetic clasp of her hand before she turned to hurry back downstairs.

Gavin stepped up close to her back. "We're coming with you, if that's okay."

She tilted her head to look up at him behind her. "It's not like he's going to hurt me." She didn't really care if they came, but didn't want them to feel like they had to.

Dean joined them and ran his hands down Poppy's arms. "Of course not. But we'd still like to come."

Poppy sighed. "Fine. Make sure the bacon doesn't burn."

Flynn sauntered over finally yanking on a shirt over his gorgeous chest. "I already turned the pan off."

"Come on then."

The guys followed her as she trooped downstairs, her feet heavy and dragging with each step, dread and irritation warring within her. Why wouldn't the bastard leave her alone? He'd been excellent at it for twenty years, why stop a good thing now?

She could feel the protective anger swelling the guys behind her as they entered the shop. It wasn't necessary, but she appreciated it nonetheless. Having them at her back was nice. Having them give her a choice was even better.

Her sperm donor sat in the back corner of the shop, away from prying eyes and eavesdropping ears. The guys gave her space as she approached her father's table, but remained close enough to listen and interfere if necessary.

Poppy refused to take a seat, preferring to stand, not planning for this to take long. "Why are you back here?"

Her father took a leisurely sip of his coffee before he set it back down. "I came with a business proposition."

She jerked, frowning in surprise and confusion. "What?"

He gestured around her shop. "I'm willing to take over the mortgage on your coffee place here. You'll still run things, of course. I have a job already in another state, but this way you don't have to worry about the stress of owning and running the place by yourself. I'll hire some extra help and they'll help you really turn this place around and make you some excellent money."

Her mouth opened and closed, then opened and closed again. "I don't understand why you're offering this."

"You're my daughter. I want to help you. And I think it'll actually make me some money too. Win win." He didn't sound like a loving father. He sounded like a smarmy asshole businessman.

"Uh huh. Right."

He patted his briefcase in the seat next to him. "I've had my lawyer draw up the papers already. All you have to do is sign."

Rage raced through her so hard and fast, her ears popped. "Get out." She pointed to the door, her voice low and hard and cold.

Shock strained her father's face. "Excuse me?"

"I said, get out. Get out of my shop, my life, hell, get out of the city. I want nothing from you. Ever. I will not sell to you or to anyone. I don't need your help or want it." Poppy didn't wait around to see if he listened.

She knew the guys would get him out of there if he didn't.

It only took five minutes for the guys to follow her upstairs.

"How dare he?" Flynn slammed the door behind them, his eyes almost as hot and wild as they were the night before. "What a fucking asshole. I can't believe he had the nerve to pull that bullshit."

Gavin shook his head. "He's a prick, but our girl handled it. A hell of a lot better than I would have. Hopefully, he got the point this time. If not, we'll make sure he understands if he tries this shit again."

"I'm fine, guys." She headed towards the kitchen. She needed more coffee.

Flynn still brimmed with anger on her behalf. "You shouldn't have to deal with this on top of everything else. He always was a selfish shit."

"Let's just salvage breakfast and forget about it for a while." Seeing her dad again reminded her of the brother and sister she had.

And she didn't want to think about them. Her and Perry's replacements. Blood or not, she didn't need them in her life. Especially if they were connected to the man who sired her. Which made her father sound like a vampire, but she hated thinking of him as her father or dad. He didn't deserve those terms.

He didn't deserve squat.

She didn't want him in her life. She wanted answers. She wanted to know why her brother, her best friend, her other half was taken from her. She needed to understand. Perry was twenty-seven years old, barely starting out in life. He had so much to offer the world. She needed to know who took him from her. Who the coward was who murdered her brother and left him dying in the street.

She should have been there with him, for him. Why hadn't she said yes when he invited her to go along? She couldn't even remember why she'd declined now. Her excuse was so unimportant, it wasn't even memorable.

A hand cupped around the side of her face broke her out of her spiral. She blinked and focused on Dean staring at her with haunted eyes. She covered his hand with her own and tried to smile for him, remembering Gavin's concern for Dean.

"I'm okay. Or, I will be. One day." She hoped.

A little of the pain disappeared from Dean's eyes. "Me too."

Poppy raised onto the tips of her toes and pressed a soft kiss against Dean's lips. She had no idea what she was doing, but something in his expression drew her in and she couldn't help herself and didn't want to. She'd meant it to be soft and quick, but Dean's tongue darted from his mouth and teased hers, making her knees weak and her free hand clutch the fabric of his shirt.

He tasted like coffee and pain mingled with hope and she couldn't get enough. She lost herself in him—-in his taste, in his touch, in his scent.

Dean hardened against her belly and she groaned into his mouth, heat pulsing low inside her. Their hands were still joined against her face, his other dug into her hip, holding her close.

Heat brushed her back as one of the others swept the hair away from her neck to trail lips across her skin, trapping her between two hard, hot bodies.

"I think I want something else for breakfast." Gavin was the one behind her and he highlighted his dark words with a nip to her ear.

Their hold on her was the only thing keeping her from collapsing to the floor in a puddle of pleasure.

Dean released her face and lifted her into his arms by her ass, causing her to wrap her legs around his waist automatically. Gavin's roving hands kept her steady as Dean carried her over to the table Flynn has already cleared off. They laid her out on it like she was their personal feast, the three of them surrounding her, staring at her like they'd never seen anything so delicious.

The sight made her shiver and reach for them. And it snapped the leashes they held themselves on. Suddenly, hands and lips were everywhere, clothes peeled away from her skin. She couldn't keep track of who was touching where, unable to keep her eyes open, focused completely inwards on the ecstasy they sent rippling through her.

Dean looked up at her from between her legs after dropping a kiss and nibble in the bend of her thigh. "Let us help you relax and forget for a little while, beautiful. Help us forget too."

They all needed to forget and find and enjoy the small moments of happiness and pleasure they came across. Otherwise, what was the point of living? Perry couldn't anymore, so she had to live for both of them.

Hopefully, he'd approve of her having a foursome on her kitchen table. She was too far gone to give a crap if he didn't. He'd made much worse romantic decisions before. He had no right to judge.

A tongue between her legs ran all thoughts of her brother straight out of her head. All thoughts of anything. Only the buzz of pleasure remained as two mouths latched onto her breasts, tongues and teeth teasing her, making her writhe beneath their touch.

No one else could bring her body alive like this. No one else ever had. Only these three.

Only ever these three.

She tried to pull them closer, touch them back, but they pulled away.

"This is about you, baby," Dean said. "We need this. Let us do this."

She ached to run her hands over every inch of them, but they distracted her with kisses and licks and nibbles. Her hands curled around the edges of the table, gripping it with desperate fingers as she tried not the lurch from the hard surface.

"We've got you, muffin." Flynn took her mouth in a savage kiss as he tweaked her nipple.

She bit his lip in response, making him growl against her lips. He pulled back and they shared a wicked smile which Dean's skillful tongue wiped from her face.

Flynn and Gavin rushed to keep her from toppling over as she arched against the climax stampeding through her, fuzzing her vision. She shook and trembled from the aftershocks, Dean never letting up as his groan vibrated through her.

Gavin stroked the side of her body and whispered nonsensical sweet words in her ear as she came down, her breaths sharp and shallow. The three of them cleaned her up and helped her back into her clothes since her limbs refused to cooperate and let her do it herself.

Dean stole her and sat with her cuddled in his lap as Flynn and Gavin made plates of now cold breakfast for everyone.

Gavin grimaced at the plate of food as he handed it to her. "Sorry it's not exactly what we planned for the morning."

Poppy shrugged with a grin. "Worth it."

Chapter 35

Close to closing time, Poppy smiled to herself as what she and the guys did together that morning ran back through her mind. She'd barely been able to concentrate all day, swamped with thoughts of them, their scent still lingering on her skin. By the time they'd finished, she hadn't had time to wash it off.

They hadn't really talked anything over about what this all meant, but Poppy preferred it that way. She wasn't ready to discuss it and take it all apart as they tried to figure out where to go from here. She was happy keeping her head in the sand for now, confident they'd figure it out eventually.

Guilt stabbed her chest as she thought of her brother. She'd been so focused on the guys and the drama with their dad, he'd been slipping her mind more and more. She was waking up without him being the first thought in her mind, she was finding more and more moments of joy.

Poppy didn't want to forget him, forget the loss. But she couldn't stop living her life either.

She closed her eyes against the pain washing over her. It came and went in waves. Sometimes she could pretend everything was fine, the next moment she wanted to ball up in the fetal position, broken on the floor. The rampaging emotions gave her whiplash.

She checked the clock for the hundredth time that day, blowing out a frustrated breath when she saw she still had an hour until closing. The guys were at work, and she found herself missing them. She shook her head at herself. No. She wasn't going to become that person. She wasn't going to cling and become needy, wanting them around constantly to reassure her. One or more of them would be by before the night was over.

They'd tried to talk her into coming to their place once they finished their shift, but she wasn't ready for that. In fact, she had something else she needed to handle tomorrow, and she didn't want them getting involved, trying to help and take over. It was time for her to finally return all the phone calls and finish handling Perry's affairs.

"Hey guys?" Poppy turned to Tam and Marie once they had a lull in customers.

"Yeah? What's up, Pop?"

She grinned at Marie's new nickname for her. She liked it. "Do you two think you can handle the whole day tomorrow? I have some things to take care of. I'll be in and out, but mostly unavailable."

Marie nodded. "Of course."

"I'm going to hire a few more people soon. I promise." Poppy felt awful for how much she'd been leaning on them lately.

Tam shrugged. "No worries. We like the paychecks when we're here all day. There's no rush."

"Are you sure?" Poppy asked. "It's a lot to handle."

"We're sure. This is our only job and we can always use the money. We've been wanting more responsibility for a while. We mentioned it to Perry a few weeks ago." Marie raised her voice to be heard over the frother.

A frown creased Poppy's forehead. "He never said anything to me."

Tam shrugged again. "You know how he was. Micromanager."

Poppy snorted. "He was that indeed."

Tam changed the filter in the coffee pot, tossing the used one into the trash. "I've also been taking business classes online. I'm no expert yet, but if you need help on that side of things, just ask."

"You two may need raises." They were worth way more than what she was paying them now.

Marie shook her head. "Nope. But we love this place and want it to succeed so we'll help in any way we can."

Warmth spilled across Poppy's chest at these two women who had become such good friends to her in such a short time. They'd only been working for her for a few months, but their kindness and good humor had wormed into her heart.

"Thanks, you guys."

Marie smiled softly. "Don't thank us. Just take care of yourself."

"Yeah. And let those hot guys of yours do it." Tam winked.

Poppy's cheeks flushed at Tam's teasing words. "I don't know what you mean."

"Uh huh. They've been in and out of here at a lot of odd hours lately." Tam looked way too interested in hearing all the dirty details.

Poppy tried to shrug it off, not sure how to explain whatever they were, not wanting to share what had happened so far. "They're just worried about me and trying to do right by Perry."

"That may be true, but their interest isn't new," Marie said.

"What are you talking about?"

Marie returned the carton of creamer into the fridge. "We noticed it right away when we started working here. The way they watch you when you aren't looking."

Tam snorted as she gathered the dirty silverware. "Or when Perry wasn't looking."

Marie leaned her hip against the counter. "You always seemed so clueless and uninterested, so we didn't say anything. But now, you've noticed. And we don't want you missing out on a good thing."

"And what good thing is that?" Poppy asked.

She struggled with seeing anything other than pain in her future, she struggled with seeing how part of the situation with the guys was a good thing.

Tam snickered. "A chance to build your own harem,"

Poppy's head jerked up to stare at her crazy friend with wide eyes and a gaping mouth. "What?"

Marie snapped her fingers. "Oh yeah. It's a big thing in novels right now. You haven't read any reverse harems?"

"No. I've never heard of it." A complete lie.

Tam huffed. "Bullshit. We know how much you love romance novels. We've seen your shelves."

Poppy's shoulders slumped. "Okay fine. Yes, I've heard of it. And have read a lot of them. But that's fiction."

"So what?" Marie asked. "If some of the heroines in those books can save the world while they're falling in love with five guys, you can easily handle it in regular life."

"Maybe." Poppy wasn't so sure. As much as she wanted whatever this was with them, the complexities of the situation had her spinning.

Marie refilled the wooden coffee stirrers into the canister. "They clearly adore you. Take the leap. You'll regret it if you don't."

If only she could silence Perry's voice in her head, telling her to think things through, reminding her the cost if she tried and it all fell apart.

The door to the shop opened before she could come up with a reply and at the sight of who was there, all the good feelings the conversation had brought disappeared.

What was her father's wife and son doing here? Why couldn't they leave her the hell alone?

Chapter 36

The woman and her son approached the counter and Poppy froze, unable to run away or hustle them somewhere more private. The only other people in here were Tam and Marie and they knew enough of what was going on, it didn't matter much to Poppy if they overheard.

Poppy searched her memory for their names. Callie and Blake. Callie was the wife, Blake was the son. The girl, Tiffany, wasn't with them.

Poppy couldn't bear to look at her father's son. He looked so much like Perry did when he was a teenager. It hurt to look at him. She didn't want a replacement brother. She didn't want her father back. It was like some horrible cosmic joke that her dad had returned and brought her two almost grown siblings. What was this bullshit? Why did her father get to live when Perry deserved life so much more?

"Can I get you something?" Marie asked.

Her father's wife hesitated. "Uh, sure. I'll take a mocha. Blake?"

Blake shrugged. "Coffee. Black. Like my soul."

Callie grimaced while Tam and Marie snorted. "Coming right up."

"Thank you."

Poppy still hadn't said anything, still stood frozen and staring, panic clawing up her throat.

Marie and Tam busied themselves making the drinks, leaving Poppy and her father's family with a semblance of privacy.

Her father's wife tapped her fingers against her leg. "I know this is uncomfortable and probably inappropriate, but I wanted to come and try to smooth things over. You father means well. He wanted to come long ago to see you and your brother, but was too afraid to. He was heartbroken when he heard the news through some distant cousin that he was too late for Perry. He didn't want to be too late with you. He's just trying to make things right."

Poppy reminded herself this woman wasn't at fault. She was just as much a victim of the man as Poppy's mother had been. As she and Perry had been.

But she wasn't going to forgive him just because Callie came to do his dirty work for him and stared at her with sad eyes. "How many days did he know about Perry's death before he finally decided to come out here?"

Callie winced. "Three days. But you have to understand. He's a very busy man and was concerned it would cause a scene if he showed up at the funeral."

Three days. "Three days to decide whether or not he was going to come and pay his respects to the son he abandoned? Why should I give him a chance? He hasn't earned it."

Callie's eyes somehow grew even sadder. "Maybe not, but maybe you should do it for your own sake if you can't for his."

Blake snorted. "Our father is a selfish ass who cares more about work and money than his family." Surprisingly, Blake defended Poppy's anger. "The only reason he's actually here is because he had some kind of business dealings in the area."

Callie gaped at her son. "Blake, that's enough."

Blake ignored her. "Don't blame my mother. She had no idea about you and Perry until our father found out about his passing. None of us knew he'd abandoned one family to replace you with another."

"I'm sorry, Poppy. I told him I'd try." Callie forced a strained smile onto her face and hurried from the shop, forgetting her coffee on the counter in her rush to escape.

Blake sighed as he grabbed his mother's forgotten cup. "My sister and I would like to get to know you. And maybe to hear about Perry. It's a bit of a mind fuck finding out we had siblings out there all this time. Do you think maybe we could come back before we leave the city if we leave our parents behind?"

Poppy couldn't bear to say no to Perry's look alike. "Uh, sure. I guess. Yeah."

"Awesome." Blake pulled out a slip of paper and slid it across the counter. "Here's our numbers. Shoot us a text when you have some time. We leave next Wednesday."

"Okay."

He waved as he headed towards the door. "See ya."

Poppy stared after him. "Yeah. Bye."

Maybe Poppy should be glad her father left them. Their mother had struggled to raise them alone sometimes, but she was amazing and strong and kind. This woman was weak and trapped and lonely and had just gotten the rug yanked out from under her.

Would her father abandon them now too and try for a third time? They had to be scared of just that now that they knew what he'd done ten years ago.

She wanted to hate his new family, but could only find it in herself to pity them. And a part of her weakened at Blake's desire to get to know her. How could she say no? None of this was his fault or his sister's.

What a nightmare this was all turning out to be.

DEAN SQUINTED AGAINST the blaze of the fire trying to overtake the pizza restaurant as gripped the fire hose, pointing the spray at the flames.

His muscles trembled as he fought to keep his aim steady, the water misting back in his face.

The lights of their truck flashed, clashing against the lights of the flames.

The cops kept all the spectators from getting too close as they filmed the disaster with their phones. Assholes. They were hoping to get their fifteen minutes, their clicks and likes while someone lost their business. While someone could lose their lives.

Worry pounded through him as he waited for Flynn and Jeff to finish clearing the restaurant and come back outside where it was safe. Dean used to be confident in all their abilities, but with Perry taken from them, he was terrified of losing another friend, another piece of his family.

Especially now since they were finally starting something real with Poppy, new and fragile as it was. Finally finding a little happiness in the midst of all the pain and loss. A sliver of light in the darkness.

Dean glanced over at Gavin at his side, making sure he was okay.

The fire was beginning to die down, but Gavin and Jeff still weren't out yet. Dean was two seconds from going in after them.

Dean thumbed his radio. "Flynn. Jeff. Status."

Only crackling static answered him.

Fuck.

"Flynn. Status." Dean's grip twisted and slipped on the hose.

They needed to get this fire out. Now.

"Flynn." Dean's voice rasped.

The door of the pizza place crashed open and two firefighters spilled through, an older man hanging between them.

Paramedics raced for them, taking the man off their hands, getting him onto a stretcher and hooked up to oxygen.

Dean was finally able to breathe again.

Chapter 37

Poppy halted in front of the door of the lawyer's office, taking a deep breath before stepping inside. She still couldn't wrap her head around Perry hiring a lawyer to handle his affairs. She'd never even considered doing that, it seemed too grown up. But that was Perry, always one for making sure he had all his bases covered, unable to enjoy life until he had everything prepared to his demanding expectations.

Considering his job as a firefighter, it made sense.

The lawyer refused to discuss anything over the phone, so here she was.

An attractive male assistant sat at a desk in the waiting room. "May I help you, miss?"

"I'm Poppy O'Sullivan. Mr. Calgon asked me to come in."

He smiled and nodded politely. "Ah, of course. Have a seat. He'll be right with you. Can I get you anything? Coffee? Water?"

"I'd love a coffee, thanks." She'd never turn down coffee.

"Excellent. I'll have it for you right away."

Poppy sat in one of the brown plush chairs as the guy went over to a side table that held bottled water and a silver carafe.

He paused after filling the cup with coffee. "Cream? Sugar? Sweetener?"

"Cream and sugar, please." She'd take coffee any way she could get it, but right now, she could use the extra hit the sugar would provide.

He finished fixing her drink and carried it over. "Here you go."

Poppy took the porcelain cup and saucer from him with a strained smile. "Thanks."

"Of course." His head tilted to the side as a low tone sounded from the phone. "Mr. Calgon is ready for you. Right this way please. Feel free to bring your coffee with you."

She stood and followed him through the door behind his desk into a neat and minimally decorated office where a middle aged man sat behind a large modern glass desk with a nameplate reminding her his name was Henry Lisbon.

"Miss O'Sullivan. Welcome. Thank you for coming in."

The assistant closed the door behind him when he exited, leaving Poppy alone with the lawyer. "I'm sorry it took so long to get back to you, Mr. Lisbon."

"Call me Henry, please. No apology necessary. It's quite common. Grief takes time and the process is different for everyone."

His words were nice, but they sounded rehearsed, like he had no real experience himself with loss.

"Thank you for that. So, what am I here for?" She'd prefer to get this over with and barrel past the pleasantries.

Henry shuffled through the papers on his desk. "Your brother made some provisions for his life insurance policy he wanted me to express to you. As you already know, he left everything to you. All the life insurance and his savings is yours."

"Right." She hadn't bothered with the life insurance for the funeral, not wanting to deal with it, so she put everything on a credit card. At least this way, she'd be able to pay them off without dipping into the shop's account.

"His policy was for $300,000."

Her cup clattered against the saucer, coffee spilling over the side. "Excuse me, what?"

"You heard correctly, I assure you."

She set the coffee on the corner of his desk, worried the cup would end up smashed on the ground. "How could he have insured himself for that much?"

And why? They were both comfortable, but neither of them were anywhere near rich. He didn't leave behind kids or a wife who would need it. She didn't need it.

The lawyer frowned at one of the pages before seemingly remembering the reading glasses perched on his head. "Between his part of the mortgage on both your business and the house he shares with his friends, he wanted to make sure he didn't leave any of you in a bad place. That's partially what I needed to speak to you about. While he left it all to you, he asked that $50,000 be set aside to give towards the mortgage of the house he lived in.

Since it was under his name, he also left the deed in Flynn Winchester's name. That's the only thing that wasn't left solely to you."

Perry really did think of everything. It pissed her off. She didn't want his death to be all tied up and easy. Nothing about this was supposed to be easy.

"Okay. Uh...what now?" As much as Perry had handled, she was still a little lost how to begin taking care everything.

"Now, you cash the check, pay the taxes on it, give the money he wanted to go to the house to the mortgage company, and I'll get the deed to Mr. Winchester."

Did Flynn already know the house was now in his name? If he didn't, she wanted to be the one to tell him instead of some stranger lawyer.

"Have you been in contact with him?" Poppy asked.

Henry shook his head. "Not yet. I wanted to speak with you first. I'll be contacting him later today."

Her head ached as she tried to get her feet under her and find some semblance of calm. "I'll let him know what to expect."

Henry adjusted his glasses on his nose. "I'll have the insurance company mail the check unless you'd like to do a direct deposit? You can fill out the paperwork here and I'll handle the rest for you."

"Yeah, I'll do the direct deposit. I'm not great at opening mail."

"Of course." He handed her a piece of paper attached to a clipboard. "Fill this out and then we'll be all done. You can expect the money in a week or so. They like to hold large sums like that to make sure they're real."

"Right." Poppy's voice came out wooden as she scrawled down her bank and personal information onto the page, her mind spinning in circles.

What was Perry thinking? Why did he prepare all of this? He was only twenty-seven, it wasn't like he was on his deathbed or anything.

"Did he ever say why he did this? He didn't leave a letter for me or anything?" If he went to this much trouble, why not leaving her an explanation?

Henry shook his head. "No letter. If he had lived longer, I suspect that would have changed. He's updated things a few times over the years."

"How long ago did he do this?" Poppy asked. When did her brother decide to prepare for his death?

"Four years ago he drew up a will with a small insurance policy. Basically enough to cover funeral costs. But he changed things after your mother passed. He said after the difficulty the two of you had taking care of things, he never wanted to leave you with the same struggles. He wanted to make sure it was all handled so you didn't have to."

"Sounds like him." The damn control freak.

He'd hidden exactly how bad things were with her mother's affairs, refusing to let her help with anything other than the food for the wake. But she'd seen his stressed out face and Gavin had let a little slip to her, but she'd left it alone, knowing it was Perry's way to cope. He needed to feel in control and deal with the logistical things.

If she had been the one to die, she'd have left him with the exact same mess. At least this way, if she died, there was no family who'd have to come in and sort through it. Though Tam and Marie would be left without a job.

Maybe she should talk to the guys and see if one of them wanted the coffee shop. She could leave it and the money to them. Should she set aside some of this money for their half-siblings for college? Perry didn't know about them, but she was certain he'd have wanted to leave them something.

It didn't look like they were hard up for money, but her father's money might come with strings for them. This way, they could make their own choices.

It was too much. It was all too much, trying to figure out what to do with all of this.

A sympathetic smile unfolded on the lawyer's mouth. "I know it's a lot. There's no rush to make any decisions. Take your time."

"Thanks." She placed the clipboard on his desk and rose. "If that's all?"

He rose as well and held out a hand for her. "It is. Thank you for coming in. And I'm very sorry for your loss."

She shook his hand. "Me too."

Poppy left the office in a fog, barely paying attention to where she was headed, on complete autopilot. Until a blue sedan caught her eye.

A blue sedan with a dented bumper.

Chapter 38

It had to be a coincidence. There was no way this was the car. It couldn't be. Her lungs squeezed as Poppy hyperventilated in front of the car. She reached for her phone with shaking hands, struggling to take photos of the damage and the license plate. It was a long shot, but what if it belonged to her brother's killer? She had to find out.

She struggled to calm herself, to think straight, to stave off the panic and excitement churning in her stomach, making her worry the coffee at the lawyer's office was going to come right back up.

Paranoia riding her hard, she emailed the photos to herself and to all the guys without an explanation. Just in case. She looked around her, searching for a place to hide and wait, to watch and plan.

There. A cropping of trees with a straight line of sight to the car. She had a book in her bag and could pretend she was out to enjoy the summer day.

Her phone buzzed and chirped with questions from the guys, wanting to know what was going on. She sent back a short mass reply, telling them she'd explain later. She didn't want to tell them what was going on yet, worried they'd converge on her and ruin her plan. Or worse, call the cops.

She'd call the officer in charge of her brother's case once she had a few more answers. She needed to see whoever owned that car. She needed to see if she knew them, recognized them. She needed to see what kind of person they were.

Trying to make it look like she was still reading, she cast her gaze around her, trying to guess which building the car's owner was inside. She was in a more secluded section of the district, only a bakery, a jeweler, a boutique clothing store, a yoga studio, a smoothie place, and a couple office buildings close by.

Were they male? Female? Young? Old? Rich? Poor? Stupid? Smart? Was it some alcoholic or party boy? Some entitled jackass who didn't care what chaos they left behind? A panicked stoner? Who was it? What kind of person left her brother dying alone in the street?

Poppy leaned against the base of the tree, idly turning the pages in her book as she kept her gaze glued to the car. She couldn't guess what sort of person drove it based on the car alone. A blue sedan was a popular choice. It wasn't a piece of crap, but it wasn't a luxury vehicle either. The fact that they were still driving around in it instead of taking the car to the shop was telling. Unless they were worried about the police questioning mechanics in the area, which according to Officer Maxwell, he'd done.

Maybe they thought it was safer driving it around unfixed until things settled down. Which it obviously was since it had been over two weeks since Perry's death and the cops still had no leads. She wasn't even sure how hard they were working to solve it. The officer in charge seemed nice and all, but maybe not the brightest. She wanted fucking Sherlock Holmes to solve this. With the money Perry had left her, she could hire a PI. Maybe they could get the answers she needed.

If she could just understand, she could move on. She could let go. Maybe even start fresh without this weight constantly hanging over her. Without someone to blame, she wasn't sure she could ever find any closure or peace.

Instead, she'd remain broken forever. And a broken person couldn't build a relationship and have a good life of love and happiness. The guys didn't deserve that, they deserved better. They deserved someone healing, someone whole.

As much as she wanted to be theirs, to leap into this wild relationship with them, she couldn't move past the hesitation, she couldn't move past the fear. It kept her stagnant, terrified. If she took that leap and everything crashed and burned around her, she'd have nothing and no one left. Those three were the only things remaining in her life who meant anything to her. She couldn't afford to lose anymore people.

But if she kept them at arm's length, accepting only friendship, wouldn't she lose them either way? If she turned them down now, eventually, they'd move on, find people who loved and appreciated them, start their normal lives. And they'd leave her behind. Not out of any meanness or revenge, but it would only be natural. They'd move on, she'd see them less and less until they became Christmas card friends.

No matter what she did, she ran the risk of losing them. And there was no one left to care what sort of strange relationship she had with them. No family left to object or judge. Their families might, but that was theirs to deal with. Not hers.

It was probably time for them to have a real conversation about expectations and how it would all actually work. What they'd discussed so far was still too murky and unclear. She and Flynn had fucked, the four of them had a damn foursome, but there had been no promises, no declarations, no decisions. They said they loved her, but she hadn't admitted the same.

Like he could read her mind from miles away, Gavin sent a text inviting her to dinner at their house. She shot him a response agreeing and returned her attention to the blue car. This deserved all her focus.

She checked the time. She'd been here an hour already and had more phone calls and paperwork to deal with back home. But she wasn't going to give up. Not yet.

Not until every store and office around her was empty and closed would she leave, assuming the car was abandoned in this small free parking lot.

She hoped and prayed it wasn't abandoned here, doubting the cops would bring out forensics to comb over the car.

A woman approached the parking lot, a yoga mat tucked under her arm, a smoothie clutched in her hand. She looked like someone Poppy would possibly be friends with, a kindness on her face, a hop in each of her steps.

She didn't look like a murderer, like someone who would get into an accident and flee the scene.

Poppy slid her phone up, using her book as a shield as she snapped photo after photo of the woman as she strode straight for the blue car. Her heart pounded like hoofbeats in her chest.

She couldn't just let her leave without saying something. Without talking to the woman. Maybe Poppy could get the woman to confess.

She had to try.

Chapter 39

Poppy swallowed past a dry mouth and jumped to her feet, hurrying over to the parking lot, putting herself in the woman's path, acting like they accidentally ran into each other.

Poppy's lip curled as green sludge spilled all over her shirt, but she shrugged it off. "I'm so sorry. I was reading and not paying attention."

The woman huffed in annoyance, visibly trying to let it go. "Dammit. It's fine. No big deal."

Poppy was impressed at the woman's level of control. "Maybe I should try yoga if it leaves you so calm."

The woman laughed. "Something like that. It's also just been a month of weird accidents like this."

Poppy couldn't believe the perfect opening the woman gave her. "I saw your car is a little messed up. That happen this month too?"

She glanced over at the bumper with a sigh. "Uh. Yeah. Minor accident. Someone backed into me."

Poppy's heart sped up. The timing fit. "Right. That sucks."

The girl shrugged. "I was able to drive away, so it could have been worse."

"Anyone else hurt?"

"No. No. Everyone was fine."

Poppy couldn't tell if she was lying or not. If she was, she deserved a damn Oscar.

"At least it still works."

The girl let out a mournful sigh. "Yeah. I haven't had time to get it fixed."

Poppy had no idea what else to ask her without it turning weird. But she needed one more thing before she could let it go for now. "Well, I'm sorry again for troubling you. I'm Poppy, by the way."

"I'm Jemma. It was nice running into you."

Poppy forced out a snort of fake amusement and a bright smile. "You too. And just remember, the month is almost over. Hope July is better for you."

"Thanks. Sorry about your shirt."

The green sludge had melted completely, leaving her sticky and gross. "It was my fault."

Poppy barely contained her rage as she forced herself to walk away from the woman. She still wasn't sure if she killed her brother, but she hadn't ruled her out either.

Once she got far enough away, she exchanged her book for her phone, dialing the officer with trembling fingers.

A voice barked in her ears. "Officer Maxwell."

"This is Poppy O'Sullivan."

"What can I do for you Miss Sullivan?" He sounded harried.

She didn't care.

"I have some information and photos I thought you might want to take a look at." She checked up and down the street before she crossed.

"From your brother's case?" His voice sharpened, focused.

She hurried past a group of shoppers before explaining. "Yes. I just came across a dented blue sedan and the owner admitted she was in an accident earlier this month."

He sighed loudly. "You should not be searching for your brother's killer on your own. It's not safe."

"I didn't go looking for her. I literally stumbled across the car." And if he wasn't going to get her answers, maybe she should start looking for them on her own.

"What kind of photos?" Officer Maxwell asked.

"Of the license plate, of the damage, and of the owner whose first name is Jemma."

"Where are you now?"

Poppy looked around her. She had about a ten minute walk back to her shop. "I'm on my way back home."

"I'll meet you there."

Why the hell would he do that? She didn't need to see him. She didn't need him to hold her hand through this hard time. She needed him to catch the asshole. He kept wanting to do these things in person when a phone call would suffice. It was obnoxious.

"I can just email them to you."

"No. I'll meet you there."

She rolled her eyes. "All right. Thank you."

"See you soon." He hung up.

He was so odd. He had no reason to meet her in person. She could easily have sent the files. Maybe he had something else to tell her, something he didn't want to explain over the phone. Dread weighed down her limbs as she made her way back to her shop. She couldn't handle much more, barely able to sludge through each day as it was.

She sighed as the front of her bakery popped into view. The gorgeous sign Perry had commissioned with the name of their coffee shop stamped in purple, Cool Beans with two smiling coffee beans carved beneath the words.

They'd decided to lean into the words play and puns and the names of their specialty drinks reflected it. Along with the goofy prints hanging all over the walls interspersed with Dean's photos.

It hadn't been worth the fight with Perry to try and come up with something a little more...or less, embarrassing. And he'd ended up being right. People seemed to enjoy the novelty of it and they needed something kitschy to compete with the chains.

In retaliation, she'd added a bunch of unicorn decor even though he claimed it didn't fit or match, but between the art, puns, and unicorns, they ended up with a charming and eclectic shop people liked to spend time in -—writing their novels, reading their books, meeting for dates and business meetings.

Poppy pushed the door open and let her favorite smells calm her. Coffee and sugary treats. She should make a pie for dinner tonight. Flynn would be thrilled. She should probably make cookies too in case he refused to share.

Tam and Marie looked up and smiled, nodding when Poppy gestured towards the kitchen. "I have a visitor coming. Just send him back there when he arrives." She shook her head at the mischief widening their smiles. "It's the cop."

They grimaced, making Poppy snort. She felt a little bad for them, so she decided to throw them a bone. "But I'm headed to their place for dinner."

That brought the sparkle back to their eyes.

Poppy shook her head as she ducked into the kitchen, her moment of amusement fading as she caught sight of the table covered in papers and her computer. Right. She still had a ton of work to do, calls to make, mail to open and answer.

With a sigh, she took a seat and dove back in, only looking up when the cop and Tam come into the kitchen.

"Miss O'Sullivan."

"Officer Maxwell." Poppy took the latte from Tam with a smile of thanks, who winked at her before returning to the main part of the shop. "I don't have the best printer, so I'll need to email you the photos I took."

His pale blue eyes searched hers. "Can I see them, please?"

"Sure." Poppy pulled them up on her phone and handed it over.

He swiped through them, his brow folded into a frown. "I'll look into this. But I have to warn you, it's not safe for you to do any investigating on your own. Whoever did this will be feeling desperate and cornered. And they could know who you are since the story was on the news and in the papers, your shop mentioned since he was part owner."

For a cop, he really had a lack of listening skills. "Like I said on the phone, I wasn't prowling the town like some kind of vigilante. I'm not Batgirl. I stumbled across it completely by accident."

It wasn't her fault she was more successful at his job than he was.

"Right." He didn't look like he bought it. "And where was this that you found the car?"

She sat back in her seat. "Over on Blecker Street, the free parking lot."

"What were you doing over there?" Suspicion was bright in his eyes.

She spoke past gritted teeth. "I was on my way back from talking to my brother's lawyer. I have his card, you can call him to confirm if you like."

He stared at her a moment before answering. "That won't be necessary. Can I email these to myself?"

"Go ahead."

He tapped at her phone and then handed it back to her. "You shouldn't get your hopes up. The damage to her car looks bad, but it could be a coincidence. The chances of you stumbling across the person who did this are rare."

"I know." And she did. But her hopes were still up. Way up.

Officer Maxwell adjusted his belt. "I'm glad you called me with the information though. But please don't go looking for your brother's killer. It's not safe."

Oh for crying out loud. Maybe if this jackass spent less time interrogating her, he'd actually solve some crimes.

"Again. I wasn't looking for them. But I wasn't going to ignore a smashed up blue car when it's been weeks and there are still no answers."

He refused to let it go. "Investigating isn't like TV or the movies. It takes time and patience. I understand you want answers and we are going to keep searching for them for you."

"How long before this becomes a cold case?" She knew they weren't going to keep looking forever. Eventually, they'd give up.

His eyes iced over. "This wasn't a robbery, Miss O'Sullivan, or a simple hit and run where there wasn't any injuries or deaths. We aren't anywhere near filing it away yet."

"Okay." She'd let it go for now.

But if she didn't get some answers soon, a private investigator might be her best option.

"Thank you for contacting me with this. I'll let you know what we find out. I'll take it from here." Officer Maxwell gave her a short professional nod and turned to leave.

"Thanks."

Chapter 40

Dean opened the door at Poppy's knock and greeted her with a short, but hard and hot kiss, leaving her breathless and craving more.

A small smile curled his lips when he pulled back. "Hi."

"Hey." She shook off the tendrils of lust and walked through the doorway, her nose twitching at the delicious smells of grilled steak.

Dean took the bag of food from her hands. "What's this?"

"Dessert. Don't let Flynn near it."

"Why not? You made pie, didn't you?" Flynn's voice sounded from behind her.

Poppy clasped a hand to her leaping chest and stumbled back a step. "Dammit, Flynn. Don't pop up like that. And keep your mitts off my pie. It's not just for you, you greedy bastard."

Flynn pouted as he inched towards Dean and the bag of desserts. "But it's been so long since you made me my own pie."

She tried not to laugh as Dean smacked Flynn's hand away. "I'll make you a special one soon. But tonight, you have to share."

Flynn let Dean carry the bag into the kitchen and turned on her, getting right into her personal space. "Oh, I don't mind sharing, muffin, if it's something really tasty. I'm not so greedy."

Poppy quivered at Flynn's flickering eyes, the innuendo in his voice. It should have been amusing or ridiculous, and if it was anyone else, it would've been, but coming from Flynn, it was arousing. It brought to mind filthy thoughts that stained her cheeks and chest scarlet.

The tension in the air crackled around her, raising goosebumps along her skin, icy heat flaring in her veins.

Gavin looked up from the stove when they entered the kitchen, stirring something in a huge pot.

She forced her focus on him instead of the heat in Flynn's eyes. "What are you making?"

Gavin banged his tongs against the side of the pot and set them down on the counter. "Corn on the cob. Dean already made the salad. Flynn did nothing."

Flynn flipped Gavin off. "I bought the beer."

Gavin snorted and Dean shook his head.

"Our girl made pie." Flynn was trying to sneak towards the bag again.

Gavin's brows shot high on his forehead. "And you haven't already stolen it?"

Flynn stopped when he realized they were all staring at him. "She said I have to share."

"I made cookies too since I didn't trust Flynn to stay out of it." Poppy slid the bag away from him and pulled out the desserts.

"You don't trust me?" Flynn gave her big puppy dog eyes.

Poppy refused to melt for him. As adorable as he was. "Not around pie. Or bacon. Or beer. Or bacon cheeseburgers."

Gavin grinned over his shoulder as he drained the corn. "Or whiskey. Or flannel."

"Or old vinyl records," Dean added.

Flynn folded his arms. "Now you are all just being pricks."

Poppy narrowed her eyes on him, forcing her expression blank. "Wait. You're willing to share me. Does that mean you love bacon and beer and pie more than me?"

Flynn gaped at her, a rather dumb expression on his face while the other two hid their smirks and snickers. "O-Of course not. I-I...well, I mean..."

She laughed. "Calm down. I'm screwing with you."

He scowled. "You little brat."

Dean and Flynn chuckled.

Poppy winked at him before she sobered. "There's some stuff you guys need to know."

Dean stepped forward, his eyes serious and searching. "Like what? Something about those photos you sent us?"

"Yeah, but there's other stuff first. I went to see Perry's lawyer today. He left money for his portion of the mortgage and he left the deed in Flynn's name. You should be getting a call from him soon."

Flynn lost all signs of humor as he stumbled back a step.

Dean frowned and rubbed the back of his neck. "I hadn't even thought about the mortgage. I forgot it was in his name. Stupid banks refusing to put us all on it."

"He left fifty thousand."

All their eyes widened as she quoted the amount.

Gavin fumbled the stick of butter, barely catching it before it smacked to the floor. "That's more than what he owes."

She was glad Perry left them something. He had loved them so much and wanted to make sure he didn't leave things harder for them. "It was part of his life insurance. I got the rest."

Gavin shook his head. "Man, he really did plan ahead, didn't he?"

"I also might have found his killer."

Dean sank into one of the chairs at the kitchen table while Flynn froze and Gavin cursed as caught the edge of his finger with the knife as he chopped a bunch of green onions.

"Are you okay?" Poppy asked, taking a step towards him.

Gavin inspected his finger. "I'm good. Didn't even draw blood."

Dean grabbed her elbow and tugged her attention back to his. "What exactly do you mean?"

Poppy explained her afternoon, leaving them even more shocked and silent as the guys carried all the food to the table already set with plates and silverware.

"It can't actually be her, right? The idea that you just stumbled across her is too wild to be real." Flynn sat down across the table from her.

Poppy slathered butter onto her corn cob. "Probably. The cop said the same thing after treating me like I was some kind of wannabe superhero, stalking the shadows for my brother's killer."

Flynn grinned around a wedge of steak. "You'd be hot as a superhero."

"Of course I would." She smiled. "Anyway. Once the money is in my account, I'll transfer it to one of you."

Dean poured her a glass of wine and slid it over to her from his place beside her. "You know you don't have to give that to us. It's more than he owed and we don't actually need it."

Poppy took a sip of the wine to wash the steak down her throat. "It was what he wanted and I certainly don't need so much either."

Gavin forked a pile of salad onto Flynn's plate, ignoring his scowl. "Maybe he saw what would end up happening."

"What do you mean?"

Gavin gestured around the table. "The four of us, together. You know, we wanted you to move in with us when we bought this place. Perry told us you wanted your own space though and that it was a bad idea."

Poppy frowned. "He never offered."

How many secrets did Perry keep from her? How many ways did he control her life without her knowing? She didn't want to be so angry with him and hurt by him when he wasn't here to punch in the face.

And was it really all his fault? She'd allowed him that control because it was easier than handling her life on her own. He wanted the control, she didn't. She hated the responsibility and the planning and thinking things through.

What was she going to do without him? Would she completely wreck her life?

Dean cut up his steak with careful precision. "I think he was worried it would all blow up if the five of us lived together under one roof. Any guy you tried to bring home we probably wouldn't have handled well. He never thought we could actually share you successfully. He thought we'd hurt you."

Poppy turned her upper body to face Dean headon. "Was he right?"

She didn't think they would, but a relationship like this would be messy and difficult. She didn't want to hurt them either.

Dean dropped his fork and knife, giving her all of his attention with black coffee eyes. "Never. If we've loved you for this long, I don't think it's going anywhere."

It took her a moment to break out of his spell to find her breath after his words took the air right out of her lungs. "What exactly do you expect from me? What about your families? What will they say?"

"We just want you to be with us. To choose all of us. And I haven't spoken to my family in over a decade, so I don't really give a shit what they say." Flynn shrugged like it didn't bother him how his parents stopped caring about him a long time ago.

If they ever had.

Her blood still boiled every time she remembered how skinny and starved he used to be. How fast he grew out of his clothes.

Gavin reached across the table to squeeze her hand. "My parents and siblings adore you and the guys. They've been expecting it for a while. You saw at the party. And I told you what my mother said."

"My parents may be a little taken aback, but they aren't a huge part of my life anymore either. Just major holidays. Sometimes. If they don't like it, that's their problem. Next?" Dean slid a finger up her thigh.

Poppy tried to focus past the desire Dean's touch burned through her. "Do you want me to move in with you?"

Gavin shook his head. "Only when you're ready and want to. I think it'd be a bit much right now."

She moved the salad around on her plate. "The dynamics of it has me a little...confused. Is there going to be some sort of schedule?"

"For who gets to fuck you?" Flynn asked. "No."

She gathered her thoughts, wanting to make sure she didn't forget any of the concerns and questions she had. "Not necessarily sex, but I'd want some alone time with each of you. I think it'd be necessary. And I wouldn't want anyone to start feeling left out. Making one relationship work is hard, but three? That's going to take some juggling. I don't understand how the three of you won't get jealous. I'd want to kill you if we started this and you touched another woman."

Dean sighed and tapped the end of his knife against the table. "How to explain this? Look, the four of us, well three of us now, we've been so close for so long, we don't really know how to live apart from each other and we don't want to. We've always shared everything and if you think about it, we've always shared you too.

"Perry always got most of your time and attention and it made us irritated as hell that he would share everything except you with us. But we shared you as our friend, as our family, as the girl we watched grow into a fun and hot woman who we all fell in love with. It sounds crazy and strange, but that sort of relationship works for us. We're never going to want to be on our own and we're never going to want to give you up. You just have to decide if you can give us up. Because if this is just grief or a fling for you, please let's end it now. You have the unique ability to completely wreck us."

Poppy could only stare at Dean with a gaping mouth. She'd never heard him say so much at one time before. She'd also never heard him open up, laying himself bare. It made her eyes burn with emotion and her thighs rub together with arousal. Too many conflicting feelings bubbled inside her.

"I'm terrified." She whispered the confession, staring down at her plate of food.

"Of what?" Gavin asked.

"That I'll lose you three too."

Flynn groaned. "You aren't going to lose us. No matter what you choose. If you want us to be your friends and family, that's what we'll be. If you only want one of us, we'll figure. it out. But if you love us all the same and want to be with us, I swear to you we aren't going to let you go. We're all in, muffin."

Chapter 41

Poppy wanted what they offered more than almost anything. The only thing she wanted more was Perry back with them. She didn't know what to say, what to do. Perry's voice wasn't in her head giving her any suggestions or warnings, she was alone, she had to decide for herself.

She finally looked up at the three men who were sitting here willing to give her everything she'd ever wished for. "I could never choose between you three. It was always you. All of you."

The three of them jumped from their seats and surrounded her, stroking and kissing and hugging any part of her they could reach. Poppy let herself melt into them, her throat clogged with too much emotion as lips pressed against her cheeks, lips, neck, shoulders, fingers.

They pulled away and Dean took her hand. "Come on. Let's go watch a movie."

She let him drag her to her feet and into the living room, the food forgotten. "No blanket fort tonight?"

Gavin shook his head. "Not this time. We weren't sure you'd stick around after we talked."

She bit her lip. "I wasn't sure I would either."

Dean tugged her onto the couch next to him. "Dare we ask what changed your mind?"

Her cheeks flushed, not wanting to talk about it, but if she was in this, she had to be honest, she had to open up to them, to trust them. "Ever since Perry died, I keep hearing him in my head, like he's some weird angel on my shoulder, warning me about choices and decisions. He kept telling me all the reasons this was a bad idea. For the first time, tonight, I didn't hear him."

Gavin sat on her other side. "So you were finally free to make your own choice instead of listening to his?"

Poppy nodded. "Yes. I'm not crazy. I know it's not actually him."

Dean cupped her face, his thumb stroking her cheek. "Oh, baby. We don't think you're crazy. You were closer to him and knew him better than anyone. He doesn't need to physically be here for you to know what he'd think and say."

"There's a part of me that's scared." Poppy pulled her feet up on the couch, hugging her knees to her chest.

"About what?" Flynn turned back from the TV, remotes in his hands.

Her arms tightened around her legs. "What if I stop hearing him? I don't want him to stop talking to me even though I'm making a decision he would've disapproved of."

She didn't want to lose this last connection to Perry.

Gavin shifted until he was pressed right up against her. "I think that's going to be up to you. If you let his "disapproval" drown him out, then yeah, you might stop hearing him. But if you decide this one time you're going to ignore his advice, he should still be there next time you need him."

The slightest tendril of hope wiggled into her chest. "I hope so. I'm not ready for him to be completely gone. Annoyed as I still am with him."

Flynn kissed the top of her head before he collapsed on the other side of Gavin. "He's always going to be a part of you, muffin. He's not going anywhere."

"Do you feel guilty that you want to be with us when you know he tried to keep it from happening?" Dean asked.

Poppy sucked on the inside of her cheek as she considered his question. "A little, maybe. I know part of him was just trying to protect all of us in case this went bad. But I hate feeling like ultimately he did it for himself. And I hate that he's gone and I can't call him on it. I can't smack him for interfering for so long."

She wanted to believe he did it all for her, but as much as she missed and adored him, she wasn't blind to who he really was. And he was always selfish and controlling.

Anymore than she was blind to Dean's occasional brooding angst and same need for control, Gavin's recklessness, Flynn's cocky immaturity and wild rage, her own laziness and lack of confidence. They were all damaged and imperfect people who had formed themselves into a family when their own let them down.

Maybe they were broken in all the right ways for them to fit together.

Each one of them had something she needed. Gavin was the one who would take leaps with her, go on spontaneous adventures with her. Flynn was the one who could tease her from a bad mood, who would get in the kitchen with her and make messes, who brought music and dancing into her life. And Dean. Dean was the calm to her storm, the anchor who kept her and the rest of them from floating away. He was the one who she could curl up with and enjoy the quiet and peace.

What did they need that she gave them?

She hoped whatever it was, it was enough.

"I've had a few moments like that myself," Gavin said. "It was something we should have addressed a long time ago, but we didn't know how you felt, so it wasn't worth the fight if you were uninterested."

"I doubt I was ready for it." She wasn't exactly confident she was ready for it now.

But she wanted to be.

Dean curved his arm around her shoulders. "We'll figure it all out, baby. We'll take it slow, one step at a time. We're in no rush and it's gonna take time for us to learn how to make this work."

"Have you ever tried this before? Sharing someone?" She almost wanted to take those questions back, not sure she wanted to know.

Gavin grimaced. "Uh, not exactly. We've never shared a serious relationship with anyone."

She didn't miss the glance they exchanged. "But?"

Gavin sighed. "But we've uh...shared a couple women. In other ways."

Her eyes narrowed. "You mean you've had foursomes before."

She hated the slice of pain it sent through her chest. It wasn't fair of her. They hadn't owed her anything. But she still couldn't bear the images his words sent flickering into her mind. She was being ridiculous. It wasn't like she'd saved herself for them.

Gavin shook his head. "No, never all of us at the same time. Do you want the specifics?"

"I'm not sure." She was leaning towards no.

"Are you all right?" Dean asked.

"I think so. It's not like I'm some shrinking virgin."

Flynn snorted. "Believe me, muffin. We wanted to kill every single guy who ever touched you."

"You guys hardly ever brought the women you dated around me. At one point I wondered if you were all sleeping together." She rubbed her lips.

Flynn peeked around Gavin with an evil glint in his eyes. "The thought of that turns you on a little, doesn't it?"

Poppy shrugged, trying not to blush "A little."

Dean chuckled, the sound wrapping around her like warm silk. "Sorry, baby. No sword crossing for us. It's all about you."

"That's a shame." It wasn't really. She wouldn't have minded if they wanted to put on a show for her or even if they had real feelings for each other, but they were more than enough for the just the way they were.

Gavin leaned over, nipping at her ear. "I think we'll be able to keep you from being too disappointed."

Her breath caught in her throat as she sank further into the couch, trying to keep from attacking Gavin at his heated words.

Flynn grinned and flipped on the TV. "All right. What are we watching?"

She tried not to gape at him in shock, struggling to believe they were just going to watch a movie like they hadn't just wound her up and left her wanting.

Dean adjusted her place on the couch until she was half in his lap, running fingers along her arm, leaning over to whisper in her ear. The same ear Gavin teased. "This thing, this relationship between us isn't just about sex. It's also about us wanting to spend time with you. As much time as we can find."

"Besides, we have an early shift in the morning," Gavin said.

Flynn turned on the latest Marvel movie and flopped around beside Gavin, forcing him almost beneath Poppy's ass as Flynn held her feet. The four of them wiggled around until everyone found a comfortable position and left the heavy conversations behind, focusing on the humor and action of the film.

She couldn't imagine a better place to be.

Chapter 42

Gavin pushed into Poppy's coffee shop, grinning when she glanced up at him with a bright smile from her spot in the corner wiping down one of the tables. Damn, she was gorgeous.

"Just in time. We're closing up. Do you want anything before we finish?"

Gavin shook his head. "I'm good. I'm here to take you to dinner."

Her brows raised. "Oh really?"

"Really. I beat the others at rock, paper, scissors."

She laughed.

He shrugged, unrepentant. "We considered bringing you out with all of us, but figured it might be better to ease into this."

She waved to Tam and Marie who were cleaning up behind the counter. "I'm headed upstairs. You guys got the rest?"

Marie nodded. "Of course. Go. Have fun."

Gavin was pleased to see her lean on her employees a little.

Poppy gestured for him to follow her as she threw her rag into the sink in the kitchen.

He tried not to stare at her ass like a creep. "We missed you the last two days. We were hoping you might want to come back to our place after the dinner and spend the night. We have two days before our next shift. Maybe you could come in late tomorrow."

Poppy pushed into her house and glanced over her shoulder at him with a small smile. "Yeah, I could do that. I've been coming in late in the mornings anyway. Actually acting like an owner instead of doing it all. I gave Tam and Marie raises and they've been huge helps getting things in order."

"That's great." And it was. They'd been worried about her taking it all on without Perry, but it looked like she finally had a handle on it.

"Yeah. I'm going to hire one more barista since I can afford it once Perry's check clears and it'll give me some time off. Working six days a week is a lot."

That was excellent news. Maybe he could talk her into making a visit to see his sisters with him sometime soon. "It is. Flynn said you talked to his accountant?"

"I did. She helped a lot and I finally feel like I'm getting a handle on things. I hadn't realized how much Perry handled while I did all the baking and made drinks and basically ran the counter and kitchen. And Tam is taking a business class, so I may eventually see if she wants to be a partner instead of just making her the manager." Poppy walked into her bedroom and started sorting through her clothes.

It relieved Gavin to see her so confident and present, but it hadn't been long since she lost Perry. It had only been a little over a week since their fourth of July weekend. He'd lost it in the shower earlier today after seeing Perry's room stripped and bare after someone left the door open.

He worried this was the calm before the storm. He didn't want her to throw herself into the shop and relationships with them instead of dealing with her grief. It wasn't healthy. This was why they'd meant to wait. It was his own fault for losing sight of it and spilling so much that night at the bar.

Gavin couldn't say he regretted it, but he hoped they weren't doing more harm than good by starting this with her so soon.

Poppy started stripping from her clothes before it really hit Gavin that he'd followed her all the way into her bedroom while they talked.

He spun around to face her wall, his blood heating. "Sorry. I'll wait for you in the living room."

"It's nothing you haven't already seen, Gav." There was a thread of laughter in her voice.

"Yeah, but this is a proper date."

"I know you're all about the clean eating, but me? I like to enjoy dessert first." Her soft hand gripped his shoulder and turned him around to face her.

He gulped as he took in her gorgeous body clad in only matching purple underwear.

She was so fucking stunning, standing there confident and at ease and wanting him.

Right there beside her bed.

"I guess dinner could wait a little longer."

A slow smile spread across her tempting lips. "Or we could grab takeout on the way back to your place."

His control snapped.

POPPY MELTED AS GAVIN cupped her cheeks and kissed her. She steadied herself with her hands clutched in his shirt as his tongue danced with hers.

This was her first real kiss with Gavin. Her first where they were alone and she was focused on him alone. He tasted delicious, like tea and honey.

His hands released her face and slid down her body to clutch her hips and pull her tighter against him. She flicked the buttons of his shirt open, wanting his clothes off. He shrugged out of his shirt once she released the last button, revealing his perfectly sculpted chest.

She stepped back to take it all in, wanting to taste every inch of him. He didn't give her long to stare, yanking her back to him and popping the clasp of her bra open and slid it off her arms.

It was his turn to stare.

Poppy grabbed his hand and tugged him towards the bed, but Gavin scooped her into his arms and tossed her onto the mattress where she landed with a bounce and a laugh.

He grinned and covered her with his body, burying his face in her neck and nibbling at the sensitive flesh there. She shivered and spread her thighs wider so he could fit against her.

Gavin explored her like she was precious, almost reverently. His slacks and the last pieces of fabric separating them disappeared, leaving them naked and breathing in short pants as their touches and kisses sped up, growing more needy and impatient.

He rolled onto his back, taking her with him until she straddled him, his cock a hard length teasing her soaked center. Poppy ground herself against him and he groaned into her mouth, his hands stroking up her sides to cup her breasts, his thumbs brushing against her nipples, making her gasp and her core clench.

Poppy batted blindly at her nightstand for a condom as she kissed him, shivering at the way his tongue stroked hers. It was almost indecent.

Once she had the condom, she ripped it open with her teeth and slid it onto him, enjoying the way he pushed into her grip, the way his eyes hooded with lust as he watched her. She was on birth control and had been for a long time, but she had no desire for kids anytime soon and she'd been foolish with Flynn. At least he'd pulled out.

She sank onto him and they both released sighs of pleasure and relief as he speared deep inside her. Poppy steadied herself with her hands planted on his chest as she began to ride him, tossing her head back as heat spread through her.

"Fuck, you look gorgeous like this." Gavin groaned and his grip on her hips tightened as she sped up.

Poppy smiled down at him, unable to believe this was actually happening, really happening.

She'd wanted it for so long and never thought she'd have any of them. But they all wanted her too. It still didn't feel real.

Gavin sat up and rolled them over again, splaying her out beneath him, never breaking stride as he pumped in and out of her, slow and hard, over and over, trapping her in his stormy gray eyes.

They way he looked at her made her feel sexy and powerful and wanted and loved.

Poppy surrendered to the climax pulsing through her as he bent to suck a nipple into his mouth. She bucked and thrashed beneath him as fireworks crackled through her veins. Her release triggered his and he stiffened inside her as she fluttered and pulsed around him.

He slumped, but kept his weight off her as he pressed a kiss to her sweaty forehead.

Gavin finally pushed off of her and out of her with a grunt, making her hiss at the empty feeling he left behind. He disposed of the condom and collapsed beside her on the bed, reaching over for her hand and tugging her into his arms.

"This wasn't quite how I planned the night to go."

She raised her head to quirk a brow at him. "Are you complaining?"

He chuckled and pressed her face back to his chest. "Not even a little. I've imagined this a million times over the years and it was leagues better than any of my fantasies."

"Same here. You should know, I want you all like you're an addiction. I love cuddling and watching TV with you, but our entire lives has been spent getting to know each other. You guys don't have to take it so slow."

"Feeling a little horny, sweetheart?" Gavin laughed.

"Little bit, yeah." She buried her face in his chest.

He teased her out, grabbing her chin to make her face him. "You aren't going to hear us complaining about it. We just didn't want you to feel like we're only interested in sex. We want you anyway we can have you. Cuddled on the couch, naked in a bed, challenging me to a bet I'm sure to lose, dancing with Dean, fighting with Flynn, kicking our asses at basketball. We want it all."

Warmth bloomed in her chest and she was sure she looked just like the heart-eye emoji. "I do too."

He smacked her ass. "Good. Now, come on. We had dessert, now let's have dinner. And no greasy takeout. We're having a proper meal. And don't forget to pack a bag."

Chapter 43

Dean sat in one of their adirondack chairs in their backyard, sipping at a glass of brandy. Gavin and Poppy had returned from their date hours ago in time to watch a movie with them before they went to bed.

Dean was feeling restless, so he'd come out here to think. He was glad Poppy and Gavin seemed to have had a good time. A really good time based on the ease they touched each other with.

But tonight, Dean was plagued with guilt. He missed his friend. He was always closer to Perry than the other two. They were all family, brothers, but Perry was a kindred spirit with his cold logic and need for control. They understood each other on a deeper level than they had with the other two.

And this situation with Poppy had gotten completely out of his control. He'd promised Perry they'd handle it carefully, that they wouldn't hurt her. that they wouldn't fracture their family. But they'd barrelled into this with all the grace of a rhinoceros.

He was terrified she'd jumped into this to drown out the pain of her grief and when she woke up, she'd regret it. Her happiness the last few days had an edge to it, like she was determined to be fine.

Fine.

He hated that damn word. And she used it liberally, trying to convince them and herself it was true.

But none of them were fine and wouldn't be for a long time. They'd lost someone precious to them. In such a stupid way. A car crash. A firefighter dying in a car crash was infuriating.

What would Perry say if he was here? He'd be furious and claim they'd taken advantage. And they had. She was vulnerable and broken and they'd let their long pent up desires make them stupid.

Dean couldn't see a way out but through. He had to hope she really wanted this. If he tried to back things off now, it would only hurt her more.

He raised his glass towards the sky. "Miss you, fucker. Really wish you were here."

He brushed the tears off his cheeks and rested his head against the back of the chair.

"Dean? What are you doing out here?"

He jerked and wrenched around to see Poppy standing in spilled moonlight, looking like some kind of glowing goddess.

He'd clearly had too much to drink.

POPPY DIDN'T MEAN TO startle him. She'd woken up after a nightmare about Perry and had crawled out of Gavin's arms and come downstairs to get some air.

Dean's eyes still had tears in them when he looked over at her. "What are you doing up?"

She rubbed her arms and looked up at the stars. "Just a crappy dream. What's going on with you?"

He turned back to face the line of trees. "Just crappy thoughts."

She ambled closer to him. "What kind of crappy thoughts?"

Dean peeked at her from the corner of his eye. "Nothing in particular."

Poppy had never tried to tease him from his brooding before and she wasn't sure she'd be able to. But she wasn't going to turn around and leave him here with wet eyes and slumped shoulders.

"So just general crappy thoughts?"

"Pretty much." His voice was a whisper in the dark.

She plopped herself into his lap. "Can I guess them?"

Poppy had a few decent ideas of what was on his mind.

His hands jerked up and clutched her hip and thigh. "Sure."

"You're missing your best friend."

"Yeah." Dean barely breathed the word.

She ran her hand up his neck into his hair. "You're worried what he would think about what we're doing."

"Yeah." He relaxed a bit beneath her touch.

"You're worried we're rushing this and I'm going to regret it."

"Yeah. Wait. What?" He stiffened and his hands clenched against her body.

She gripped the back of his neck and made him face her. "I'm not going to regret this. I know I've been a bit crazy lately with my mood swings, but this relationship with the three of you wasn't something new I decided I wanted. I fell in love with all of you when I was twelve years old. It's never been anyone but you three for me. Maybe Perry's death finally gave me the courage and the push I needed to take the leap. And maybe we are moving fast, but this has been a long time coming. I can't promise I won't freak out and get overwhelmed any more than you can promise you won't come out here to brood or Flynn can promise not to come home with bruised knuckles or Gavin can promise not to go do something reckless."

Dean cut off the rest of her speech with his lips against hers. She turned in his lap and threw her arms around his neck, pressing into him.

He took complete control of her mouth, demanding entry, one of his hands fisting her hair, the other digging into her ass.

She wondered if she should feel weird or ashamed over being out here with Dean after having sex with Gavin and falling asleep in his arms. But this was part of being in a relationship with three men. It would take some time to get used to, but Dean clearly needed her right now. And she needed him too.

Dean stood with her in his arms and set her down on the ground and took a step back.

Confused, she stared at him.

His mouth was set in a stern line. "Strip. Now."

She shivered at the dominant command in his tone. She shouldn't be surprised he liked games of control in the bedroom. What did surprise her was how her body reacted. With little thought and no resistance, her hands went directly to the hem of her shirt and lifted it over her head, leaving her only in a pair of lacy underwear.

Poppy dropped the shirt to the ground and reached for the waistband of her underwear, shoving them down her legs and stepping out of them and waited for what Dean would do next.

Her nipples pebbled beneath his perusal and goosebumps spread across her skin.

Dean stalked towards her, circling around her, looking her up and down. "Don't move."

Even with the slight chill in the air, heat flushed through her. The moonlight glinted against Dean's dark skin, highlighting his mysterious air.

She curled her hands into fists as she fought the need to yank him to her. She was way too curious and excited about discovering what he had in store for her.

Poppy had expected romance and candles from her artist, but she should have known better. She knew the darkness he had raging inside of him. She knew his desperate craving for control so similar to Perry's but was more focused on the internal than the external.

Perry needed everyone and everything orderly and in its place. Dean focused it inwards on himself.

She wanted to see his careful control shatter more than anything.

Dean stepped up right to her back, not touching her, but she could still feel him. "Are you ready for me, baby?"

"Yes. Please."

A pleased growl rumbled from his chest. "On your knees. Now."

Poppy sank into the dewy grass and Dean's hand fisted in her hair, drawing her head back until all she could see were stars. A moan slipped from her lips and floated away into the night, her body tense and trembling with nervous anticipation.

She was already so close, teetering on the edge, and he hadn't even touched her yet.

What was he doing to her.

"You look like some kind of magical creature, kneeling out here with moon and starlight glittering across your skin." He released her hair and came around in front of her, his eyes as black as the night sky.

Poppy eyed the bulge in his pants and licked her lips.

Dean cupped himself. "You want this?"

"Yes."

"Touch yourself. Your tits."

Poppy kneaded her breasts, plucking at her nipples while his gaze seared her skin. He rubbed at his erection while he watched her, his breathing calm, the only sign he was affected was the way his cock strained the zipper of her jeans.

She peered up at him through her lashes as she slid one hand down her stomach and into the wet heat of her core.

Dean cursed and yanked her up by her arms, crushing his lips against hers in an almost bruising kiss.

He pulled away with a gasp and a groan, pressing his forehead against hers, his breaths ragged. "Fuck. I've wanted you for too fucking long I can't torture you like I need to. Not tonight."

A smile curled her lips. This was exactly what she wanted. Him out of control, desperate for her. "Good. Put us both out of our misery. You can torture me next time."

"Oh baby. You have no idea what's coming to you." With a dark smile, he laid her onto the grass, looming over her with a flash of teeth as he yanked off his clothes.

Dean slid his hand between her legs, a rough noise ripping from his throat. "You're soaked for me."

"Always." Poppy spread her legs wider in wordless invitation.

He pulled a condom from somewhere like he was a damn magician and sheathed himself in it. Instead of sinking into her, he teased her clit, making her gasp and toss her head back into the grass.

He played her body with expert strokes, bringing her right to the precipice, but refusing to let her fall over.

"Please, Dean. Please."

"What do you want, baby?"

"I want you. Always you."

She cried out when he filled her with one hard thrust, shattering around him, her hands ripping up clumps of grass as the stars above her shimmered and brightened, her body jerking and shaking.

Dean pulled out of her, making her frown. "I'm nowhere near finished with you, baby." He flipped her over onto her hands and knees, yanking her ass into the air.

Poppy whimpered when he sank back inside her, reaching deeper from this position.

He pistoned in and out of her, no longer going slow and careful, no longer teasing and holding back.

Dean was completely unleashed and she loved it.

The night embraced them as he fucked her under the midnight sky, the music of chirping insects acting as their soundtrack.

One of his hands dug into her hip and the other roamed over her body, pinching and stroking and squeezing.

He whispered her name into her ear with a rasp in his voice, making her moan and arch back against him.

Heat lashed through her with such ferocity, she thought she would burn to ashes before he was through with her.

Her head drooped as he plucked at her clit, everything inside her boiling over and exploding in ecstasy. Only his grip on her kept her from collapsing facedown into the dirt as he finished, his body curled around hers, their sweaty skin sliding against each other.

"Fuck, I love you." Dean groaned the words and got them both to their feet and over to the chair where he pulled her back into his lap.

She nuzzled into him, a sleepy smile on her face when he kissed her forehead and threaded their fingers together.

A comfortable silence fell between them as they calmed, still caught in the spell and magic of the night.

Chapter 44

Gavin raced towards the building roaring with flames, his heart drumming in time with his steps. Dean and Flynn were on the hose and yelled after him to be careful as he followed Marcus and Jeff inside.

"Fire Department. Call out." They screamed it again and again trying to be heard over the shriek of the fire as they searched through the house.

Sweat filled his gear as he pounded up the stairs to the second story. The parents' screams for their child still trapped inside rang in his ears. He had to find her. The other two children had gotten out, but one had been left behind. Half his squad was holding the terrified and panicked parents back, leaving them short-handed.

"Fire Department. Call out."

They didn't have long before the building collapsed beneath them. They needed to find this kid. Now.

He kicked open a door across the hall from the one Jeff was clearing and it was clearly a young girl's room.

"Fire Department. Call out." He peered through his mask and the billowing smoke, searching for any sign of life, wincing at the heat trying to melt through his gear. "Is there anyone in here?"

A small sob caught his attention and he got on his hands and knees to peek under the bed. There. A young girl was curled up, shaking and crying and terrified.

He held out his hand. "Come on. We need to get you out of here. Your parents are waiting for you."

She reached out a trembling arm and took his hand, letting him pull her out from under the bed. Gavin lifted her into his arms and carried her into the hall, calling to the others he had her. Jeff and Marcus went ahead of him back downstairs, clearing the way.

The last step buckled beneath Gavin's feet and he went down, twisting to take the brunt of the impact, curling the girl close into his chest.

Jeff and Marcus tried to catch him, but they were only able to grab the girl before Gavin hit the floor, pain radiating through him as something snapped in his wrist and a piece of flaming wood sliced into his shoulder.

POPPY HUMMED AS SHE prepared the baked goods for the following day. The guys would be off tomorrow, and she wanted to have things in order so she could spend some time with them.

The insurance check had hit her account that morning and she needed to transfer the money she owed the guys over to their mortgage account. She hadn't had a chance to even message them about it yet today, her shop had been packed and then her half-siblings had come in and she'd taken a break to try and get to know them.

They were sweet kids, kind of sad and lonely. She'd given them her number and social media information so they could keep in touch, but it was still hard being around them. They were a harsh reminder of her loss and she had a hard time separating everything.

Her phone rang with Dean's ringtone and her face flushed as she remembered what they'd done the other night. Something she wanted to do again. Soon.

She answered the call on speaker so she could keep working. "Hello?"

"Hey." His voice was businesslike and strained, making her freeze. "Don't freak out. Everything's fine. But Gavin is in the hospital."

She leaned her palms against the counter as her head spun. "What?"

"There was an accident at work. He's okay, they're just running a couple tests to make sure he didn't break anything. But I wanted you to hear it from one of us before you found out some other way."

She took deep, even breaths to calm her skittering heart. "Where are you?"

"You don't have to come. He should be released soon."

Frustration pushed out some of the fear. Of course she was coming. Gavin was in the damn hospital. "Where are you?"

Dean sighed. "St. Theresa's."

"I'm on my way." Poppy hung up before he could argue any longer.

Her pulse thudded in her ears as she scrambled for her purse and made sure her ovens were turned off. Moving on autopilot, she locked up and ran outside to her car she hadn't driven in weeks.

But Gavin needed her and St. Theresa's was too far to walk to. She'd just have to deal.

Poppy fought to keep her breathing steady and focused on the task in front of her as she threaded through rush hour to get to the hospital. *He's okay. He's okay. He's okay.*

He's alive.

Gavin hadn't left her. He was still with her. With them.

She kept that mantra running through her mind, over and over, as she searched for a place to park in the ER parking lot.

He's alive. He'll be fine.

Terror strangled her as she ran through the entrance, easily spotting the group of soot and ash covered firefighters in the waiting room.

She jogged over to them, panting. "Where is he?"

Jeff grabbed her upper arms, steadying her. "He's fine. He's being seen by a doc. Flynn and Dean are with him. He's going to be just fine. Minor scratch and burn. Probably a sprained wrist."

She gulped and nodded over and over again. "Okay. Okay. When can I see him?"

Jeff released her and fumbled for his phone. "We should be getting an update soon and I'll text and let Dean know you're here."

Brian stepped forward to pat her shoulder. "He's a hero, Poppy. He saved a little girl tonight."

She didn't give a shit. Not right now. Maybe she'd be impressed and awestruck later. But right now she was scared and angry and it was all hitting too close to home.

She couldn't lose anyone else. And the men she was in love with had one of the most dangerous jobs in the world.

How was she supposed to handle that?

Dean poked his head through the door. "Poppy. Come on and I'll take you to see him."

FLYNN LOOKED UP FROM his spot on the edge of Gavin's bed as Poppy entered, her face pale and strained, her eyes panicked and wide.

They should have waited to call her once Gavin was home from the hospital. She shouldn't have to see this. Not so soon.

Gavin smiled at her. "Hey sweetheart."

Flynn grabbed Poppy's clenched hand, drawing her closer. He wanted to hug her, but he worried if he did, she'd shatter. "They gave him some painkillers, so he's a little loopy."

"What's the word?" Her eyes were glued to Gavin, her voice shaky.

He wasn't exactly feeling calm and steady himself. While he and Dean stood helpless outside, all sorts of nightmares ran through his mind.

And Dean had kept himself separate and stiff, barely speaking, refusing to come close.

"It's just a sprain. He'll be fine in a week or so and the burn and scratch was minor. He didn't even need stitches."

Flynn hoped his words would wipe the worry off her face, but it remained.

"Good. That's good."

Dean leaned in the doorway behind her, watching with folded arms and a clenched jaw. Flynn exchanged a frustrated glance with him, both of them waiting for the setback this could cause.

Poppy was a woman with deep abandonment issues and this could really make it hit home how easily she could lose them.

But as they watched, Poppy seemed to shake off her fear and climbed into the bed with Gavin, who snuggled into her with a smug grin.

Flynn rolled his eyes. Dude was milking it. Not that he could blame him. Now that Flynn had gotten a taste of her, he couldn't get enough. He wanted to always be kissing her.

Flynn moved off the bed and into the chair next to it, slinging his leg over the arm as he tapped at his phone, texting Gavin's mom an update.

Dean didn't move from his spot in the doorway, like he was standing guard.

This had freaked them all out. It reminded them that life was short as hell and all that cliched crap.

Flynn glanced over at Gavin and Poppy whispering together on the small bed. Satisfaction swelled in his chest, seeing them cuddled together like that, exchanging secrets and kisses.

It would be completely perfect if only the hole Perry left didn't leave something missing from their family. Finally having Poppy in the way they had wanted her for so long helped, but it didn't heal any of them.

Hopefully, time would.

Chapter 45

Poppy tried to keep the darkness from washing over her, she tried to fight it, but it was a strong force, determined to drag her into a living nightmare, to drown her in what ifs and fears and regrets.

Gavin was back home, bandaged up and safe and headed back to work in a few days. Poppy kept it together long enough to get him settled, assuring herself he was fine before she returned to her own home. He needed rest and the other two needed to get back to their shift.

Which gave Poppy the perfect chance to escape and try to regroup. She didn't want to infect them with the haze of despair surrounding her.

She trudged upstairs and deadbolted the door behind her. Even with their keys, the guys wouldn't be able to get through the other locks. And she needed to be alone for a bit. She needed a timeout to come to terms with all the changes in her life and what it meant.

If she could handle it.

She'd thrown herself into a relationship with three men, her three best friends without thinking it through enough. Maybe as a way to forget and ignore what she lost. Maybe as a way to console and heal herself.

But it wasn't fair to put that on them. It wasn't their job to heal her, to fix her. They were already struggling to fix themselves. They could be there for her and she could be there for them. They could go through it together so they weren't alone in their pain. But the healing had to be done themselves and with time.

After showering and changing into soft and cozy pajamas, Poppy flopped onto her bed, hugging her pillow to her chest, breathing in the scent of Gavin still clinging to the fabric.

Her body started to shake as worst case scenarios raced through her head. Gavin could've died. Every time they went to work was she going to spend the time terrified one of them wouldn't return? Or all of them?

She'd never really feared for them before, caught in the childish fantasy that they'd all live until they were old and living in the same nursing home.

But then Perry died and not in some heroic blaze of glory. Instead, he'd died alone, bleeding in these street at the hands of a drunk driver.

Even if the guys had safe jobs, she could still lose them. And she was in too deep with them already for it to do anything other than completely shatter her.

Poppy fell asleep to dreams of fire and blood.

The next morning, she dragged herself out of bed and downstairs. Tam and Marie eyed her with concern, but she waved them off, focused on work, going through the motions. She was numb, feeling nothing but a hopelessness and a dull ache in the center of her chest, nothing inside her but a yawning, empty crater.

Officer Maxwell called and it jerked her out of herself as she hurried into the kitchen for privacy. "Hello?"

"Miss O'Sullivan?"

"Yes. This is she." Please, let him have answers.

"I'm calling about the information you gave me."

Took him long enough. "All right."

She paced back and forth in the kitchen as she listened to him.

"I'm sorry, but it turned out to be a dead end. The person and car in question had a record of the accident. It was a few days after your brother's death and it was a simple accident where everyone walked away. She's innocent."

No. It had to be her. Poppy need it to be that Jemma person. She needed closure, answers, justice, a chance to move on.

Her eyes closed and her chest ached as she pushed words from her mouth. "I see. I'm sorry for bothering you with it."

"You did the right thing, ma'am. It was a long shot, but worth looking into." Officer Maxwell's voice swelled with pity.

She didn't want his damn pity. She wanted him to do his job. "Right."

"I'll be in touch once I have more for you."

"Of course. Thank you for calling." At least he didn't show up this time. Poppy didn't want to see his stupid face.

She hung up and slid down the cabinets to the floor, burying her face in her hands, her eyes dry and burning, the fog rushing back through her, numbing her. With a groan, her hauled her aching body back to her feet and returned to the shop, a disconnect between her body and emotions.

The rest of the day passed in the same way. She stayed in the background at work, letting Tam and Marie handle the customers, she ignored the texts and emails from her new half-siblings, she brushed off the guys when they called and texted, claiming busyness.

That night, she baked enough for two weeks, trying to combat the pressure in her chest and her head she couldn't banish. She couldn't even cry anymore, her tears had dried up, leaving her insides as barren as the desert.

The kitchen door swung open and Poppy looked up with a frown. Tam and Marie had left over an hour ago. Did one of them forget something?

It was the guys.

"What are you three doing here?"

DEAN'S JAW HARDENED as he took in Poppy's dull eyes staring at them in confusion. Her multicolored hair was a mess, strands stuck to her face and there were sheets of cookies and scones and pastries covering every inch of the counter.

He was glad Tam had called them.

Poppy was spiraling. Badly.

"We're taking you home," Dean said. "Tam and Marie are going to handle the shop for the rest of the week." They'd offered when they called him, concerned for her.

A restless shrug jerked her shoulders. "Okay."

Worry stiffened Dean even further at Poppy's lack of hesitance or argument.

After exchanging stressed out glances, the three of them cleaned up her kitchen, fed and watered her cat, packed a few of her things, locked up, and herded her out the door.

She followed where they led without comment, completely pliant and willing to do and go where they wanted. It was like leading around a robot.

Since she still wasn't comfortable riding in a vehicle, they walked back to their place, Poppy wrapped in one of Flynn's arms.

Dean didn't know how to help her, how to reach her. He tried to grasp for any bit of control over the situation, but that was the thing about Poppy. She was impossible to control. It was impossible to guess what she'd choose or do next. She was always a surprise.

She was the only surprise he'd ever enjoyed.

"We fucked this up, didn't we?" Gavin asked under his breath as he strode at Dean's side behind Flynn and Poppy.

"I don't know." Dean hoped not, but only time would tell.

Gavin's steps clopped heavy against the sidewalk. "I fucked this up. Me getting hurt triggered all this."

"It wasn't your fault. I had a feeling this was coming again sooner or later. For all of us. Next week it may be Flynn. Or me. Or you. We've all been so busy since his death and so much has changed, it's going to all start hitting us." Dean had a small moment the other night and Poppy was able to bring him out of hit.

He hoped he'd be able to do the same thing for her.

Grief wasn't a straight line. It wasn't orderly. It wasn't something that could be controlled. It was a wild fire razing everything in its path and right when you think you have a handle on the destruction, a single spark lights it all up again.

Dean hoped they could tame the fire rampaging inside of her. He hoped hers didn't spark theirs.

Chapter 46

Poppy laid in bed, staring at the wall, muffled sounds from the guys barely reaching her through the silent scream ringing in her head.

She had no idea what day it was, how long she'd been here, what time is was.

And she didn't care.

The door opened behind her and Gavin stepped into her view with a coffee and a water he sat on the table beside the bed. He didn't say a word, just climbed into the bed behind her, letting her know she wasn't alone, letting her know he was still here with her.

Ever since they brought her back here, this was how it went. She was rarely alone, but they didn't force conversation or anything else on her. Sometimes all three of them smooshed onto the bed with her, other times it was just one of them. Sometimes they brought in one of their computers to watch movies, sometimes Flynn brought his guitar and worked on one of his songs. They kept her plied with coffee and water and the pastries from her shop.

They didn't seem to care their girlfriend had turned into a zombie who couldn't get out of bed, who no longer showered, who could barely do more than grunt and zone out in a light doze.

Perry constantly whispered in her mind, taunting her. Reminding her he tried to keep her from the mess she found herself in. He reminded her he knew what was best, that he had always been there to keep her from making decisions that could ruin her life.

The screaming helped drown him out, but his voice kept worming into her brain like a dagger. It wasn't really him. It was the worst part of him with none of the good to balance him out.

Poppy really worried she might be losing her mind. She was supposed to be stronger than this, she had plenty to still be happy about, grateful for. But she just might be broken. Too broken to be what the guys needed. Too broken for love.

She had failed them all.

FLYNN'S FISTS POUNDED into the heavy bag, his chest and shirt already soaked in sweat as he tried to pour out the rage and worry and pain twisted and snarled in his chest.

Poppy had gone so deep, lost inside herself, they couldn't reach her to pull her out.

Flynn hated feeling so helpless and useless with no idea how to bring Poppy back to them. He hated the vacant expression on her face, the torture in her eyes.

She wasn't crying or talking or doing much of anything. Two days of this and Flynn wanted to burst out of his skin. Dean had sent him to the gym so he could burn off some of his anger and restlessness.

They only had another day before they headed back to work, but he didn't know how they could leave her alone. One of them would have to call in. Since Gavin was still injured, he was the best choice.

Or maybe they could see if Stacy could come stay with Poppy.

Thankfully, Tam and Marie were handling the shop and taking care of the demon cat who still hated the guys.

Flynn's knuckles ached and his lungs burned when he finally stopped beating at the punching bag. He leaned his forehead against the bag, his chest heaving.

He missed his friend. Perry would know how to help her. How to help all of them. He and Dean had led their little family and with Perry gone, Dean seemed lost, unable to regain control. Gavin was trying desperately to keep them all upbeat and fed. And Flynn was just angry. So angry. About everything.

Perry's death was ripping them all apart and Flynn wasn't sure they were going to get through it whole. They were fracturing and he didn't know how to stop it, how to heal the gaping wounds spilling blood all over his family.

Chapter 47

Poppy was sick of the dark side of Perry constantly hissing at her, bringing her deeper into the black waves of grief. His ghost had become the devil on her shoulder, spreading doubts and fears through her.

She fumbled for her phone on the nightstand next to the bed, planning to drown out Perry's ghost with his real voice.

But when she dialed his number, a robot told her his voicemail box was full. She knew his code, so she dialed in to listen to them, her pulse speeding up.

Maybe she shouldn't listen to these, to whatever words people had decided to leave in his box. But she needed to clear up some space and just deleting the messages seemed wrong.

The initial ones were before his death, coworkers leaving information, bill collectors wanting to talk to him, his dentist reminding him of an upcoming appointment.

Her first tear fell when Flynn's laughing voice yelled in her ear, asking Perry where he was. "You're an hour late, dude. Hurry up and bring that sister of yours with her. I have a surprise I think she'll enjoy. Stop hiding her from us."

He must have been talking about the unicorn cocktails.

She saved that one, unable to delete it.

The next few were unimportant, easy to delete.

Then Dean's voice whispered through the phone. "We can't do this without you, you fucker. This wasn't how it was supposed to go. Dammit, man. Poppy's destroyed. We all are. We miss you. We love you. And we'll take care of her. Whatever it takes."

Poppy clapped a hand over her mouth to muffle her sob.

The message she'd left him played next and hearing the hopeless grief in her own voice made nausea roll in her stomach.

Flynn's fury rang down the line, making a matching one rise in her chest. "You piece of shit. You didn't wear a seatbelt? What the hell were you thinking? You know better than that. How many car accidents have we been called to and witnessed what happens to idiots who don't wear their seatbelts?" Flynn's words started coming out strangled, tears in his throat. "You've broken us."

The pillow was soaked beneath her cheek and the bed shuddered around her as their pain sank into her.

"Hey Perry. It's me, Gavin. This is stupid, leaving a message you'll never hear. But it feels a little less stupid than talking to the sky like you're hanging out on some cloud with a harp in your hands.

"It's been two weeks since your funeral. I didn't actually mean to call to leave a message for a ghost. I called you without thinking about it. I don't even know what to say. We're all plowing through as best we can. We fucked things up and admitted our feelings to Poppy sooner than we meant to. It was my fault. I couldn't keep my damn mouth shut." Gavin paused, silence loud in Poppy's ear.

Poppy tried to mop her face, but the tears kept flowing.

"She wants to be with us. Can you believe that? Did you know and keep it a secret from us all these years? You and your secrets. I want to be pissed at you, but it's hard when you can't fight back. I miss fighting with you. Hell, I miss *you*. I hope you aren't too pissed that we've started something with Poppy. You agreed to it...before. Can't take it back now. Ugh. Horrible joke. I need to hang up now because I sound like a complete jackass. But wherever you are, I hope you found some peace. I hope you aren't alone. I know how much you hate that. And I want you to know, Poppy isn't alone. No matter what, she'll never be alone. We've got her. She's everything to us and that will never change."

Poppy couldn't listen to anymore. She hung up and let the phone fall to the carpet, digging her palms into her eyes as she released the storm raging in her chest.

Guilt swelled within her. She was so selfish, so focused on her own pain and loss, she left the guys to muddle through on their own while trying to take care of her. It wasn't fair of her.

She had to snap out of this funk and let them be there for her and be there for them in return. They should be able to lean on her as much as she leaned on them. But now their grief was on hold while they held her hand through it all.

Poppy knew what she needed to do.

And she needed to do it alone.

THE GUYS HAD BARELY left her alone since they brought her home, but it was early in the morning, still dark, and they were all passed out, Flynn snoring softly beside her.

She eased from the bed, grabbing her phone, keys, and Perry's hoodie the guys had so thoughtfully packed for her.

There was something she needed to grab from her shop on the way.

In the living room, she scrawled a note for the guys, letting them know she was okay and would be back later in case one of them woke up before she returned. She'd put them through enough, she didn't want to worry them further.

Poppy slipped out of the house like the ghost Perry had become, hurrying down the dark streets back to her shop, clutching the hoodie tight around her against the early morning chill in the air.

Back at Cool Beans, she grabbed what she needed and locked back up behind herself. The place looked great. Tam and Marie had taken good care of it while she disappeared on them. They deserved more than the piddling raise she'd given them.

The sun peeked its face over the horizon, lightening the sky with dark streaks of purple. Poppy walked the streets alone, only the occasional car passing by her. She liked the town like this, quiet and still and asleep with only the fading stars and waking birds to keep her company.

Poppy paused when she reached the gate to the graveyard. It was her first time visiting since the funeral. But it was time.

Time to say a more proper goodbye.

The gate creaked as she opened it like something out of a horror movie, but she'd already lived through enough real horror, it didn't scare her.

She followed the path towards Perry and her mother's graves, her steps growing heavier the closer she got.

At her mother's grave, Poppy kissed the tips of her fingers and pressed it against the top of the stone. "Miss you, Mom. Love you. Dad's an asshole, by the way."

She knelt in front of Perry's grave, the dirt still fresh, the flowers left wilted and brown. She grabbed the stems and tossed them away, brushing grass clippings and leaves off the stone.

Once it was clean, she placed the framed print of the definition of petrichor Perry had given her. She had the design saved on her computer so she could print off another, but she wanted him to have this one.

Poppy sat back on her butt, crossing her legs in front of her. "Hey, Pear Tree. I have not been doing too well since you left me. Our bastard father showed up and wanted to buy our place. Apparently I can't handle it on my own. Which I have my doubts as well, but I'm going to prove that asshole wrong. Oh, and we have two half-siblings. They're okay, but they're not you and it makes me resent them a little. It's you I need. I need you here so I can tell you how pissed I am at you. All these secrets you kept. From me, from the guys. You tried so hard to keep us apart. For years. Why?" Her voice cracked and she paused to rain tears onto his grave.

Frustration and agony twisted inside her as she stared at the engraved words on the stone. Loving son, brother, and friend. Like those three things were all he was, his entire person shrunk down to one single phrase.

She should have chosen better, something with more zing. She should have used a pun. Maybe she could order a new one once she figured out the perfect words.

"You were so selfish. You kept them from me and me from them, hogging us all for yourself. You wanted to be the center of everyone's world. I know it's because our father sucked and left us and started a new family. I get it. I see it all now. I was so desperate not to lose you, I let you get away with too much. I let you control me since you seemed to need it so much and I was happy not having the responsibility. So it's as much my fault as yours. I forgive you for it. And I love you anyway. I love you so damn much."

She sniffed and wiped her face with the sleeve of his hoodie, clambering to her feet.

"But I'm not going to feel guilty or sorry for taking comfort in the friends you left behind who miss you too. I'm not going to shove them away over worry over what you might think. They're the only ones who understand. They're my family as much as they were yours and I love them. And I think they love me too."

She finally said the words out loud, finally admitted what she'd known since she was a angst-filled teenager, unable to see anyone but them.

"We do, baby."

Poppy spun around with a wet face and hands clutching her chest to see the guys all standing behind her, tears and love in their eyes.

Gavin smiled. "We love you."

She ran a few steps towards them, slamming into their embraces.

Flynn kissed her cheek. "Come on, muffin. Let's go home."

Poppy glanced back over her shoulder as she let them lead her away. "Goodbye."

She felt lighter. She wasn't over it by any means, none of them were, but maybe she'd taken her first step.

And her first step had brought her back to them.

She had a long road ahead. But she was learning how to live in a world he no longer walked in. Maybe one day, she'd stop trying to call or text him without having to remember it all over again. Maybe one day, she'd have answers of who killed him and she'd get to see him find justice. But she had to move on with her life without it. She had to keep going. If anything her life so far had taught her, there was rarely any justice found in death.

Chapter 48

A little over a year later...
Poppy's eyes filled with tears as the scent of petrichor rose from the ground, rain splattering around her.

Arms slipped around her from behind and Dean's voice brushed against her ear. "You all right, baby?"

Of course it was Dean. He was always the one who found her when she was sad. He seemed to sense it. And the backyard had become a special place for the two of them, a place they escaped to when they needed to be alone.

She had special places with all three of the guys.

"Yeah. Just missing him."

His arms tightened on her middle, Dean completely uncaring he was getting soaked right along with her. "You always miss him when it rains."

A sad smile trembled on her lips. "I probably always will."

He kissed the crook of her neck. "It hits me whenever I smell bleach."

Poppy released a wet chuckle at the reminder of her clean freak brother.

"Come back inside, baby. Flynn just brought home enough food to feed our entire squad."

"Of course he did." She let Dean tug her out of the rain.

Gavin waited for them right inside the back door with towels and dry clothes. "You two okay?"

Poppy nodded. "We're okay. Hungry."

She and Dean toweled off and kicked their shoes into the corner before following Gavin into the kitchen.

Gavin's mouth curled with disapproval. "Good. Flynn went overboard."

"We've all been working up an appetite moving Poppy in with us. We need the fuel if we want to welcome her properly later tonight." Flynn winked at her. "I still can't believe it took you so long to agree to move in with us."

"I liked living above my shop." And as much as she loved being here with the guys, Perry's room was still vacant and depressing.

It took her time to ready herself for that step. But she spent so much time here, it started getting a little ridiculous for her to keep putting it off.

She'd finally agreed at the Independence Day party. She told them beneath a sky of fireworks and stars how much she loved them and wanted to go to sleep and wake up with them every day.

It had taken another month for them to sort everything. Tonight was her first night in her new home.

At least Cyclops had finally come around and accepted the guys. After months of patience, the cat would finally allow them to pet her.

Sometimes.

Tam and her boyfriend decided to move into Poppy's old place now that she was a partner. Poppy named Marie as the manager and they'd hired four new employees.

Cool Beans was thriving and so was Poppy.

Some days were harder than others, but she didn't let those days win.

Gavin pulled her into his lap as they sat around the table and Flynn passed out the food. Poppy snuggled back into him as she sucked on the coffee-flavored milkshake Flynn bought for her.

She smiled at her guys as they chatted and stuffed their faces with bacon cheeseburgers. Except for Gavin and his boring salad.

Poppy waved the milkshake beneath Gavin's nose. "Want a taste?"

"Nope. I'm waiting for a taste of something a little sweeter."

She shivered and pressed back into him, rubbing against his building erection. He nipped at her neck and she gasped, the noise attracting Flynn and Dean's burning attention.

"Dinner over already?" Dean asked.

"It'll all keep or reheat." Flynn plucked Poppy's milkshake from her hands and popped it into the freezer.

Gavin stood with Poppy in his arms and carried her upstairs to her new room. It wasn't much different than before, just her things moved in.

He dropped her onto the bed and her guys surrounded her, touching, tasting, kissing, stroking. Clothes disappeared and they slid into bed with her.

This. This was what she'd longed for when she was nothing but a foolish kid, and so many years later, her wish had finally come true.

She wasn't alone. And she never would be.

THE END

Thank you for reading, and I hoped you enjoyed Poppy's story. If you did enjoy or even if you didn't, I would really appreciate it if you left an honest review on Amazon. It helps so much in determining what to work on next.

ABOUT THE AUTHOR

AN EXPERT IN PARKOUR, Helene Gadot moonlights as a Nail Polish Namer and occasional ghostwriter. She lives with her husband and trio of rugrats in the South. Helene has a serious coffee mug and throw pillow addiction, and when she isn't reading or writing, she's probably shopping online or watching Marvel movies online.

GADOT ALSO WRITES URBAN Fantasy as Harley Gordon[1].

---

1. https://www.amazon.com/Harley-Gordon/e/B01I5KOIYA/ref=sr_ntt_srch_lnk_2?qid=1542665207&sr=8-2

Also by Helene Gadot

KINDRED SOULS SERIES:
Her Assassins
Her Prince
Her Dragon
Her Bonds
Omnibus with new content - coming soon

ACES & KNAVES SERIES:
Crash
Boom
Zap - holiday novella coming late 2018

MAGIC & DREAMS SERIES:
Wicked Fae
Wild Fae - coming early 2019

STANDALONES:
Petrichor

ANTHOLOGIES:
Shifting Destiny

Printed in Poland
by Amazon Fulfillment
Poland Sp. z o.o., Wrocław